LOVE LEGACY

Pinebrook University Book #1

MK Owens

Book Cover by Maldo Designs (@smaldo.designs)

Copy and Line Editing by Cassidy Hudspeth (@cassidyhudspethedits)

Contents

Book Playlist

THE OFFICIAL PLAYLIST FOR LOVE LEGACY

1. Slumber Party (feat. Princess Nokia) – Ashnikko

2. JOY (Unspeakable) (feat. Pharrell Williams) – Voices of Fire

3. Bad Girl – M.I.A.

4. Baby's On Fire – Die Antwoord

5. Drunk Affairs – Vinlisa

6. Escapism. (Sped Up) – RAYE, 070 Shake

7. Float (feat. Seun Kuti & Egypt 80) – Janelle Monae

8. These Four Walls – Khamari

9. Me & U – Cassie

10. Wonder Woman – LION BABE

11. I'm Tired (with Zendaya) – Labrinth

12. Let Me In – H.E.R.

13. Lipstick Lover – Janelle Monae

14. everything – Kehlani

15. Fall In Line (feat. Demi Lovato) – Christina Aguilera

Listen to the full playlist at mkowensbooks.com

Content Tags and Trigger Warnings

Tropes/Content Tags:

- Black Cat x Golden Retriever Vibes

- Opposites Attract

- Love at First Sight

- Gay Awakening

- Found Family

- Religious Deconstruction

- Sapphic Romance

- Tattooed and Pierced FMC

- Queer Representation

- Racially and Ethnically Diverse Characters

- Neurodivergent Characters

- Anxiety Representation

- ADHD Representation

- "I Only Have Eyes For You"

- College Romance

- Greek Life

- Strong Female Friendships

Content/Trigger Warnings:

- Homophobia

- Transphobia

- Religious Trauma

- Parental Abandonment

- Thoughts of Self-Harm

- Discussion of Self-Harm

- Mention of Childhood Abuse

- Mention of Previous Suicide Attempt

- Stalking (Not Between MCs)

- Intimate Partner Violence (Not Between MCs)

- Verbal Abuse (Not Between MCs)

- Religious Deconstruction

- Devout Religious Practices

- On Page Panic Attacks

- Open Door Sex Scenes

- Underage Drinking

- Binge Drinking

- Marijuana Usage

- Sexual Assault (Off Page, Not Involving the MCs)

For all the queer adults that had a mini existential crisis of faith and identity when coming out...
This one is for you.

1

Sage

"So, Sage, did you call her?" Cora asks me as she searches through the hanging rack in my closet.

"Call who?" I respond, checking the rush schedule on my phone. In two days, Kappa Theta Alpha will begin welcoming potential new members for Rush Week, and Cora is helping me pick out something to wear for each day of our schedule.

"You know the British girl? That you met in Costa Rica? The one with the amazing tits?"

I chuckle, thinking back to our Costa Rica trip. Every year since we were freshmen, I've traveled to a resort in Costa Rica with Gabby and Cora, my two roommates, Maeve, my sorority sister, as well as my foster sister, Theia, and her boyfriend, Aaron, for a few days during the summer.

And every year, I inevitably hook up with some woman staying at the resort. This year, however, there were not one but two equally attractive women in rotation. The Brit Cora is talking about and a sweet little redhead from Dallas, Texas.

"I remember her, Cora. And no, I have not called her. I actually liked the redhead better." To be honest, though, I was never going to call either of them. I never do.

"Oh, the Southerner? She was super sweet. A little too sweet, if you ask me. What was her name... Stacy? Kacey? Lacey?"

"Her name was Misty. And before you ask, no, I haven't called her either," I answer, rifling through the growing stack of clothing on the bed next to me. Cora may not be into the idea of Greek Life, but she has one hell of an eye for fashion. Especially when it comes to blending the sorority standard look with my own personal style.

Cora finally steps out of my closet, grabbing the pile of clothes off my bed and heading into the hallway. While she isn't a member of Kappa Theta Alpha, our third roommate, Gabby, is. During Rush Week, we usually put up a temporary clothing rack in the hallway of our apartment. This way, it's easier for us to coordinate what we're wearing ahead of time. As Cora starts hanging up my picks, she stops to turn and look at me.

"Sage, you know you're my best friend in the world, so I say this with love. But you're a hoe."

"I second that!" Gabby shouts from the front door, returning with food from our favorite off-campus spot, Happy Sprout.

"Gee, thanks, guys. I'm really feeling the love from both of you." I head to the kitchen to grab my lunch. I ordered my usual black bean and mushroom burger with lettuce, onions, and chipotle mayo.

Happy Sprout is a small, family-owned cafe that focuses on plant-based foods. While I'm not a vegetarian, Cora is, so this became our go-to spot for food early on. "I'm serious, Sage. Your revolving door of women could put some of the frat guys' to shame."

"Ouch," I mumble around a mouthful of my burger. As much as their comparison hurt, they were right. I had developed a bit of a reputation as a player on campus. I've hooked up with most of the queer women and even experimented with a couple of the straight ones.

I'd like to think I'm not hurting anyone. I'm pretty upfront about my expectations in that I have none; I don't expect things to go beyond that one hookup. I tend to lose interest quickly if there's not a deep connection, and I've been in splash pads deeper than the feelings I have for these women.

"Why are you allergic to dating?" Gabby asks with a raised brow.

"I'm not. I just haven't found the right woman I want to date," I answer half-heartedly, fidgeting with the ring I wore on my right hand. I was starting to feel a little uncomfortable with being the focus of the conversation.

"Bullshit," she counters, "if that were the case, you would've found her by now." And Gabby is completely right. If I were genuinely open to a relationship, I probably would've found one by now. But relationships are messy, and that's a struggle I don't know if I'm ready to take on. As I try to come up with an acceptable response, Cora jumps to my rescue.

"What I think Gabby is trying to say..." she starts, giving the other woman a pointed look, "is we just want to see you happy, Sage. You deserve more than a string of one-night stands." Cora gives my arm a squeeze, settling my fidgeting.

While the three of us have been best friends for a couple years now, my friendship with Cora goes so much deeper. We actually met in high school, online, in a support group for children of adoption. Our friendship was almost instantaneous, and when we found out that we were going to the same college, that bond grew stronger. If anyone could understand my hesitations about entering a relationship, it would be Cora.

I went into the foster care system at twelve when my mom started caring more about the bottle than me. My dad passed away before I was born, so at that point, I had no one. My foster parents came into my life when I was fourteen, and just before my sixteenth birthday, they tried to adopt me. Unfortunately, it didn't work out due to a series of clerical errors, but they treated me as one of their own all the same.

Cora was adopted from Japan as an infant by her parents. They tried for years to have biological children, and when that was unsuccessful, they decided to adopt instead of surrogacy. She has two younger siblings who were also adopted. Cora was part of the adoption support group long before I was, and even though our situations were different, we shared a similar struggle—reconciling that our biological parents left us for one reason or another and the death of a parent.

My dad passed before I got the chance to know him, but Cora's mom, her adoptive mom, died from breast cancer when she was a teenager. Losing your mom when you need her the most? That shit hurts, and the pain never goes away. Cora still has a hard time talking about her. Her mom went to Pinebrook U in the nineties, so attending as a student brought up many emotions that she packed away. Our freshman year was rough for her, but Gabby and I were here.

Those girls are my sisters for life and I couldn't ask for anything more.

Theia

Can you come over? I could use some help getting the apartment set up. *prayer hands emoji*

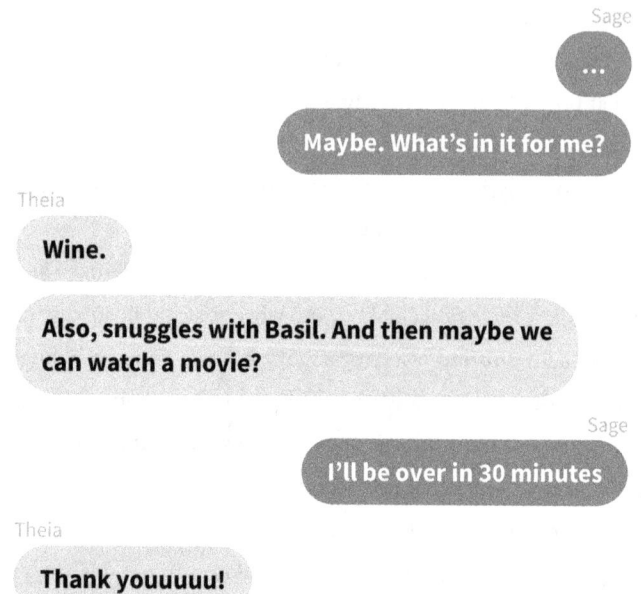

Theia was my older sister—foster sister, I mean. It was her parents, Melody and Ken Davis, that took me in. Theia's four years older. She was a junior in high school when her parents first fostered me. We spent two years together under the same roof before she left for college, but those two years were enough.

Theia had always wanted a younger sibling, and that was part of the reason why her parents became fosters to begin with. Our connection was different, and I think that's why her parents made the decision to adopt me. We became the best of friends. Thankfully, Theia was a *cool* older sister. She'd take me on trips to the mall, let me hang out with her and her friends... Maybe it was because I was a foster kid, but she made every effort to make me feel included, no matter what.

It was tough at first when she left for college. I was bullied in high school, but when Theia was around, nobody messed with me. Class President, Salutatorian, the women's basketball team captain—she was the perfect student. All the teachers loved her, and the students equally respected and were intimidated by her. No one would even think of messing with Theia, and I was afforded the same protection by association. Once she left though, all bets were off.

Pinebrook University is only two hours from our family home in New Jersey, so thankfully, Theia came home for every holiday (even some of the smaller ones like Valentine's Day), and at least one weekend a month to spend time with me and our parents. Her visits, plus transferring to a different high school, helped a lot, and before I knew it, it was time for me to apply for college.

I applied to one school—Pinebrook University.

Should I have cast a wider net? Sure. Did I have any idea what I wanted to do? Not a clue. Before I was placed with the Davises, going to college wasn't even on my radar. I wasn't sure if it were something I would be able to afford, and hearing these horror stories of adults in their forties and fifties still paying off their student loans, I was going to pursue a different path. Maybe cosmetology? But when they tried to adopt me, they made it clear, if I wanted to go to college, I'd have their full support, emotionally and financially.

So, of course I picked the school that would have me close to my sister. My freshman year of college was high school all over again, minus the bullying. Theia took me under her wing to show me the ropes around campus. I mean, she was the one who convinced me to rush a sorority in the first place. She was president of Kappa Theta Alpha her senior year, which inspired me to run my senior year. Theia was the blueprint, and I got to follow in her footsteps, with her right there with me.

Since Theia decided to get her master's, and now PhD, at Pinebrook University, she's still here on campus with me. We're not too far from home, but since she's still enrolled, I can drop by on a random Tuesday, especially since Theia's new apartment is in the same complex as mine.

It takes me all of five minutes to walk over to her building, but first, I had to change into some comfortable clothes and grab a couple pints of ice cream. I knock on the door, sending Theia a text that I'm here as well.

"Sage. If you're going to knock on the door, you don't have to also text me. You're so annoying." She rolls her eyes, opening the door.

"You know you love me," I say, giving her a quick hug as I enter her apartment. "I brought ice cream!"

Theia takes the bag from me, bringing it into the kitchen to open. "Did you get the—"

"Banana's Foster Cashew Milk Ice Cream? Yes."

She pulls the pint out of the bag, doing a little happy dance. "I freaking love you." Theia puts the pint and my dulce de leche ice cream into the freezer.

"So what exactly do you need help with?"

Meow.

I turn toward the soft mewing sound to see Theia's orange tabby, Basil, laying down on the top shelf of his cat tower. "Basil! Hi, baby, how are you?" I coo, reaching out to lift him and snuggle him to my chest. Basil was a young cat, only about two years old. Theia adopted him last year and we always joke that he's basically my cat.

Since I'm over on a regular basis, he stays glued to my side anytime I step through the door. Basil's basically a dog trapped in a cat's body. He's extremely playful and relatively high-energy for a cat. He's social as well and loves physical touch, which is why he's snuggled into my chest right now, purring very loudly.

"Sage! You came over to help me, remember?"

"Sorry, but he's such a precious baby," I say, giving her an apologetic smile as I stroke my hand along the fur on his back.

"I unpacked the best as I can. The furniture store is supposed to be coming by in an hour or so to deliver some furniture. I have to clear space for them, assemble my bookshelves, and then unpack the rest of my things," she explains, running down the list that she has sitting out on the counter. Ever organized Theia; she has a list for everything.

"Why isn't Aaron here helping you?" I ask, sitting in one of the folding chairs she has in the living room.

I notice her freeze in her tracks ever so slightly before continuing. "Aaron started his job at the law firm this week, so he's a little busy. I figure between you and me, we could handle assembling the small furniture."

I eye her carefully, feeling like there's more to the story, but I don't press. "It's a shame Mom and Dad are in Austin. Otherwise, they'd probably insist on helping."

Theia laughs. "Oh, definitely! You know Dad would make us stand back and 'take notes on his techniques' as he puts everything together for me."

I put Basil down on the floor and he scurries off to hide in the bathroom. Theia and I start working on assembling her small furniture pieces, only stopping when the furniture delivery men come to the door. We move out of their way, hanging out in the kitchen as they bring in all the furniture in pieces and assemble them in the rooms Theia directed them to. Once they left, we resumed our work, and after a few hours, she had a fully assembled apartment. Sure, the walls were bare, and she could use some decorations, but functionally, her apartment was ready.

Seeing that it was later than we anticipated, Theia decided to order us some food from the Italian restaurant off campus to be delivered to her apartment. She was still in the shower when the food was dropped off, so I unpacked everything, leaving the food on the kitchen counter. Thankfully, we finished unpacking her moving boxes, so I pulled a couple reusable plates from the cabinet, rinsing them in the sink quickly before wiping them off. I fixed myself a plate, grabbing some of the napkins and utensils they included in the bag, before sitting down on the couch.

Theia eventually emerges from the bathroom, holding a towel under her dripping hair. "Hey, Sage, are there any boxes we haven't unpacked?"

I scan the main living space of the apartment before shaking my head. "No, I don't think so, why?"

"And you haven't come across my blow dryer?" she asks. I shake my head again.

"Shit. Ugh, that means one of my old roommates probably has it. I needed my diffuser, now I wasted all this product," she groans, gently squeezing some of the water out of her hair with her towel.

"Can't you just let it air dry?"

Theia laughs as she starts braiding up her hair. "No, Sage, I can't just 'let it air dry.' I mean, I could, but my curls would not come out right. The safest bet right now is just to braid it back until I get my hands on a new diffuser. I just wish I knew this before I got into the shower. I would've just put in a leave-in and could've been done like thirty minutes ago."

I've always been envious of how Theia's curls look, but when she tells me how labor-intensive it is to maintain them, I'm grateful I have short, wavy hair. Theia's biracial, her dad is black but her mom is white. She takes after her dad mostly. She has his curl pattern but her mom's light brown hair color. She has her mom's blue-green eyes but her dad's features. She's lighter skinned, but I think most people would guess she's black before they think she's white. Theia's absolutely stunning.

"Hey, just so you know, you need dish soap, a sponge, and some paper towels." I take a bite of my pasta. "I left you a list of things I thought you might need in the kitchen."

She circles the island, reading my note before fixing herself a plate. "I'll make a run to Target tomorrow, kill two birds with one stone." She takes a seat next to me, turning on the TV. We spend the rest of the night watching *Beaches & Bombshells*, our favorite dating show, grabbing our pints of ice cream from the freezer to eat. At some point, Basil wedges his way in between us on the couch, stretching out so that his head was in my lap and his back legs were in Theia's.

I'm not sure how many more nights like this we'll get when classes start back up, but for now, I'll take any sister bonding time I can get.

2

Naomi

"I'll be fine, Granny Mae. I promise you that," I say, balancing my phone between my shoulder and ear as I carry my suitcase down the hall to my new apartment. I knew she was worried about me, moving to a new state and university three years in. Sure, it was my first time on my own, but she, of all people, understood why I was getting away.

"Now, sweet pea, I love you. I understand you needed a fresh start, I just wish you had stayed closer to home. I would've helped you with tuition at the University of Georgia or Spelman."

"Granny, I couldn't ask you to do that. You're already paying my rent up here; I can't ask for rent and tuition."

"You don't have to ask me for anything! You're my favorite grandbaby. It's what grandmas do."

"Granny Mae, I'm your only grandbaby," I say, rolling my eyes, knowing full well that she can't see me. "Hey, Granny, I have to go. I'm finally at my apartment."

"Okay, honey. Make new friends and take a lot of pictures for me."

"Alright, I will. Love you." I hang up the phone, taking a deep breath.

12B.

I guess this is where I'll be living for the next year. I turn to knock on the door, pausing for a moment. The apartment manager gave me keys when I signed the sublease earlier this week, but she warned me that my roommates had already been living in the apartment from the previous academic year. It felt weird barging into someone else's space. The door flies open before I get the chance to knock, a smiling redhead standing in the door frame.

"Hi! You must be Naomi, right? I'm Maeve, one of your new room-mates," the woman says, holding her hand out.

I shake her hand. "Yes, ma'am, Naomi Williams."

"Oh my god, I love your accent!" she says, grabbing the handle of my suitcase and dragging it into the entryway of the apartment. I follow her lead, stepping inside.

Looking around, this is exactly what I pictured a New York apartment to look like. Granted, we're in the Hudson Valley and not actually in New York City, but this apartment captures that same aesthetic. Coming into the apartment, the wall to my right is exposed brown brick extending down to the far side. The wall at the end of the apartment is taken up by a large rectangular window, letting in a flood of natural light. To the left, the wall of the entryway opens up to the open concept floor plan, and the kitchen and living room are separated by a small breakfast bar.

The kitchen is full of stainless steel appliances, with a simple, black, single-serve coffee maker tucked into a corner. The upper cabinets are made of shiny white material, the counters are butcher block, and the lower cabinets are black wood. A large white sectional fills the living room, leaving enough space for a wood and black steel coffee table and a tall bookcase in the far corner. There's a large TV mounted on the wall opposite the couch. It's such a sleek and modern place, and I can't believe it's mine for the next year.

"So Naomi, our other roommate, Alex, should be back soon with some food. I'm not sure if you're hungry, but we ordered sushi if that's alright?"

"I've never had sushi before, but I've always wanted to try it."

Maeve's mouth drops open at my confession. "Never had sushi? Where'd you move from, the middle of nowhere?"

"Close enough. A small town in Georgia. Two thousand five hundred people, two stop lights, you'd miss it if you blinked."

"Wow. Well, you're in luck then because we got a sampler platter. You'll be able to try a bunch of different rolls," she says, heading toward the fridge. "Would you like anything to drink? We have water, coffee, soda, protein shakes, probiotic soda, wine, cider..." Maeve digs through the fridge, pulling out a small soda can for herself.

"Water is fine," I say, taking a seat at the counter as she slides a water bottle toward me.

"So I'm not going to ask you too many questions right now because I know Alex's going to want to know your story, but what's your major? I'm Biology, pre-vet focus. She's a linguistics major with minors in Spanish and Mandarin."

"Well, at my old school, I was a business major, but Pinebrook had a lot more options when I enrolled. So I'm going to switch to the Global Management BA program."

"And do you know what you're going to do with it? I mean after college. I know I plan to go to veterinary school, and I think Alex said she wanted to work at the UN as an interpreter or something."

I shrug. "Well, originally, the plan was to take over business operations for the mission organization that Daddy's parish is partnered with, but now, I'm not so sure that's what I want to do."

Maeve rubs her chin, squinting her eyes at me. "Mission organization... So you're like *religious* religious?" she asks, eyeing the cross around my neck.

I smile sheepishly, taking another sip of my water. "That's a long story and one that'll need something stronger than water." Maeve laughs, and shortly after, the front door opens.

"Hey, I've got the food! Is the girl here yet? Oh, it's you," a brunette says, rounding the corner from the hallway. She puts the two takeout bags on the counter before turning to me. "Hey, I'm Aleka, but most people just call me Alex."

"Aleka... That's a unique name," I say with a smile, getting up to help them with the food.

"Thanks, it's Greek. My dad moved here as a teen from Patras, my mom's from Xanthi, though she moved here as a baby," Alex replies, taking out the different containers of sushi rolls and other side dishes. Maeve gets out a couple plates and little dipping bowls for us. "So Naomi, we ordered a few different rolls: California, Spicy Tuna, Salmon and Avocado, Philadelphia and Spider rolls. We also ordered Crab Rangoon, Rock Shrimp, Edamame and Pork Shumai," she says, pointing to each item once we've unbagged it all.

"Naomi here has never had sushi."

"No freaking way!" Alex responds as she hands me chopsticks. "On second thought, I'll grab you a fork," she says, taking back the chopsticks.

"Yes, please," I reply, fixing myself a plate with one of everything before sitting at the counter. Maeve pours some soy sauce into each of the dipping bowls before handing one to me and Alex.

I dip one of the spicy tuna rolls into the soy sauce before putting it in my mouth. Once I finish chewing, I look up to see Maeve and Alex staring at me.

"So...?" Maeve asks, eating her own sushi.

I give her a reassuring smile. "It's delicious." Both women relax once I answer.

"Okay, good. Just wanted to make sure we didn't ruin your first night with food you hate," Alex says.

"Now that we got your first taste of sushi out of the way, tell me this long story about you and religion," Maeve says, pouring a glass of wine.

I point to the glass. "Is that for me?"

She nods, sliding it across the bar counter to me. I take a big swig before taking a deep breath.

"Okay, so where do I start? I transferred to Pinebrook University right before my senior year because I got kicked out of my old school for one too many honor code violations with no remorse." Maeve and Alex both gasp.

"Kicked out?"

"Honor code violations? For what?"

I laugh cynically, taking another big swig from my glass of wine. "Let's see. First, I wore a skort to class during the summer. Then, I got a second violation for insubordination because I posted on Instagram about how ridiculous the policy was. I got my third violation because someone took a photo of me and my boyfriend studying in his dorm and sent it to the Dean of Students. According to policy, after three violations, we're supposed to go through a 'restorative conference' and then the Conduct Review Committee would reevaluate my standing. I told them they could take their policies and shove it where the sun don't shine, and they dismissed me with the status of Non-Return."

Maeve and Alex just stared, looking at me as if I had five heads.

"Over a skort?"

"Studying in a dorm?"

"What's a restorative conference?"

"What does non-return mean?"

"What outdated ass school did you go to?"

They both fire off a bunch of questions, and I wait for them to finish before I respond. "I went to High Valley University."

"Oh! Well, that explains everything," Maeve says as she starts to clean up the leftovers from dinner.

"Wait, isn't that one of those super-religious schools?" Alex asks, taking a seat next to me and refilling my wine glass.

"Yep, nicknamed 'the BYU of the South'," I respond, drinking more wine.

"So why the hesitation on whether or not you're religious?" Maeve asks, leaning on the counter in front of me.

I look down at my wine glass, chewing on the inside of my cheek. "It's not that simple. My daddy's the lead pastor for our congregation. I grew up in the church. I'm religious, but I'm starting to realize that some of the things that I was taught aren't quite right."

"What do you mean?"

"Well, take my violation for wearing a skort. Why does my choice to wear knee-length shorts over a floor-length skirt affect my education or my relationship with God? Why is it that women are treated as less than men and it's okay? I know y'all didn't sign up for my identity crisis, but there's just some things I need to work through on my own with religion. And until I do, I don't know where I stand."

Alex pats my arm reassuringly. "Well, you don't have to figure it out just yet. And we can help! You know, show you what it's like outside the religious bubble."

I smile, finding comfort in the two women. "Thank you. I appreciate that!"

"Speaking of the quintessential, secular college experience, Rush starts this coming week!" Maeve says, going to sit down on the couch.

I turn around on my stool. "What's Rush?"

"Oh, my young padawan, you have much to learn," Alex says, taking our glasses and washing them in the kitchen sink.

"Padawan? What's that?"

"You've never seen *Star Wars*? Alex, add that to Naomi's experience list," Maeve says with a laugh.

Alex takes a notepad from one of the kitchen drawers and actually starts making a list. "So Rush is the one week a semester when all the sororities get together and try to recruit students to join their organization. Pinebrook does things a little differently because instead of forcing you to go to multiple houses, each sorority does their own individual rush. It's less overwhelming this way and takes up less of your time."

"Okay, I've heard of sororities, but I'm not sure what they do. I've heard some horror stories about hazing, do the sororities here do anything extreme?"

Maeve shakes her head, giving a small shrug. "Nothing extreme, but I have heard a rumor that one of the sororities will essentially kidnap you in the middle of the night to take you to your member initiation."

Now it was my turn to be shocked. "That's slightly terrifying."

"Yeah, but it keeps you on your toes!" Alex says with a laugh, scribbling on the notepad. "Okay, so for your experience list, I have: learn how to use chopsticks, rush a sorority, and watch *Star Wars*. Anything else I should add?"

I bite my lip. "I want to make out with someone!" I say in a rush.

She raises a brow. "I thought you said you had a boyfriend?"

"Ex-boyfriend, I guess. It was an arranged relationship with the expectation that we'd get married when we graduated, but I haven't talked to

Josiah since I left High Valley. He blamed our sanction for being together in his dorm on me."

"And you guys never kissed?" Maeve asks, completely surprised.

"We shared a kiss once or twice, but he never let it go much further than that. I remember the one time we accidentally kissed with tongue, he went to confession the day after. So yes, I would like to have the normal college experience of kissing and making out."

Alex chuckles. "Well, the normal college experience goes a little further than that, but we'll start out slow," she says, adding *make-out sesh* to the list.

"I'm going to leave this list on the fridge. If you can think of anything else you'd like to add, just add it. And that goes for you too, Maeve. And then Naomi, as you do the things on the list, just cross them off! It'll be cool to see how many new things you try this year before we graduate."

"About that... Since I'm transferring in so late, I have to take an extra year. Pinebrook won't let me graduate until I've completed thirty credits here, and I can't do that in one year," I say.

"Well that's fine, just more time for you to try out new experiences," Alex says with a wink as she tapes my list to the fridge.

I'm optimistic. Already, I'm feeling more at ease with my two new roommates than I had felt in a while at High Valley University. Maybe moving from Georgia to New York to attend a brand new university wasn't such a crazy idea after all. I'm excited for what Pinebrook University might have in store for me.

3

Sage

"**G**et up, Oregano. It's time for Day One of Rush!"

I roll my eyes, twisting onto my back in bed. Like normal, I've been awake for the last hour. I always have a hard time sleeping coming into Rush Week. Call it nerves, call it excitement, but alarms are pointless during this week. That never stops my roommate and sorority sister, Gabby, from dubbing herself my personal alarm system. She gets a kick out of the fact that my name is an herb, so any time she's messing around with me, she starts going down the spice rack for inspiration.

I lay in bed for a couple minutes more before getting up and heading down the hall to the bathroom. "Gabs, let me in. I just need to brush my teeth and wash my face." The deadbolt slips back into the door as she unlocks it, and then I hear the shower curtain move. I enter the bathroom, walking over to the sink to freshen up.

"Are you excited? First day of Rush as president," Gabby projects from behind the shower curtain.

"Eh, mixed emotions, honestly. I'm excited, sure, but nervous. And kind of sad. It's our last Rush Week," I say, garbled, my mouth full of toothpaste. I rinse my mouth before I start to wash my face.

"Word on the street is that we have at least one upperclassmen PNM," she says, turning off the water and sticking her arm out the shower curtain. I roll my eyes, handing her a towel from the hook on the back of the door. "Do we know anything about her?"

Gabby steps out of the shower, wrapped in her towel, grabbing a smaller one from the linen closet and towel drying her short, curly hair. "She's a late transfer, Maeve's roommate. Her name's Naomi. Maeve said she transferred from High Valley U," she says, giving me a mischievous grin.

"No fucking way. Isn't that one of those uber-religious universities run by a mega church?"

Gabby nods, putting mousse in her hair before finger-styling the short locks. "Yup. She says she's basically been living under a rock. Didn't know what *Star Wars* was and never had sushi."

I gasp, drying my face off. "How is that possible?"

"That's what I said when she told me. She's from Georgia apparently, here on a scholarship and taking an extra year. Might be worth extending her membership if she gels well with us. She'll be able to put at least another year into the organization before graduating."

"A church girl? I don't know. The way we do things might not mesh well with her beliefs. Especially our sister bonding night."

"Maeve said Naomi's trying to branch out from her religion and have a bunch of new experiences this year. Who knows, she might surprise us," Gabby says, finishing off her hair with a little oil and styling butter.

"Well, we've got maybe twenty minutes before we have to head to the house. Go get dressed," I say, heading back to my room.

"Back at ya!"

I grab one of the outfits Cora set aside from me in my closet, throwing it on the bed. A white halter v-neck bodysuit, camel-colored tapered dress pants, and black ankle strap heels. I get dressed, putting on a gold chain, a thin watch with a small face, and my dad's gold class ring I had resized to fit my middle finger. Looking in the mirror, I run a brush through my previously straightened hair, pulling the top half of my hair back and twisting it into a smaller-sized claw clip. I apply some light natural makeup before grabbing my phone and purse and heading out into the living room.

"Okay, let's go meet some underclassman!" Gabby says, standing up from the couch. She is wearing a red short sleeve button down blouse, white dress pants and tan gladiator sandals.

On the first day of Rush Week, we usually dress in business casual for members. Tradition states that to make a good first impression on potential new members, we should dress to impress, so we've kept this tradition up through the years, even as we've modernized some of our recruitment practices.

Some people regard sororities as sexist and archaic cults, but joining Kappa Theta Alpha was honestly one of the greatest decisions I made when I came to Pinebrook University. As a foster kid, I always wanted to find some sort of community, a family, and KTA gave me exactly that. Granted, I met my two best friends through a freshman housing lottery, but my KTA sisters are my ride-or-dies.

Over the years, we have acknowledged that our practices were a little outdated, and since have updated our policies. We got rid of some of the more cloak-and-dagger traditions, bowed out of the whole preference system that our Panhellenic Council used, created new traditions, and removed any of the religious and "traditional" wording in our bylaws and

rituals. We've been trying to make the sorority a more inclusive organization, and I think we've been doing a good job. I mean, where else do you
get to see an out-and-proud lesbian serving as president?

Gabby and I drove over to campus, heading to the Kappa House. We did
the bulk of our setup the night before, decorating the house for the group
of young women who were about to show up. But we still had to set out
our refreshments and make sure all the sisters were ready.

We head into the sorority house, entering the kitchen. The house is
decorated from head to toe in our sorority's colors: pale pink, yellow, and
white. There are balloon arrangements, streamers wrapped around the
banisters, and arrangements of pink carnations, our flower, set up in the
house.

In the kitchen, we have our usual caterers set up a spread of the members'
favorite foods, as well as large pitchers of our signature sparkling pink
punch made of pink lemonade, grapefruit juice, and Sprite, with muddled
strawberries and raspberries. The spread includes veggie burger and turkey
burger sliders, mini mushroom and spinach quiches, veggie sushi rolls,
cheese pizza, ham and cheese sandwiches, brownies, chocolate chip cookies, and mini fruit tarts. Is it standard recruitment refreshments? Definitely
not, but it gives just a bit of insight into who we are as people, and year after
year, everyone says they love Meet The Sisterhood Day.

I grab a plastic champagne flute, filling it with punch. I take a sip as I
connect my phone to the house Wi-Fi, tapping into the smart home network. I start my Rush Week playlist and shuffle it, the sound of "Bad Girls"
by M.I.A playing low through the speakers installed around the house. My

phone pings, a text from our Recruitment Chair, Raven, indicating that she was on her way with the group of PNMs interested in our sorority.

Since we do things differently than the rest of the sororities, and because we're not a national organization, we aren't involved with the Panhellenic Council's recruitment process. We have our recruitment events earlier in the day, so if anyone wants to participate in formal rush, they have the chance to do so. But we do stick around for those who are solely interested in Kappa Theta Alpha so that they can continue to spend time with the sisters. We usually have about a quarter of the PNMs stay.

Maeve comes into the kitchen, wearing a short, soft pink wrap dress in our sorority's colors. "Nervous for your first Rush as president?"

I grimace. "Why does everyone keep asking me that?"

"So, that is a yes?" She laughs, grabbing a veggie burger slider off the table and taking a bite.

Her roommate, Aleka, enters the kitchen as well. "Hey, save some snacks for the PNMs," she says, steering Maeve away from the table and handing me my name tag. I pin it to my top, grateful she remembered them. I knew I was forgetting something last night while we were prepping.

"Sorry we're a little late, we had to drop Naomi off at Rush registration first."

"So you convinced her to rush?" I ask, a little surprised, given the background that Gabby shared with me this morning.

Maeve nods. "We did. I don't expect her to stay with the other orgs past day one though."

"Well, you guys vouched for her, so assuming she connects with the rest of the sisters, I don't see an issue with offering her membership if she's not interested in one of the traditional orgs."

"We have guests!" Raven calls out from the other room, the low chatter of the other women carrying through the house. I touch up my lip gloss in the hallway mirror, taking a few calming deep breaths. Gabby comes up behind me, patting me on the back. "Show time, Madame President."

I playfully roll my eyes. "Come on, let's meet the PNMs."

We head into the entryway of the house, looking at the group of about forty women standing in front of us. "Hi, everyone! Welcome to Kappa Theta Alpha. I know you're going to speak with a lot of women and sororities this week, so we're going to try to keep this brief and save more of the information about the organization for later in the week.

My name's Sage Carpenter and I am President of this chapter of Kappa Theta Alpha sorority. This is Maeve, our Vice President; Stephanie, our Secretary; Gabriella, but we call her Gabby, our Treasurer; and then last but not least, you all know Raven, our Recruitment Chair and Panhellenic Council delegate.

KTA is a smaller sorority. Our chapter here at Pinebrook has maybe thirty active members at any given time, and we have five thousand active members and alumni nationwide. Pinebrook is the home of KTA, it's where we were founded thirty years ago, but we have fifteen other chapters scattered around the northeast and midwest and two chapters in California. All of this to say, we do things a little differently around here. We try to foster a welcoming and inclusive sisterhood, and part of that is keeping our membership small.

If you guys choose to stick around, you'll see what we're about. There are some snacks and drinks in the kitchen if you're interested, with vegan, vegetarian, and allergen-friendly options. The sisters will be walking around to mingle with you all, and if you have any questions, just look for any of the executive board members. We all have pink name tags, the rest of the sisters have yellow. Enjoy!"

I step back, heading toward the stairs. I like watching over the upper floor railing during Rush. It gives me a bird's eye view of the interactions between sisters and PNMs and allows me to make my own observations

about the PNM's compatibilities before I meet them myself and talk with
the other sisters. Maeve joins me upstairs, watching the PNMs with me.

I scan the room, making mental notes of PNMs I want to talk to, and
that's when I see *her*. She was practically radiating as she spoke with Raven.
Her dark brown curls are voluminous, forming a halo, framing her face.
She wore a bright yellow, off-the-shoulder sundress, showing off her ample
cleavage and highlighting her curvaceous body. From this angle, I can't see
too much of the lower half of her body, but as she moves through the room
with Raven, I can tell there are thick thighs and thick legs hidden under the
skirt of that dress. I watch her converse with Raven and another one of our
sisters, Kelly. This woman lights up as she talks, her laugh carrying through
the room over the rest of the sound of conversation.

"Maeve, I am no better than a man."

"What makes you say that?" She chuckles, looking at me. I point toward the woman I was ogling. "That one? Total smoke show. Like she's
absolutely gorgeous."

Maeve's chuckling turns into a full-blown laugh. "Oh man, are you
serious? Sage, that's my roommate."

"Wait, your roommate? As in…"

"The super religious one that just transferred here? Yep, that's Naomi."

"Damn," I say, disappointed. I probably shouldn't be hitting on PNMs
anyway, especially ones that are considering joining my organization. It's
definitely an ethical grey area, and Maeve just made my moral dilemma a
lot easier for me.

"We should head down there. It's not polite for the president to ignore
the PNMs." She grabs my arm, pulling me toward the staircase. We head
down to the ground floor, mixing in with the crowd. I bounce from person
to person, joining the small groups that have congregated. I mainly stay
quiet, listening to the PNMs talk about themselves. A couple are eager to

learn about the sorority, so I answer their questions, fill them in on our organization's history, and tell my story of how and why I joined.

After an hour or so of mingling, Raven calls for everyone's attention. "Alright, time's up! If you're still open to rushing the other sororities, please come with me. Otherwise, you're welcome to continue mingling with the sisters of Kappa Theta Alpha and you can leave at any time," she calls out before heading out of the house. Most of the women follow her out, but a smaller group of seven women hang back, continuing to mingle with the sisters, including my newest obsession, Naomi.

I linger in the kitchen, snacking on some of the remaining appetizers, including the miniature version of my favorite veggie burger from Happy Sprout. "Man, I love these sliders," I mumble around a mouth full of food.

"I didn't get to try the sliders before, but I did love the pizza."

I jump a little, startled by the noise behind me.

"Sorry, didn't mean to startle you. I guess these shoes aren't as loud as I thought they were."

God, that voice. That accent. The voice is velvety soft and rich, warming me from head to toe. I turn toward the voice, and of course, it belongs to my lady love.

"Naomi, right? Maeve told me you were coming to rush today," I say, wiping my hand on my pants before holding it out. "Nice to meet you."

She takes my hand in hers, holding it in a light grip as she shakes my hand. "Nice to meet you, Sage."

I wish I had recorded that. I could listen to Naomi say my name over and over again on an endless loop.

"Nice to meet you too. So what do you think of the sorority?" I ask, crossing my arms across my chest and leaning back against the kitchen island.

"Y'all are really nice!" she drawls. "And you seem like you've made a nice community here too."

"Yeah, it was nice finding an organization that accepted me for who I was. You don't find too many women like me in sororities."

She squints her eyes toward me, trying to size me up. I've seen that look before. From teachers, parents of friends, and colleagues. It's the *what's wrong with you* face. And the answer varies depending on who's asking—gay, tattooed, neurodivergent, a foster kid—take your pick.

"What? Do you mean covered in tattoos?" she asks, her eyes roaming my body, taking in the many fine-line tattoos covering my arms and hands. She did have a point, I was covered in more ink than most of my peers, but she was incorrect.

"No, I mean gay. Many sororities still have a lot of work to do regarding their LGBTQ inclusiveness. It's a bit backward, in my opinion. An organization for women, but my interest in other women disqualifies me from membership? Pass."

"So is that how you ended up in Kappa Theta Alpha? It was the only sorority willing to accept you?"

I chuckle softly, shaking my head. "No, I actually received a bid from another sorority. The one that the girl I was seeing casually was in."

"How'd you end up here then?"

"Gabby, my roommate, joined Kappa Theta Alpha when we were freshmen, I accepted the bid from the other sorority. But things went sideways very quickly. Turns out the woman I was seeing wasn't out yet. So I let it slip to one of my new sisters that we were seeing each other, and she told someone else, who told someone else, who told the president, and it was a chain reaction. She got brought up on standards violations within the chapter and was ultimately blacklisted from their national organization. I then had my bid revoked and was blacklisted from rushing any of the other sororities on campus."

"Except KTA because they do things differently."

I wink at Naomi. "See, you're catching on. Since we do continuous open bidding, technically, anyone can rush our sorority at any time, assuming we haven't hit our membership quota yet. We always try to reserve one or two spots within our sorority for this purpose.

Once she was a fully initiated member that spring, Gabby fought for KTA to extend a bid to me during COB. Originally, they didn't want to. I mean, who would want to take on a blacklisted pledge? But once they found out why I was blacklisted, they offered me membership. They would've offered it to my ex too, but there were other hoops she had to jump through in order to join another organization, and she didn't do any of it.

I joined Kappa Theta Alpha that spring semester and I've been fighting the good fight ever since," I say jokingly.

"Wow... Well, that's their loss, then, because it seems like Kappa Theta Alpha hit the jackpot with you. Everyone that stayed wants to join your sorority from what I heard, even a couple of the girls that left to go to the other houses are still interested." Naomi sips her punch, checking her phone. "Shoot, I have to take off. I have a meeting with my academic advisor about my transfer status and degree progress. I'll hopefully see you the rest of the week?"

"You can count on it, Naomi. I hope you do decide to join KTA. We'd be happy to have you," I say, giving her shoulder a small squeeze as I walk her to the door.

"Bye, Sage," she says with a wave before heading out the door. I close it behind her, turning around to see Maeve and Gabby converging on me like hungry wolves.

"So...?" Gabby asks, bouncing with anticipation.

"Sage has a massive crush on her," Maeve answers before giving me a wink. As much as I'd like to deny it, I wear my heart on my sleeves, and both Gabby and Maeve know me well enough to know when I'm lying.

"Shut up, really? So does this mean she's in?" Gabby asks Maeve, completely forgetting about me standing right there.

"I think so. We still have to put it to a formal vote with the rest of the exec board, but I don't see why we can't offer her membership."

"My vote is yes," I chime in, reminding them of my presence.

"We know," they say in unison, heading back to mingle with the rest of the sorority and PNMs.

Maeve was right, though. I do have a big crush on Naomi, and I'm going to do everything I can to get her to want me too.

4

Naomi

There's a soft knock at my door, then a second, more forceful one right after. I roll over in bed toward the door, fully awakened. "Come in!"

Maeve pokes her head in, holding up a pale pink-colored envelope. "I believe this is for you." She holds it out to me, stepping into the room.

I throw the blankets off, sitting up in bed and taking the letter from her. "What's this?" I ask, turning the envelope over in my hands. It's the same shade of pink as the Kappa Theta Alpha colors, and my name is printed on the front in gold calligraphy. *Fancy.*

"Just open it," Maeve says, bouncing on her toes excitedly. I raise an eyebrow, watching her drink her coffee with already too much energy for the day. I open the envelope, taking the card out. It's equally as ornate as the envelope. The card is cream-colored with the Kappa Theta Alpha crest on the front and the sorority name in the same gold calligraphy underneath.

I open the card, skimming it quickly before reading it out loud for Maeve's satisfaction.

"Naomi, we've had an amazing time this week getting to know you and the rest of the interests. You embody the values that we hold close: Sisterhood, Leadership, Inclusivity and Charity. If you are interested, the members of Kappa Theta Alpha would love to extend an invitation for you to join our sisterhood."

Maeve tries to hide her mega-watt grin behind her hand. "So... Are you going to join us?"

I smile, grabbing one of my pillows and chucking it at her legs, avoiding her coffee mug. "You're so annoying. Yes, I would love to join your sorority."

"Yay! Okay, you have approximately...forty-two minutes to get yourself ready. Wear some kind of light-colored bottoms, like a lighter wash denim or white pants. Top doesn't matter though, we'll give you a T-shirt when you get to the house. Alex will drop you off. I have to be there in fifteen," she says, checking her watch.

I wasn't even paying attention to the fact that Maeve was already fully dressed. She had on a pair of distressed, light-washed, straight-leg jeans, a cropped, light yellow T-shirt with the Kappa letters across the chest in gold, and a pair of her white running sneakers. "You look cute. I'll see you in a little while."

Maeve smiles, leaving my room in a hurry. I get up, heading toward my closet and pulling out a pair of white, high-waisted skinny jeans and a plain grey T-shirt. I get dressed, putting on a pair of tan gladiator sandals along with my outfit. I take my bonnet off, letting my hair down. There were no rush events yesterday, so I managed to squeeze in an appointment at a braiding salon in Manhattan I found on social media.

It was pricey, but they did a fantastic job. I got Senegalese twists done, and they curled the ends and added gold clips and other charms to the braids. It was much different than the basic box braids I'm used to getting in Georgia, but I'm extremely pleased with how they came out.

I pull the front sections of twists back, using a gold claw clip to hold them in place. I keep my makeup simple, putting on some mascara, a peachy lip and cheek tint, and then a pinky-nude gloss. I put on my gold cross necklace and a few simple gold bracelets before grabbing my purse and heading into the living room.

Alex was waiting for me in the living room, dressed similarly to Maeve. She was wearing the same yellow Kappa T-shirt, tied up and knotted at the waist, with a pair of loose, white, split-leg pants and flip-flops. "Ready?"

I nod. "Is this okay to wear today? I know Maeve mentioned some kind of dress code."

"It's perfect. And I love your hair! I don't think I saw you last night when you go back from the city."

"I think I came back after you left for Matt's house." Matthew is Alex's current boyfriend. According to Maeve, she is a bit of a serial monogamist, always dating someone new, but Alex really seems to like this guy. And he is completely opposite her usual type, but maybe that's for the best. From what I've heard, Alex tends to date athletes, but Matthew is a total nerd. Don't get me wrong, he is equally as built as some of the student athletes on campus, but he works out for fun.

Matthew is a computer science major and an expert coder. He actually made a small fortune in high school from a Smart Home app that he created and sold to Philips. He's a tech and video game nerd through and through, but he Alex are so evenly matched with their laid-back mentalities and outgoing personalities.

"Ah, yeah, probably. I think I left around dinner time. Matt was doing a twenty-four-hour video game marathon charity stream yesterday, and it ended at seven. I went over there to cook him some food and clean his apartment because I knew he was going to crash hard."

"Aw, look at you. You're basically a whole wife already," I say jokingly.

Alex shoves me gently as we head out of the apartment. "What can I say? I really like him."

We got to the Kappa Theta Alpha house to see that the driveway was already full of cars and the yard full of women. Alex parked her car on the street outside the house before getting out. "Okay, you stay out here with the rest of the pledges, and I'll see you in a little bit," she says, leaving me to head into the house.

There were about ten of us hanging out in the front yard. "I think we might be their biggest pledge class in years," says a woman to my right. She holds her hand out to me. "I don't think we've met yet. I'm Penny! Well, Penelope, but no one on this planet other than my grandma calls me that."

I grip her hand lightly, shaking it. "Naomi. Nice to meet you."

"Oh, *you're* Naomi? They've been talking about you all week," she says, gesturing toward the house with her head. "You must have had some kind of an in, because rumor is, you were an automatic yes from Day One. Which says a lot. I mean, I'm a KTA legacy, and even I wasn't an automatic."

I tilt my head in confusion. "A KTA legacy...?"

"Oh my gosh, and you don't even know what a legacy is, how precious." Penny gives me a cloyingly sweet smile. "When you're a legacy, it just means that your parent attended the school or joined the organization before you. So my mom was a KTA sister at this very chapter twenty-one years ago."

I fight the frown forming on my face. *This girl is a piece of work.* "Ah, I see. I am not a legacy, but Maeve and Aleka are my roommates. They're the ones that convinced me to rush in the first place."

You could practically see the color drain from Penny's face. "You're roommates with Maeve. Like, the Vice President Maeve?"

"Yep!" I say, popping the P.

Penny scrambles to come up with some excuse or apology, but she's cut off by the sound of the front door opening. There stood Raven and Sage, also dressed in their yellow KTA T-shirts. Raven had cut hers into a tank top paired with some lightweight, tan cargo pants. Sage somehow turned hers into a tube top that laced up in the back, pairing it with a white tennis skirt. The outfit showed off all her tattoos, the dark ink contrasting against her pastel outfit.

"Hi, everyone, and welcome to Kappa Theta Alpha. If you're here, I assume that means that you've chosen to accept our invitation to join the sisterhood. We are delighted to have you. If you could follow us into the house, we're going to hold a brief ceremony first, and then bid day will be underway," Sage calls out, leading us into the house.

We head down the hall to a large room set up with a projector, a few rows of chairs and a table up front. "This is where we hold our weekly chapter meetings," Raven explains, gesturing for us all to take a seat, "though if we don't need the projector, sometimes we'll just gather around in the living room or kitchen."

"We do, however, use this room for all our membership rituals. The first of which being your pinning." Sage takes a wooden box from the table, opening it to reveal ten pins sitting in the velvet lining.

The pins were a gold cloud, maybe an inch long, with the Kappa Theta Alpha letters and four small gold stars, all on a pink background. She takes a moment to explain the symbolism of the pin, from the non-traditional shape to the four stars, which represent the core values of the sorority.

Sage hands out the pins with Raven's help, carefully instructing us not to put them on yet. She then begins the pinning ceremony, having us recite the vows of membership back to her as she reads them, line by line, in a call and response. Once done, she tells us to put the pins on.

"Congratulations. You are all now associate members or pledges of Kappa Theta Alpha. There's a membership intake process to go through before you are initiated as full members of KTA, but from now on, we consider you one of us. Raven will reach out in the coming week with all the information on the membership intake process."

"But now, you guys can head down the hallway and go to the backyard. There's plenty of sisters out there ready to congratulate you!"

We all file into the backyard to see a big group of Kappa Theta Alpha sisters gathered together under a big banner that says *Welcome Beta Nu class!* There were many more members present today than there were during Rush, maybe another ten or fifteen sisters? They all had matching yellow letter shirts, and some of the sisters were holding signs with names written on them and gift bags.

I scan the group to see Maeve and Alex waving at me, holding the sign with my name on it. I walk over to them and they engulf me in a massive group hug. "Welcome to the fam, Naomi!"

I hug them back. "Thanks, y'all!"

Maeve hands me the pink gift bag in her hands. "Open it!"

I take the pink gift bag from her, pulling out the tissue paper on top. In the bag is a light pink T-shirt similar to the one they are wearing. It has white Greek letters across the chest, with *Beta Nu* underneath. Also in the bag is a twelve-ounce metal tumbler sublimated with the sorority's letters in gold and a plush dove.

"A dove?" I ask curiously, lifting it from the bag.

"It's our animal. You learn more about the symbolism during your membership intake process," Alex says with a wave of her hand. "Now give me that and go change into your shirt. You can use one of the bathrooms in the house if you don't want to do it out here."

I give her an appreciative smile, heading into the house. On my way to the bathroom, I bump into a familiar tall blonde. "Oh, sorry, Sage."

She catches me by the waist, righting me before I stumble backward. "Naomi, hi. Congratulations again on joining Kappa Theta Alpha."

"Thank you for the invitation. Rumor has it that I was an automatic acceptance."

"I don't know about automatic, but you were definitely a favorite. Aleka and Maeve were pulling hard for you."

"They've been pretty good to me so far. I know they wanted me to have the quintessential college experience, and what better way to do that than join a sorority?"

"You've got a point there," Sage says, her hands still lightly gripping my sides.

"SAGE! Did you get lost?" a voice calls out from the backyard.

She steps back from me, dropping her hands at her side. "Right, I was on ice duty. Let me get that before they send a search party after me." Sage starts walking back toward the kitchen before turning.

"I'm glad you decided to join Kappa. I look forward to seeing you around," she says with a wink before heading off.

I make my way to the bathroom, locking the door behind me. I change out of my plain T-shirt and into the Kappa shirt, tucking the front into my jeans. I come out of the bathroom and almost bump into someone else. I look up from the shirt in my hands to see a woman a few years older standing before me.

"Sorry, I guess I should be more careful about watching where I'm going. You're the second person I've bumped into today."

She smiles, waving my apology off. "Don't worry about it. I was completely absorbed in my phone," she says, tucking the device into her back pocket. "My name's Theia. Nice to meet you."

I smile. "Naomi. Are you an alumni?"

Theia shakes her head, pauses, and then shrugs. "Kind of? I'm a PhD student here at Pinebrook. So I graduated and officially became an alumni three years ago, but I still hang around at the house and attend sorority events when I can."

"That's awesome! You must be really close with the current sisters then."

She laughs. "Yeah, though not entirely by choice. My younger sister is part of Kappa Theta Alpha too."

"Oh, who's your sister?"

"Sage."

My jaw drops. "Wait, you guys are sisters?" I ask, trying to process. I never would've guessed they were related, let alone sisters.

"I know, we don't look anything alike. Sage is my adopted sister."

"Ah, that makes more sense." Sage was a beach blonde, Malibu Barbie, and Theia might as well be Logan Browning's doppelganger.

"She spoke a lot about you this week."

"Really?"

She nods. "Yep. I think Sage has a bit of a girl crush on you. But don't tell her I told you that," she says, putting her finger to her lips.

I mime zipping my lips shut and throwing away the key. "Your secret's safe with me, Theia." I grin.

She smiles back at me, reaching out and lightly touching my elbow. "Let's grab a coffee soon, yeah? I'd love to sit down and get to know you."

"I'd like that," I say as Theia walks away.

I finally head back out into the backyard, beelining toward Maeve and Alex. Maeve has her phone out, taking photos. She takes a photo of me in my Kappa T-shirt before handing her phone to someone else and asking them to take a photo of the three of us. I stand in the middle, Alex and Maeve on either side of me, pushing in tight and pointing to the writing on my shirt.

We take another photo with them sandwiching me in the middle of a big group hug. This is what I longed for: genuine friendship. And I think I finally found it with my roommates, now sorority sisters.

5

Naomi

*C*lass dismissed.

I absolutely hated my Organizational Behavior professor. Imagine the most bored you've ever been, add in the somberness of a funeral and the joy of a colonoscopy, and now you know what it's like to sit through one of Professor Connors' classes. And of course, it's the one class I don't share with any of my new friends. I just keep my head down, do the work, and hope that the class passes quickly.

I gather up my notebook and laptop, packing my things away.

"Hey, Naomi, right?"

I turn, looking up to see a very, very handsome man. "Well, hello there. Yes, that's my name. Who are you?"

The man holds his hand out to me. "The name's Elijah. Nice to meet you." I take a moment to check him out, sizing him up. He's good looking, conventionally attractive. He has wavy blond hair, piercing blue eyes, and a smattering of light freckles across his cheeks and the bridge of his nose. Elijah is extremely tall, probably 6'4", and built. He's wearing a polo and jeans, but his clothes stretch across his body, muscles bulging underneath. He honestly looks like he stepped off the page of a Ralph Lauren ad.

"Nice to meet you, Elijah," I say, shaking his hand. "Can I help you with something?"

He smiles, shaking his head. "There's that southern hospitality. You have a really strong accent. It's cute."

I blush, shifting my bag on my shoulder. "Thank you, but why'd you approach me today? We haven't talked all semester."

"Well, you caught my eye a while ago. I've just been waiting for the right time to approach you."

"Oh, really?"

"Of course. You're beautiful, extremely smart, and I want to get to know you better. Maybe buy you coffee?" Elijah asks, leaning against the lecture hall table behind us.

I think it over for a moment before nodding. "I'd like that."

"Are you free right now? I've got about an hour or so before my next class."

"I was going to study at the Kappa house, but I can always study later. Let's do it."

He grins, standing up straight. We walk to the door of the lecture hall, Elijah holding the door open for me. "Well, thank you."

We take the ten-minute walk from the business program building to the coffee shop at the center of campus to make small talk about our classes. Turns out, Elijah is a double major in marketing and business analytics. He is majoring in business to prepare to take over his father's company. The position is his without the degree, but he wants to make sure he won't run the company into the ground. We have a lot of similarities in that sense.

We reach the busy coffee shop, squeezing into the small space. Elijah gets in the line to save our spot while I walk up to the counter, trying to get a better look at the menu.

I scan the list of unique drink names, trying to find something tea-based that looks interesting, when I spot a familiar name—Earth Matcha. That is Sage's favorite. She swears it's one of their best specialty drinks. And it's coffee-free.

I walk back to Elijah, pleased to see that the line has advanced a bit. Once we reach the register, we order an Earth Matcha for me and a boring iced coffee with a splash of cream for him.

We grab our drinks, heading outside to sit on a bench across the street at the Student Center.

"So you moved from Alabama, right?"

I shake my head. "Georgia."

"Georgia! I knew it was one of those deep south states. Why'd you move up to New York? That's a big change."

"It is. I was kicked out of my old school. I needed one willing to offer me a full scholarship as a transfer student, and Pinebrook University was the only school that would."

"Whoa, kicked out? What did you do? No, don't tell me. I bet I can figure it out." He thinks for a few minutes, observing me. I smirk, knowing there's no way he'll guess correctly.

"I got it. You're secretly a pyro. You 'accidentally' set fire to the science building. Bunsen burner accident."

I laugh. "What about me screams pyromaniac? Or makes you think that I've ever used a Bunsen burner? I'm a business major."

Elijah laughs with me. "Well, we all have to take an intro science course for core foundations credits. Who knows, maybe yours was a chemistry class?"

"Nope. I took a botany course. I like flowers." I say, being careful not to reveal too much.

"So, no to the firebug charge?"

I shake my head. "Definitely not, Big Guy," I say, bumping him with my shoulder.

"Well then, tell me, Sunny, what did you do to get kicked out of school?"

I look around dramatically, feigning like I'm about to share a big secret. Then I lean in to whisper in Elijah's ear. "I was caught studying in my ex-boyfriend's dorm room. With the door open."

Elijah's eyes go wide, and then he freezes, his brow furrowed in confusion. I can almost hear his brain short-circuiting as he tries to process what I just told him. "What?" is all he manages to get out.

I laugh as he tries and fails to make sense of it all. "I was kicked out of High Valley University. We were not allowed anywhere but the common rooms of opposite-sex dorms. I wasn't allowed to be in his room. And they gave me a choice: apologize and go through counseling, or leave."

"And you told them to fuck off and came here?"

"Something like that, yeah," I say softly.

"And your boyfriend? What did he do?"

"Ex-boyfriend," I say, emphasizing *ex*.

"He decided to go through with the punishment. Tried to tell me that I should just go along with it as well. Since that was the 'godly woman' thing to do. To stand by my man and submit to his guidance." I roll my eyes, annoyed by the memory.

"Brutal. So I guess that means you're back on the market?"

"I don't know if I was ever really off. Josiah and I were essentially an arranged marriage. Our parents' plan was for us to get married when we graduated. They were grooming us to take over the church's operations."

"Well, now, what do you want to do?"

"I'm not sure. I'm majoring in Global Management. I don't think I want to work with a mission organization, but I do love the idea of continuing some kind of non-profit work."

"A noble calling."

I shrug. "Charity is one of the seven virtues. It's how I was raised."

Elijah smiles. "I can respect that. You've gotta stay true to your values."

He checks his watch, standing up. "Shoot, I have to get going for my next class. I'd love to see you again though."

"Likewise. Here, give me your number," I say, pulling up my contacts app and handing my phone over to Elijah. He does the same, passing his phone to me. I enter my phone number, putting my name as *Sunny* before handing it back to him.

Elijah smirks, likely reading the contact entry. "See you later, Naomi," he says, heading back toward the academic buildings.

I check my phone as I head toward sorority row, laughing when I see Elijah's number is saved under *Big Guy*. Clearly, he had the same idea as me.

After a short walk, I reach the Kappa Theta Alpha house. I head inside, going into the kitchen to rummage for a snack. I find some apple cinnamon muffins in a container on the counter. Not seeing a note indicating that they're for someone specific, I grab one.

I sit at the kitchen table, opting to spread out in here instead of going to the study room. The KTA house has a large room called the Quiet Room, which we use to study.

It's a sound-proofed room on the main floor of the house, with a large table in the center, a monitor for presentations, and desktops around the perimeter of the room. It's a great place to study if you need complete silence, but I hate the isolation. So I usually just sit in the kitchen, throw on my noise-canceling headphones, and hope for the best.

I was sitting, working on today's assignment from my Organizational Behavior class, when I started hearing shouting, even cutting through the music playing on my headphones.

I pause my music, take my headphones off, and close my laptop, curious about the commotion in the other room.

"Aaron, I told you I'm getting my PhD. I was making great progress with my advisor on one of her papers, and I want to continue working with her."

"Theia, you don't have to do your PhD. Come back to Jersey with me. I'm making great money. You don't have to work. You can just stay at home."

"I don't want to stay at home! What part of that are you not getting? This is what I want to do."

"Don't you dare raise your voice to me! Maybe you need to come home after all since you seem to have forgotten your place."

"My place? Aaron, a relationship is supposed to be a partnership, not a dictatorship. I'm not going to just bend to your will and follow orders from you. I'm a grown woman. I can make my own life choices."

"Do you have any idea how this makes me look? Being back at home while my girlfriend is off frolicking somewhere else, doing who knows what. For all I know, you could be hooking up with someone here. Maybe that's why you don't want to leave."

She gasps. "How dare you accuse me of cheating? That's your MO, Aaron, not mine. Or have you already forgotten about Jessica?" She turns to walk away, but the guy, Aaron, grabs her forearm tight, stopping her in her tracks and pulling Theia close to him.

"Ow! Let go, Aaron, you're hurting me," she says, but that just seems to encourage him as he squeezes tighter.

"How many fucking times do I have to say I'm sorry before you drop it?" he hisses, his face close to hers.

"Then don't accuse me of cheating on you! If I wanted to get back at you for what you did, I would've done it last year when I found out."

"Isn't that what you're doing now in your own little way? Punishing me by staying away from home for this stupid little degree?"

Theia tries to pull herself free from Aaron, but his grip on her arm is relentless. "It has nothing to do with you. I'm doing this for me, regardless of how you feel about it."

He raises a hand as if he's going to strike her and that's when I step in. "Hey, Theia, I need a favor from—oh, sorry." I stop mid-sentence, feigning like I didn't realize I was interrupting. Aaron's grip loosens and Theia takes the opportunity to free herself from his hold.

"That's alright, he was just leaving. Right, Aaron?" She shoots daggers at him, and he takes the hint, his eyes narrowing.

"Sure. We're not done talking about this though," he says, grabbing his keys and heading out the front door of the sorority house, slamming it behind him.

Theia lets out a large sigh of relief, cradling her arm to her chest and rubbing her forearm to soothe the ache. There are already red marks from Aaron's grip.

"Naomi, right? What did you need?" she asks, turning toward me.

"Are you okay, Theia? Are you...safe?" I ask hesitantly. We didn't know each other well at all, but I'd seen abusive men before, and Aaron was a field of red flags. Plus, we were sorority sisters now, and I felt like I should check in.

She sighs again, this time completely deflating as she sits down on the couch. I tentatively take a seat next to her and look over to see her blinking back tears.

"Yes... No... I think so? I don't think he was actually going to hit me. Aaron's usually not like this, I promise. Things have just been tough for us since I decided to stay here," she says softly, barely above a whisper.

"Aaron went to Pinebrook too?"

She nods. "Yep. We met at a sorority fraternity mixer when we were juniors. It was a 'famous duos' theme, and every KTA member was assigned a fraternity brother as their partner and one-half of the duo to dress up as. Except we weren't told who our partners were. So we just showed up and had to find out who we matched with. It was kind of like a blind date on steroids. But Aaron was the SpongeBob to my Patrick. Went on a few dates after and we've been together ever since."

"Weren't you initiated seven years ago? He just graduated?"

"I joined KTA as a freshman. Aaron and I graduated with our bachelors three years ago. I took a year off to travel and do some research in South America with one of my undergrad professors who was on sabbatical. Aaron went straight into law school. He just finished his JD in May. I finished my Masters in Biology."

"So when he graduated and got a job, he thought you were just going to come home?"

Theia nods. "Apparently so. I thought he would get over it once he started his law firm job in New York City, but he freaked out when he realized I came back. Today was the first time he was able to drive up to campus and see me in person. I've been dodging his calls this past week," she says sheepishly.

"Theia, you shouldn't be afraid to talk to him. That's not a relation-ship..." I say softly, looking at the marks darkening on her arm. "Let me get you some ice for that."

I get up from the couch, heading into the kitchen. Theia follows me quietly, taking a seat at the island in the kitchen. I open the freezer drawer, reaching in to grab a medium-sized ice pack for her. I wrap it in a dish towel before handing it over.

"Thanks," she says, giving me a small smile and wrapping the ice pack around her arm.

"Theia, does Sage...know? About what Aaron's been doing?"

She shakes her head adamantly. "No, absolutely not. And she *can't* know," she says pointedly.

"Theia, you need to tell someone. Other than me, I mean."

"I can't tell Sage. You can't tell Sage."

"Why not?"

"Because she'll tell our parents! And I can't have them worrying about me. Not about this... They love Aaron," she murmurs.

"You think they wouldn't believe you—" She holds a hand up to silence me.

"Naomi, I know you mean well, but can you drop it? Please?"

I want to continue pushing the issue, but the look of desperation on Theia's face stops me in my tracks. She looks so scared, terrified even. She needs help, but it's not my secret to share.

I nod, giving Theia half a smile, before grabbing a piece of paper and scribbling my number down. "If you need anything, anything at all, no matter the time or place, call me, please. But I promise. Your secret's safe with me."

For now...

—

6

Naomi

Raven

Hope you don't have plans for tonight! Tonight, we're going out for some sister bonding. Just your class and a handful of the sisters.

Sage

Meet us at the house at 7:00PM sharp.

Jk. But, if you're not at the house by 7:30, we will leave you behind and you'll have to find your own ride there.

Raven

> **Dress code is Dress to Impress**

Sage

> **No dress code is Vegas Club Wear.**

Maeve

> **Since you guys can't make up your mind, wear what's comfortable for you and what you would wear to party in.**

Sage

> **What she said.**

I have a couple of hours to get ready before I have to meet at the Kappa Theta Alpha house. I go to my closet and look through the options before quickly realizing that none of them fit what Maeve suggested. "Alex!"

My roommate comes running, poking her head into my room. "Is everything alright, Naomi?"

"You know about this sister bonding night, yes?"

She nods.

"So you must know the 'dress code' then? I have nothing that fits into that description."

Alex steps into my room. "Are you asking me for what I think you're asking me for?"

I sigh, flopping onto my bed. "I need you to take me shopping."

Alex cheers. "Yes! I've been waiting for this since you moved in."

"Really?"

"Absolutely! Naomi, I love you, but you dress like my grandmother. You have a bangin' body, but your clothes aren't doing you any favors."

I playfully roll my eyes, but Alex was right. Almost everything I own was picked out by my mother at some point. "Well, we've got a couple hours before I have to be at the Kappa house. We are going to the mall and I am giving you free rein to put together five outfits for me."

Alex was practically vibrating at this point, bouncing up and down because she was so excited. "Alright, I can be ready to go in fifteen minutes," she says, running out of the room.

I laugh to myself, getting up to get dressed. I throw on a pair of green joggers, a white T-shirt, and a pair of running sneakers. I grab my crossbody bag and sling it across my chest, throwing my twists into a ponytail. I meet Alex in the living room and we walk out to her car, heading to the mall.

"Come on, Naomi, let me see!"

"This was a mistake, giving you free rein. I feel naked."

"You're being dramatic, come on out!"

This was the fourth store we've stopped at, and everything has been way out of my comfort zone. Alex convinced me to buy two outfits: a pink, satin, midi-length shift dress, a pair of navy paper bag pants, and a low-back yellow halter top. Everything else though has been too revealing for my personal comfort, and even that halter top was pushing it.

For instance, the outfit Alex had me in now—a short, high-waisted, medium-wash denim skirt and a sheer, strapless, black, lace body suit. The cups of the bodysuit were lined, thankfully, but between the boning and low neckline, this outfit left very little to the imagination. I take a deep breath, stepping out of the dressing room stall to show Alex. "That's cute!"

I look in the mirror, tugging at the hem of the skirt, knowing full well I can't pull it down any further. "I'm uncomfortable," I grumble.

"What part of it makes you uncomfortable? The body suit? The skirt?"

"Both."

Alex thinks for a second. "Try the pants with this bodysuit."

"Which ones? The brown leather or the black ones?"

"Brown. Those are the straight-leg ones, right?" I nod. "Then yes, those."

I turn and go back into the dressing room, quickly shedding the skirt and putting on the brown leather pants. This pairing was actually really cute. And now that I had full-length pants on, I didn't feel so exposed anymore. I walk back out of the stall, turning around for Alex.

"Better?" she asks, with a small, smug grin on her face.

"Much."

"So, for you, stay away from short skirts, but you're willing to take risks with the top? Got it. Don't bother trying on the other stuff I gave you. I'll be right back," she says, heading back into the store.

I wait for a few minutes before she comes back with a new top, and a new outfit entirely. "Okay, try this top with the black leather pants, and then this outfit I think you'll like."

And Alex was right. These two outfits knocked it right out of the park. Using the skinny-fit, black leather pants I already had in the dressing room with me and paired them with a cropped, puff-sleeve polka-dot top that ties in the back. The last outfit was more casual: a short-sleeved, mint-colored button-down and heavily distressed boyfriend jeans. Finally, we found the five outfits we came here for, and it only took two and a half hours.

After checking out at this store, we head home. Shopping took much longer than I thought it was going to, so we were cutting close if I wanted to have enough time to change and do my makeup before heading over to the sorority house.

Once we reach our apartment, I head to my room, throwing the shopping bags. I grab the strapless, black, lace bodysuit and brown leather pants from the bag, changing out of my lounge clothes and into the outfit. Then, I quickly do my makeup, adding a winged black liner and deep red lipstick to my usual mascara and cheek tint. I put a few gold cuffs in my twists before grabbing my small, black leather crossbody, slipping on a pair of black leather pumps, and heading out.

Alex drives me to the Kappa Theta Alpha house. She wasn't joining us tonight, but the sorority house was on her way to her boyfriend's place. I thank her for the ride before heading inside the house.

"Damn, Naomi, that outfit is fire!" my pledge sister Kaylee calls out. I head into the kitchen where everyone's gathered, waiting to head out.

Maeve's jaw drops, seeing my outfit. "Alex convinced you to let her take you shopping, didn't she?"

I laugh, fidgeting with my hands a bit. "I actually asked her to. I realized I didn't have anything that fit the dress code."

"Well, I think you look amazing," Sage says from behind me, startling me. She comes around me into the kitchen.

"Back at you!" She looked stunning, as always. Sage was wearing a pair of black leather shorts, a red satin blazer with the sleeves pushed up, and a black bra top underneath, with over-the-knee black boots. I wish I had half the confidence she did.

"Okay, is everyone here and ready?" Maeve asks, looking around. It looks like it'll just be the Beta Nu Class, Maeve, Raven, Sage, Theia, and Stephanie tonight.

Sage nods. "I think we're just waiting on our ride at this point."

"Ride?"

Raven grins. "Yep, our ride. You guys didn't think we were just going to carpool to our destination, right? We said dress to party, and we don't want anyone to worry about driving home tonight."

"Don't feel any pressure to drink if you don't want to though. I'm not drinking and I think Theia's staying sober tonight too," Stephanie chimes in.

Theia nods in agreement. "I'm actually going to drive myself there, so if anyone needs to leave early for any reason, there will be alternate transportation available."

"Technically, Kappa policy is not to drink in letters and not to sponsor alcohol-related events. The focus of tonight is *not* drinking, our event for tonight just happens to take place at a bar. So by all means, drink, don't drink—just let loose and enjoy yourself," Sage says, looking around at our group.

A hand shoots up, and of course it belongs to Pain-In-the-Butt Penny.

"You don't have to raise your hand, Penny."

She lowers it before speaking. "You guys still haven't told us what we're doing tonight."

Sage and Raven look at each other, seemingly communicating telepathically. "I guess at this point, we can tell them what we're doing," Sage says.

"We are going to a bar! There's a drag show happening at one of our favorite bars tonight, and we figured it's the perfect way to let loose. We get to see the show, dance a bit, have some drinks and food, and spend time together as sisters."

Maeve steps in close to me. "You're okay with this, right? Going to a drag show, I mean," she murmurs under her breath.

I shrug. "I think so? I've never been to one before," I whisper back.

"Do you know what drag is?"

"Like RuPaul's Drag Race, right? Never watched the show, but I've seen commercials, so I think I've got the gist."

"Good. And if you ever feel uncomfortable, let Stephanie or Theia know, and they'll get you back to the apartment."

"I think I'll be okay, but thank you for looking out for me, Maeve." She leans in, giving me a small side hug.

There's a loud honk from the street outside the house.

"And I believe that's our ride!" Sage declares, ushering us all out into the front yard.

I follow the crowd, heading outside to see a party bus parked on the street in front of the house.

"Surprise!"

"All this for us?"

"Y'all will quickly learn KTA is over the top in the best way possible."

We all make our way onto the bus, taking seats on the benches along the perimeter. There was a bar set up near the front and two poles in the middle of the bus. I end up sandwiched between Sage and Raven on the bench at the end of the bus .

While the bus is still parked, Maeve rounds the bus with a platter of clear shots, passing them out to each of us. "They're tequila shots. If you want something else or just want water, let me know."

Once everyone's settled with their cups, Sage raises hers. "I'd like to propose a toast. Don't worry. This will be the only time tonight I get sappy. I'm not an emotional drunk." She laughs. "To the Beta Nu class. Each of you women are wonderfully unique and inspiring in your own way, and we're so lucky to have you in this organization."

"To Beta Nu!" Raven cheers, downing her shot. We all follow suit, downing our shots. The bus pulls out, the driver blasting music over the speakers. Based on the song selection, I'd take a guess and say one of the sisters had their phones hooked up to the bus sound system.

After a couple more drinks and almost a dozen songs later, we pull up to the bar. Now, I understand why they decided we'd all take the party bus tonight. This bar was in the city, about forty-five minutes from campus. While Pinebrook University was a small school with a fairly large campus, the town it's situated in has nothing. Usually, if you want to do anything besides going to frat parties or bowling, you have to travel a little bit.

We all head into the club, one of the doormen escorting us to the booth that the sorority had reserved. We all crowd in, and again, I end up next to Sage, this time between her and Maeve. A waitress comes by and takes our drink orders. It looks like we still managed to get to the club early because the drag queen still hasn't started her performance yet.

"Hey, you guys should be able to leave and re-enter without having to stand in line until the end of the drag show, so if y'all are hungry, the taqueria next door is open until like four AM," Stephanie states.

Sage shifts next to me as she takes off her blazer, laying it over the back of the booth seat. Sage's left side is pressed close to me, her full-sleeve tattoo on display.

"I like your tattoos," I say, leaning in close to Sage, trying to talk over the sound of the music playing.

She grins, leaning in too. "Thanks, Naomi. Can I just say again you look amazing? Like seriously, that outfit compliments you so well."

I blush a little. "Thanks. It's a little more exposed than I'm used to, but I needed to try something new." I tug up on my body suit, trying to pull up the low neckline.

"I'll keep an eye out, let you know if anything's too exposed," she says, nudging me with her elbow.

"Thank you."

Our drinks arrive right as the drag show begins. I grab my Tequila Sunrise before heading over to the makeshift 'stage,' which was just a sectioned-off part of the dance floor. We gather around, watching the drag queen, Rachel Tension, come out and put on a show, doing her performance to a medley of Doja Cat songs.

She makes her way up to a little platform near the DJ booth, dancing along. She points to Sage and me, motioning for us to join her on the platform.

"Me? Oh no. I can't," I say, shaking my head.

"Come on, Naomi. It'll be fun, let's carpe diem this bitch!" Sage shouts, grabbing my hand and pulling me with her. We climb onto the platform as well, crowding in with Ms. Tension. The three of us dance together, Sage pressed against my back and Rachel Tension behind her.

Our sorority sisters cheer us on from the dance floor. "Go, Sage! Go, Naomi! Go, Sage! Go, Naomi!" I could feel the bass of the music pulsing through my body, and as much as I wanted to get lost in the moment, I couldn't get out of my head.

I feel so anxious on this platform. This outfit isn't me, clubbing isn't me, and being up here isn't me. My heart gradually begins racing, the blood pounding in my ears drowning out the bass of the speakers on the platform next to us. My skin begins to crawl, and suddenly, my bodysuit feels too restrictive.

Once the song finally ends, I bolt from the DJ platform, heading straight for the front door. Once outside, I lean against the exterior of the building, bracing myself on the wall. I gulp down the fresh air, trying to catch my breath. I rub my hands on the wall behind me, the brick cutting into my palms, into my fingers, grounding me back in the moment. My heart rate begins to slow, but I still can't hear anything. Everything sounds so muffled at the moment.

I've had only a handful of these episodes before, all within the last year, during everything that happened at High Valley. The last one? When I told my parents I was accepted to Pinebrook University and I would be moving to New York.

I mentioned something about these episodes to my grandmother, she said it could be anxiety, that my mama dealt with something similar when she was younger. She suggested I should see someone about it, but when I tried to bring it up to my parents, my daddy just said I should pray on it.

Normally, I'm okay with managing my stress, but every once in a while, I get extremely overwhelmed. Like today...

I feel a hand grab my arm, jolting me out of my thoughts. I look up to see Sage outside with me, her brow furrowed with concern.

"Hey, are you okay, Naomi? You bolted out of there pretty quickly."

I take a deep breath, centering myself, before answering, "Hey, Sage, sorry about that. I'm fine, I was just—"

"Having a panic attack?" she finishes for me, giving me a sympathetic smile. "My roommate Cora gets those from time to time too."

I bite my lip, nodding. "Yeah, I just—I just needed to get out of there and get some fresh air."

Sage holds her arms out. "Is it okay if I give you a hug right now?" I step into her arms, wrapping mine around her waist. She squeezes me tight, resting her cheek against the top of my head. "I'm sorry for pulling you up there with me. Next time I'll check in with you before I just force you out of your comfort zone."

"Thanks for checking on me, Sage," I say after a moment, muffled since my face is buried in her chest.

"Of course, my Georgia peach, that's what sorority sisters are for! Now are you good to head back inside, or do you want to hang out here for a little longer?" she asks me, leaning away just a bit so that she can look me in the eye.

"I think I'm okay." I pull away, taking a tissue out of my purse to dab under my eyes.

"Awesome, because the drag show is over and I can already hear them playing my song," Sage says, doing a little salsa dance and eliciting a laugh out of me. She throws her arm around my shoulders as we walk back into the club to join the rest of our sorority.

7

Sage

After I checked on Naomi and made sure she was alright, we both had made our way back into the club. She was currently dancing her heart out on the dance floor with Maeve, and I was sitting next to Theia back in our booth. *God, my feet are killing me.* As cute as these boots were, I always forgot they are horrible for going dancing in. They didn't have as much cushion and support in the soles as I needed, and they trapped the sweat from my feet and ankles. I was taking a moment to give them a break before my ankles swelled, because then, I would be done for the night.

Theia's phone pings for what seems like the billionth time and I glance over to see Aaron's name flash across her screen before she quickly clears the notification. Aaron is her fuck knuckle of a boyfriend, and lately, he's been getting a bit too possessive and controlling for my liking. "Is that Aaron blowing up your phone right now? What does that asshole want?"

She tenses but tries to play it off with a roll of her eyes. "You know how men are, he's just trying to make sure that I'm safe tonight."

I look her straight in the eyes. "No, no, I don't know 'how men are.' I'm gay as fuck, remember?" I say with a laugh.

Theia laughs too, some of the tension releasing from her body as her shoulders come down from her ears a bit. "Right, silly me. He's just still adjusting to this whole long-distance relationship dynamic."

Now it was my turn to roll my eyes. I snort. "Yeah, two hours is so long distance. One and a half if he comes straight from work."

Theia playfully shoves me. "You know what I mean. This is the first time in the almost six years we've been together that we haven't been in the same city together. He's not used to it yet."

Her phone buzzes again, and this time, Aaron is calling her, but she declines the call.

"What about your gap year in Costa Rica? You guys weren't together then."

"Yeah, but this is different. He was busy with law school then and I was quite literally unreachable by phone unless you had the compound's satellite phone number, which I did not give him."

"So then why doesn't he just live with you and commute from campus?"

Theia shrugs. "Your guess is as good as mine. I don't think he wants that long of a commute. Either that or he's still hoping I'll change my mind about the PhD program and come back to Jersey with him."

Her phone buzzes again with yet another call from Aaron, and I grab it, having had enough of the harassment. I decline the call for Theia and power her phone off, silencing all further notifications.

"Sage! What did you do that for?" Theia asks incredulously, her eyes wide in surprise.

"The non-stop buzzing was irritating me. But now you can enjoy yourself." I stand, holding my hand out to her. "You coming, Sis?"

She shakes her head, laughing to herself as she takes my hand, pulling herself up to stand. "You're crazy, you know that?"

"And you love me for it!" I reply, heading to join Naomi and Maeve on the dance floor. We take turns, alternating between dancing with the sisters near the DJ booth and heading to the bar for drink refills. Now that the drag show was over and it was approaching midnight, the club was packed. Thankfully we still had our booth, but it was getting harder and harder to track down our waitress for drink orders.

I had all but given up and decided to just come straight to the bar myself. Thankfully, I'm extremely tall, and with these boots on, I easily exceeded six feet. I had no problem making eye contact with one of the bartenders over the crowd of people that's formed around the bar, signaling to him for two more. I had switched to Vodka Sprites once the crowd started filtering in, so he was able to make them quickly, sliding them off to the side close to the back of the bar. I grab the cups, bumping fists with the bartender and sliding him a twenty, telling him to keep the change.

As I make my way back toward the girls, I see a familiar head of blonde hair making its way through the crowd from the entrance. *Oh fuck, fuck, fuck, he's here. How the fuck did he know where we were?* I pick up my pace, reaching Theia and Naomi quickly, passing Naomi one of the Vodka Sprites. "Theia, don't freak out, but Aaron's here, and I'm guessing he's looking for you."

Theia does in fact freak out, her eyes going wide and her chest heaving as her heart begins to race. "How the hell did he find out we were here?"

"You didn't tell him?"

"No, I specifically left that out. I just told him I was going out tonight with the sorority for bonding with the newbies."

Aaron spots me and then Theia, his eyes narrowing. He is *pissed*. His face is mottled, various shades of red, and that vein in his forehead is bulging as he stomps over to us. "Theia, what the fuck? Why is your phone going straight to voicemail?"

Theia grimaces. "Not here, Aaron, we can talk about this later. Just please go."

"No! And what the hell are you wearing? I thought this was just 'bonding with the girls,' so why are you dressed like a cheap whore?"

I gasp, taken aback by how my sister's boyfriend speaks to her. "You have no right talking to Theia this way!"

He gets into my face, the two of us eye to eye with me in my heels, and I can smell the alcohol on his breath. "What the fuck, did you drive here drunk?" I ask, my tone dripping with disgust.

"Stay out of this, you stupid bitch," he growls. I pull back to really let him have it, but I feel a pair of hands on my wrists, holding me back.

"Sage, don't, it's not worth it. I'll talk to him," Theia says, pleading with me with her eyes. I step back, nodding, giving her space.

"Don't cause a scene," she says to Aaron through clenched teeth.

"We're fucking leaving," he demands, grabbing her wrist tight and pulling her, practically dragging her out of the club with him. I go to follow them, and Maeve stops me. "Sage..." she warns.

"I'm not going to do anything, I'm just going to make sure my sister is okay," I say, shrugging her off and heading toward the exit. I haven't even made it outside yet and I can already hear their screaming match.

"Aaron, you can't just show up here like this!"

"You stupid bitch, I wouldn't have come if you picked up the phone when I called you!"

"I should be able to have a night out with my sister and friends without having to be at your beck and call!"

"I'm sure you'd like that. I bet you would've gone home with someone tonight if I hadn't shown up. Dressed like a slut!"

"I'm just wearing clothes, Aaron, for Christ's sake! God, when did you become so insecure? Just because I went out dancing doesn't mean I'm trying to pick up anyone tonight. I'm with you!"

"Then fucking act like it! Come home, and stop with all this nonsense."

"Are we back on this shit again? I don't know how many other ways I can tell you I'm not dropping out of the program."

"If you really loved me, you wouldn't make me do long-distance!"

"It's not about you! I'm doing the PhD program for me because it's what *I* want! I'm sorry your small dick ego can't handle that."

And that's when I hear it, a sharp *crack* sound. I round the corner to see Theia cowering away from Aaron, holding her face, and him still standing over her with his arm raised.

"Get the fuck out of here, Aaron!"

He turns on me now. "Stay out of this, Sage!"

"Hey, asshat, you have two options. You can either leave of your own free will and stay the fuck away from my sister, or I can call the cops on you. Choice is yours," I say, crossing my arms.

He glares at me, but once he notices I'm not backing down, he scoffs. "God, you're such a bitch, Sage. Go to hell!" He retreats down the alley, presumably toward where he parked his car.

"I'll meet you down there, fuckwit!" I shout after him, giving him a double middle finger to his back. A loud sniffle from behind me turns my attention back to Theia, and I turn to see her leaning against the brick exterior of the club, sobbing into her hands.

"The, are you okay? Did he hit you?" I ask, walking back over to her. She nods from behind her hands, unable to say the words. My heart shatters seeing how broken she looks. I pull her into my arms, wrapping my arms tight around her. "Theia, I'm so, so sorry. I should've stayed with you." I hold onto her, rubbing soothing circles into her back, letting her cry it out.

Naomi, Maeve, and a couple sisters round the corner and stop in their tracks once they see us. Naomi steps toward us, concern etched on her face. "I've got her, you guys just head back in."

"They actually just did an announcement for last call. We came to see if you guys wanted anything or if you were ready to leave."

"If you guys are ready to leave, you can head back without us. We're going to take Theia's car back when she's ready."

"Are you sure?" Maeve asks. "We can wait for you guys and come back for her car in the morning."

I nod. "I'm positive. I'll text you guys when we make it back to Pinebrook," I say, still rubbing Theia's back.

Naomi gives me a small smile and gently squeezes my arm. "Let me know if you two need anything, Sage. I'm praying for Theia."

"Thanks, Naomi," I say softly as they all take off, heading toward the party bus.

After a bit, Theia's sobs subside. The only sound coming from her now is a soft sniffle. "Come on, Theia, let's get you some water and ice."

We head back into the club to find a lot of people clearing out. Perfect. I walk Theia over to the bar, taking a seat on one of the stools.

"Sage, you know we're closing. You missed last call," one of the bartenders says to me. Thankfully, I know him. Dominic graduated from Pinebrook two years ago, the year after Theia. He was actually my orientation leader when I was a freshman, and we stayed in touch through the years. He was the one to introduce me to this bar since they threw a lot of queer-friendly events.

"Dom, we're not trying to buy drinks. Theia's been through it tonight. We just need waters. And maybe a clean towel with ice in it?" I ask him, giving my best puppy dog eyes.

"Jeez, what happened?" he asks, eyeing Theia as he pours some water for us and grabs a clean towel from one of the cupboards behind the bar.

"Something that never should have happened," I murmur, turning to my sister and lifting her chin so I could get a good look at her face. Her cheek was extremely red, already beginning to swell a bit. She averts her gaze, chewing on her bottom lip.

"Shit." I take the makeshift ice pack from Dom and gently press it to Theia's cheek, holding it in place. She takes the ice pack from me, holding it herself and looking down at the bar. She couldn't even look me in the eye.

"Theia," I say softly, "we need to talk about what happened."

She shakes her head.

"Yes, we do. Has he done this before? Hit you, I mean?" I ask, keeping my voice low.

Theia shakes her head again.

"How long have things been this bad? With the shouting matches, I mean? How did he even find you here?"

"He tagged my car," she says in a small voice, barely above a whisper.

"He what?"

"Last time he visited. We got into a big fight about me staying at Pinebrook. Before he left, he put a Tile tracker under the mat in the backseat of my car."

"He's been stalking your location?"

"Apparently, for a couple weeks now."

"Theia... That's not healthy or safe for you if tonight's any indication."

"I–I don't know what happened. This isn't like him. The screaming matches, raising a hand to me, driving drunk? That's not Aaron. I think the stress of the new job is getting to him."

I look at her incredulously. "You cannot seriously be making excuses for him right now? He just assaulted you, Theia!"

"I know what it looks like, but I don't think he meant to do it. He loves me."

"Theia, that's not what love looks like. He put his hands on you."

She wipes her eyes, trying to compose herself. "I'm not going make any decisions tonight. I'm going to sleep on it, give him some time to sober up and think about what he did, and then I'll talk to him another day."

I sigh. "Theia, don't do this."

"Sage, we've been together for almost six years, and this is the first time he's done *anything* like this. I think I owe it to us, owe it to myself not to do anything rash. Maybe if I talk to him, I can convince him to see someone. We can do couples counseling. I can't just give up on the history we share."

"Theia, just promise me. If he so much as raises his voice at you, degrades you or raises a hand to you, you will leave."

She pauses, chewing her lip.

"Theia!"

"Alright, alright. I promise," she says, holding her pinky up. I link my pinky with hers, kissing my thumb as she kisses hers. It's the pinky promise she taught me when I was first placed with her family, and we reserve it for only the most serious of promises. "I won't let Aaron hurt me again."

8

Sage

I enter the sorority house armed with multiple bags of goodies. While I don't live in the Kappa house (despite tradition), I do have a set of keys to the house, as do the rest of the executive board. The front door has a numerical keypad, and every member gets the code. All members have twenty-four-seven access to the house, but certain spaces are locked at all times. The basement being one of them. We mainly use the space as storage for all our rush supplies, but there are also a few other items and appliances down there, including the target of my focus—the large, industrial-sized sink.

As I walk through the house, I notice Naomi sitting at the dining room table with her roommate, Maeve. She flips through the textbook in front of her, chewing on the end of her pen in concentration. *She's so cute.*

"Hey, Naomi, looking to take a break? I could use a spare set of hands right now," I ask, giving her a wide smile. *Could I do this on my own? Absolutely. Am I taking every chance I can get to spend one-on-one time with the gorgeous woman in front of me? Yes, I am.*

She looks up, returning my smile before closing her textbook and leaving her pen to save her place. "I've been working on this assignment for a couple hours now. I can afford to take a little breather." Naomi stands, walking toward me.

This woman is effortlessly beautiful. Even with her hair up in a curly top knot, glasses on, wearing an oversized T-shirt and leggings, she still looks every ounce as beautiful as she did all done up at Rush. "What do you need help with, Sage?"

A small shiver runs through my body, hearing my name on her lips. *God, I wonder what it would sound like to hear her moan my name.* With a small, imperceptible shake of my head, I release that thought before pointing to her shirt. "Is that a shirt you care if it gets ruined?"

She looks down at the shirt. It has some sort of vegetables on it, with the year *2016* and a cross. "Is that a VeggieTales shirt?" I ask with a laugh.

She smiles sheepishly. "I like it, it was the Vacation Bible School theme that summer." She pauses, considering my previous questions before nodding. "On second thought, yes, it's fine if this shirt gets messed up."

"Fabulous! Follow me," I say, handing her one of the bags before leading her down to the basement. I put the bag down on the folding table next to the sink, emptying the contents.

"So what are we doing today? Tie-dyeing T-shirts?" she asks as she checks out the gloves, bottles of dye, clips, and brushes.

"Not quite. You are going to help me dye my hair," I say, sectioning the top part of my hair and clipping it up.

"But this is blue and purple dye!" It's cute how surprised she is. I should have known she probably hasn't had many friends with vibrantly colored hair.

"Yep! I've done the normal colors—ginger, brown, red, black, and my natural blonde. I wanted to switch things up and do a vivid color for once." I then unzip my sweatshirt, revealing the old cheap sports bra I usually wear to dye my hair.

Naomi gasps, looking right at my chest, noticing the barbells poking through the thin fabric of the bra. "Wait, are those *nipple* piercings?" she asks, whispering the word nipple. She's already started coming out of her shell, but it's cute that she still gets embarrassed by certain things. Like the word nipple.

"Yep. Got them done when I was...nineteen? First piercing I got done, actually. After my ears, of course. Then I got lost down the rabbit hole of body mods," I explain, putting gloves on and mixing up my dye. I pin my bottom section out of the way, taking out the top. I start applying the lavender dye to the top, fully saturating the hair. "I just need you to make sure I'm not missing any pieces in the back. And then help me rinse the dye out."

Naomi nods, looking at the back of my head. "Did it hurt?"

"Did what hurt?"

"The piercings," she says, gesturing to the ones on my chest.

"Oh, like a motherfucker. But it was so worth it. Mine healed quickly, and now they're so sensitive. Which is always a plus during a hookup."

I can see Naomi blushing profusely out of the corner of my eye, so I pivot the conversation a little. "Ever think about getting a piercing?" I ask, pinning up the purple-coated hair before applying the darker blue dye on the bottom section of hair.

She shakes her head. "Nope. Mama always said that piercings are a sign of the devil. But now I'm not too sure if I believe that, especially since she's the one who pierced my ears as a baby. I don't think *those* kind of piercings are right for me, but maybe another one in my ears? Or even a small nose stud if I'm feeling wild?"

I smile, pinning up the bottom section of my hair, setting a twenty-minute timer, and taking my gloves off. "Well, if you do decide to get a piercing or a tattoo, just let me know! I know a guy, and I can get you set up with an appointment. I'll even go with you."

Naomi smiles at me, running one of the spare rags I brought under the water. "Thank you, I'd like that. Now look at me, you got dye all over you." She grips my jaw gently, using the rag to clean along my hairline, wipe my ears, and remove the stray dye from my neck.

Having Naomi this close to me has my brain and heart working in overdrive. Her signature coconut vanilla scent floods my nostrils, and it takes the last little ounce of self-control I have not to inhale deeply. My resolve is hanging on by a thread, hands balling into fists at my sides. All I want to do is reach out, grab Naomi by the hips, and pull her into me. It's quiet for a few minutes as she wipes all the extra dye, the only sound coming from the still-running water in the sink.

"All set," Naomi says softly, looking up at me. She doesn't pull back, the two of us still standing chest to chest. My eyes drop down to her lips, wetting my own in the process. She inches closer to me, her lips parting. A loud ding sounds, the timer on my phone going off and dissolving the moment.

Naomi steps back, clearing her throat. "I guess it's time to get you rinsed."

I take a moment to collect my thoughts and emotions before grabbing one of the spare folding chairs stored down here and dragging it over to the sink.

"Okay, so this is the important part. We have to rinse the bottom of my hair completely before we rinse the top, otherwise the dark blue will bleed right into the lavender," I say, taking a seat at the sink. Naomi guides my head back to the water, using the handheld faucet attachment to rinse my hair. She works in silence, carefully working her fingers through my hair.

The water may be tepid at best, but Naomi's fingers on my scalp burned, leaving a scalding trail in their wake, the warm sensation building equally in my core. I shift in the seat, rubbing my thighs together to try and alleviate the ache growing between them. The slight tug on my hair as she works her fingers through the strands only adds to my arousal.

Clowns. Zombies. True crime murder scenes. Frog dissections. Malaria outbreaks. Vaginal births. I try to occupy my thoughts with plenty of un-sexy things, distracting myself until Naomi finishes. "Okay, you are all set," she says, patting my hair dry with the towel.

I fake a little cough, regaining my composure before getting up. "Thanks, Naomi, I think I can take it from here," I say, giving her a smile. Hers drops a little, but she quickly regains her composure.

"Well, I'll just be in the kitchen if you need anything," Naomi offers, quickly heading back upstairs. I sigh, watching her retreat. I clean up my mess from the dye before heading up to the second floor of the sorority house.

Usually, executive board members live in the house, but I opted to stay in my regular apartment with Gabby and Cora. We've all lived together since we were freshmen, so it felt weird to spend my senior year without them right down the hall.

I still have a room in the house I keep stocked with a few spare outfits and toiletries. It comes in handy if I need to take a quick shower between events on campus or if there's a wardrobe emergency between classes.

Right now? I'm grateful to be able to take a cold shower. I put my freshly dyed hair into a bun before stripping down as the shower warms. I step into the shower, breathing a sigh of relief as the warm water hits my skin. I use a rag to rub the spare body wash into my skin. *Coconut vanilla*. Of course, the soap shares a scent similar to that of Naomi.

I take a deep inhale of the soap, my mind flooding back to her. *Her soft skin. Her delectable curves. Her luscious lips. That head full of pillowy curls.* My pulse starts racing, my arousal beginning to build again. All I can see is Naomi, feeling the ghost of her skin brushing against mine.

My hand works its way down my front, searching until my fingers reach that sensitive spot between my legs. A shudder runs through my body as my knuckles graze my clit. My fingers slowly begin to circle the sensitive bud as my other hand reaches up to tug on the barbell in my right nipple.

"Oh fuck..." I let out a shaky breath, increasing the pace of strokes between my legs. I dip a finger into my cunt, then a second, picturing it's Naomi's fingers inside me. Curling my fingers, the change in angle has me brushing against that soft, spongy spot that has me seeing stars.

I continue to finger fuck myself, rubbing my clit with my thumb, imagining that I'm riding Naomi's hand. I reach for the wall, as I pick up the pace, attempting to hold on as I ride out my orgasm. Turning the water off, I slump against the shower wall, trying to regain my composure.

Stars dance across my vision as aftershocks of my orgasm have me trembling. I don't think I've climaxed that hard in a long time, and definitely not at my own hands, while thinking of a friend.

I get out of the shower and put on spandex bike shorts, a halter tank with a built-in bra, and a large T-shirt. Delaying returning to Naomi, I take my time blow-drying my hair straight and giving it some volume. With no plans for the rest of the day, I decide not to put any makeup on.

"Can't hide up here forever..." I mumble to myself, grabbing my bag and heading back downstairs.

"Ta-da!" I enter the kitchen, catching the attention of Naomi, Maeve, and Gabby, who are all sitting in the kitchen. Gabby must have just gotten out of class because she wasn't here before when I came in.

"Damn, Sage! I love that color combo on you," Maeve says, reaching out to run her fingers through the layers of my hair.

"So that's why you were gone for so long... It looks nice!" Gabby says, raising an eyebrow. Considering that Naomi returned to the kitchen long before I did, I have a sinking feeling she knows I was doing more than just blow-drying my hair. I give her a small shake of my head, hoping she won't push it any further. She nods, mouthing, *"Later."*

"It really does look good, Sage," Naomi says softly, looking up at me from the kitchen table. I give her a wide smile, brushing the back of her neck as I pass.

"Couldn't have done it without you," I say with a wink, grabbing a bottled iced coffee from the fridge. She blushes, her hand reaching up to rub the back of her neck where my fingers touched.

Gabby checks her phone. "Hey, Sage, we have to head out. Exec meeting in thirty at Happy Sprout, and we still have to swing home to grab our laptops and the PNM files."

I nod, grabbing my belongings off the kitchen table. "Alright. See you in a few, Maeve, and thank you for your help today, Naomi. If I don't see you guys before then, I'll see you at the Halloween party. Make sure your costumes kill it." I give them both a wave, heading out the house to the car and tossing my keys to Gabby.

"You drive."

"I'll drive...if you tell me what happened with you and Naomi," Gabby says, holding the keys out with a smirk.

I sigh. "Fine, just get in the damn car."

We both get in, and she starts the drive back to our apartment. "So...? What happened?"

"Nothing happened, Gabs."

"Bullshit, Sage. I've lived with you for the last three years, remember? I know how long it takes you to shower and do your hair. You were gone for double the amount of time. Plus, Naomi looked flustered when she came up from the basement."

Guess I'm not getting out of this one. "Naomi and I had a...moment."

"What kind of moment?" Gabby asks, her eyes darting between me and the road.

"A *moment*. As in a 'I thought we were going to kiss' moment."

"Naomi? Kissing you? Are we talking about the same church girl that was literally wearing a Veggie Tales T-shirt today?"

I laugh dryly. "Yep, that's the one. I know it sounds ridiculous, all things considered, but I'm telling you, there was so much tension. And then her running her fingers through my hair to rinse the dye out didn't help either."

"So when you went upstairs to take a shower, you were—"

"Masturbating in the shower, picturing it was Naomi fingering me? Yup," I say, covering my face out of sheer embarrassment.

Gabby starts laughing uncontrollably as she pulls into the parking lot of our apartment complex.

"What's so funny?" I ask, completely confused.

"Just admiring the irony of it all. We were just talking at the start of the semester about how you need to start developing deeper connections instead of hooking up with all the eligible women on campus. And of course, the first woman you feel deeply connected to is fundamentally unavailable. You've got it bad for Naomi."

I let out a large sigh. She was completely right. In the cruelest kind of joke from the universe, I'm hooked on a woman I can't have.

9

Naomi

I wake up with a dull pounding in my head. *Ugh, I'm never drinking again.* When Alex and Maeve told me how crazy Kappa Theta Alpha parties got, I didn't quite believe them. I went to the Homecoming party the sorority threw, but I had maybe one drink and left early without any issue.

Last night, however? Last night was a blur of shots and costumes. I blame the hangover, but the details of last night were a little hazy. I pull the pillow tight over my head, trying to drown out all my senses. The warm, rich smell of coffee wafts through the air, luring me out of bed. I throw on my bathrobe over my pajama set before heading down the hall to the kitchen.

Maeve is standing at the stove, already dressed for her morning run. She's making breakfast—eggs and bacon—from what I could see, and there was a steaming cup of hot coffee sitting on the breakfast bar. I grab the cup, taking a cautious sip and letting out a small moan as the acidic beverage hits my tongue.

"Oh, that was for Alex. I've got a kettle of tea warming on the stove for you."

"This morning, I need coffee."

"Aye, aye, captain," Maeve says, plating up some food for me and sliding it across the bar. Alex comes shuffling into the kitchen, and Maeve makes another cup of coffee, adding vanilla creamer before sliding it across the counter to Alex.

"You guys look awful," she says, handing Alex a plate of food before grabbing a protein shake for herself out of the fridge.

I narrow my eyes at Maeve, glaring over the coffee mug. "Didn't you go out last night too? How are you still upright? Let alone getting ready to go on a run."

"My night was...a bit of a mess, to say the least. I didn't end up drinking much or staying out very late."

"Liar," Alex interjects, "that's a hickey on your neck. And a fresh one at that." She points to the darkening red smudge along the column of Maeve's neck, partially obscured by one of her French braids.

"I didn't even notice that," I mumble, noticing that there was at least a second one poking out from under the strap of her sports bra. Maeve blushes a deep red.

"Things got...interesting last night. But apparently, I'm not the only one," she says, turning her attention toward me. "Ready to cross *make out sesh* off your college experience list?" She holds out a pen to me.

I bury my head in my arms, groaning. "Ugh, don't remind me. Did Alex tell you?"

"Guilty."

Maeve comes over to sit next to me. "Hey, what's wrong?" she asks, sensing my internal conflict over the kiss.

"Everything! It's all wrong. Sage is my friend, and I'm not a lesbian."

"Well, you were the one that kissed her, not the other way around," Alex points out.

"I know that. I don't know why I did that. I mean, I do. I *hate* pickles. But it wouldn't have been that bad just to take the shot and get it over with. I don't know what got into me and compelled me to kiss her. I blame the alcohol. I did drink a lot," I ramble on, my thoughts spiraling out of control.

Maeve puts a hand on my arm to settle me. "Naomi, do you think that maybe, subconsciously, that you wanted to kiss Sage? I mean, you have been exploring things outside of your faith and reevaluating what it means to you. Maybe this is just one of those things?"

I shake my head, my stomach lurching. I bury my head in my arms again. For a moment, I had forgotten about my hangover, but it just came back with a vengeance. "Ugh, I'm never drinking this much again."

Alex passes me a bottle of cold water, and I take a few large gulps. "I'm not gay. I think I would know if I was. I like men. Josiah and I dated for like five years," I say, returning my focus to Maeve's questioning.

"And notice how quickly you were willing to drop him after everything that went down at High Valley. I mean, you said it yourself, you guys only kissed a couple times in your entire relationship," Alex points out, drinking her coffee.

"No, we only kissed a couple times because it was against our faith. We really weren't even supposed to do that until we got married."

"Sure, it could be that. Or maybe deep down, you didn't really want to be with him. Or any man," Maeve suggests. "Look, I understand your disbelief, Naomi, but we've all seen you with Sage. There's more than just a friendship there. At least on Sage's side, for sure. She's practically in love with you."

"Maeve's right. I watched you two kiss last night. You can't fake that kind of chemistry. I know it might be hard to accept, but I think deep down, you might have feelings for Sage. What that means for your sexuality, well, that'll come in due time."

I shift in my seat uncomfortably, switching back to drinking my coffee. "Enough about me. How was your night, Maeve? You haven't told us how you ended up with that hickey."

Maeve blushes, now her turn to hide her discomfort in her protein shake. "So you weren't there, Naomi, but Alex, do you remember I told you about those guys I was...involved with on the last Kappa Costa Rica trip?"

"The football player and his best friend, right? Yeah, I remember them, what about it?"

"So that guy, Emory, that I've been seeing casually? He's the best friend. Turns out they are also Pinebrook students."

"Oh, so you and Emory were together last night?" I ask, finishing off my bottle of water.

"Not exactly..." Maeve says, turning a deep scarlet shade.

"Shut up! Oh my god, you hooked up with the football player last night!" Alex says excitedly.

"His name is Noah and he's so fine! Tall, dark, handsome, and super-tatted."

"How many?" I ask, thinking about Sage's tattoos and how they cover a significant portion of her body.

"More than Sage. Like he's almost completely covered from the neck down. And you guys, this man is huge. Like a hulk of a man. He can, and does, easily toss me around."

Alex squeals. "So what does this mean? Are you going to keep seeing Noah? What about Emory?"

Maeve shrugs. "I honestly don't know where this is going. I really like them both, but obviously, I can't date two men at the same time. Right? I mean, that only happens in romance novels. That's not something that people do in real life."

"Well, some people are polyamorous. You can be with multiple people if you want to. Assuming they all consent to the dynamic, of course. I wouldn't judge you if you wanted to be with both Noah and Emory, I mean, you can't control who you fall for," Alex says, looking at both of us.

Maeve sighs. "Originally, we were going to talk about it last night. Or maybe fool around and then talk. But then something happened..." she says, trailing off. "You guys can't tell Sage what I'm about to tell you. Hell, I don't even know if I'm right about what I saw."

"Promise."

"Maeve, you're making me nervous. What happened? What does it have to do with Sage?"

She takes a deep breath. "I think Aaron tried to rape Theia last night. I can't be certain of it, but they disappeared upstairs together at the Lambda party we were at, and then next thing I know, I see her come running down the stairs, her clothes stretched and torn, and Aaron's trying to follow her with a bloody nose. He could barely stand upright, otherwise he probably would've caught up to her."

Alex gasps. "Oh my god, Theia, is she okay?"

"I'm not sure. I was with Noah when we saw them, and when I finally could follow after Theia, she was gone. Aaron never left the house though, so I know he didn't catch up with her. I texted her this morning, but she's probably still asleep. I was going to drop by her apartment today and check in on her."

I chew my bottom lip, thinking back to the fight I overheard between Theia and Aaron shortly after I joined Kappa Theta Alpha. Maybe if I had spoken up earlier, this wouldn't have happened. "I overheard a fight between Theia and Aaron about a month ago at the house. It was really loud and got really heated. I think he hit her," I say softly, feeling guilty.

"And you didn't say anything?" Alex asks.

"Theia asked me not to! I had just joined the sorority and wasn't really close with anyone yet. I didn't know what else to do. But in hindsight, though, I wish I had told someone."

Maeve sighs. "So Aaron might have been abusing Theia for a while. Do you remember what they were fighting about?"

"Vaguely? From what I remember, I think they were fighting about Theia being in the PhD program. She wanted to further her career, and he wanted her to drop it and move back home so they could settle down. He said there was no point in her participating in the program since she was going to be a stay-at-home mom anyway."

Maeve drums her fingers on the counter, thinking for a moment. "We have to tell Sage what's been going on with Theia. I mean, this is a pattern of abusive behavior, and Aaron's been escalating, if I'm right about what happened last night."

Alex bites her lip. "Maybe talk to Theia first. Confirm your suspicions, *then* talk to Sage. Or maybe convince Theia to do it herself. Someone should tell her though."

Maeve nods. "I wonder if Sage has her own suspicions. If I remember correctly, I think Aaron's the reason Theia left the drag show early. Sage went after her that night."

"But if she doesn't know about the other instances, Theia might have passed it off as a one-off," I say.

Maeve checks her watch. "It's noon. I should probably head over to her place now," she says, packing a Tupperware container full of leftover scrambled eggs and sausage and a travel mug of coffee into her purse. She grabs her keys on her way out the door. "I'll keep you guys updated."

Alex and I start cleaning up the kitchen, making another pot of coffee, when my phone starts ringing. I check the caller ID: Sage.

"Sage is calling me! What do I do?"

"What do you mean what do you do? Answer it, Naomi!"

"I can't! I'm not ready to speak to her yet."

"Nay, you can't avoid her indefinitely. Sage is your sorority president. Don't you have a chapter meeting this week? You're going to have to see her at some point."

"And I will wait until then to talk to her," I say, putting my phone down and letting it go to voicemail. My phone pinged, indicating a text came through.

Sage

> **Naomi, pick up your phone.**

> **We need to talk about last night.**

> **I know you're ignoring my call.**

> **Maeve says you were home and wide awake when she left the apartment. Pick up the phone please.**

My phone rings again, Woman by Doja Cat flooding the kitchen as I stand firm, ignoring Sage's second call. Alex gestures to my phone, and I shake my head, crossing my arms. Was I being stubborn? Absolutely, but I just wasn't ready to talk to her yet. Not until I've sorted out my own feelings surrounding the whole situation.

The ringtone cuts off, and more pings come through my phone, likely from Sage. After a few minutes, I finally check the device.

Sage

> **Please pick up Naomi.**

> **I'm not mad at you if that's what you're thinking.**

> **I just want to talk to you.**

> **Fine. If you won't answer my calls, and you won't respond to my texts, I'm coming over.**

That last text was sent six minutes ago.

"Dang it, she's on her way over!" I say, running to the bathroom.

Alex chuckles. "I told you, you should've just picked up the phone."

I check myself in the mirror, trying to figure out how I could clean up the trainwreck that was staring back at me in under five minutes. I throw my hair up in a messy bun, not even bothering to try and work through the knots in my hair. I fell asleep without my bonnet, and even with my silk pillowcase, my rough sleeping turned my curls into a nest.

I quickly brush my teeth, swishing a little mouthwash. I also quickly wash my face, cleaning up any eye crusties or traces of drool.

Okay, I might not look great, but at least now I don't look like I just woke up from a twelve-hour nap. I head back into the kitchen to see Sage sitting at the breakfast bar. How does she look this good all the time? She was wearing olive green skinny cargo pants, a white V-neck T-shirt, a blue denim vest covered in patches, and black high-top Converse. Her hair is in its naturally wavy state.

She was deep in conversation with Alex about something somewhat serious. Alex gestures in my direction, letting Sage know that I'd returned. She turns in her stool to look at me, giving me a sad smile. "Hey, Naomi. You're a hard woman to get a hold of."

I shrug, pulling my robe tighter around me. "Really? I think I might have left my phone at the house. I haven't seen it all morning."

She raises an eyebrow with that signature smirk, looking down toward my waist. I follow her gaze and see it—my phone sticking out of my robe pocket. I smack my forehead gently. *Stupid.* I don't know why I thought that excuse was going to work. "What do you want, Sage?" I say, sounding annoyed.

Sage winces at my tone. "Naomi..." she pleads. "I just want to talk to you. One on one. Face to face. In private..." she says, glancing over at Alex.

Alex holds her hands up in surrender. "You don't have to tell me twice. Good luck, Naomi. I'll be in my room. With the TV on. And the volume turned up loud," she says, heading out of the room.

I turn my attention back to Sage, shifting my weight from leg to leg, not wanting to say the first word.

Sage sighs, standing up and walking toward me. Standing toe-to-toe she reaches out to hug me, but I take a step back, wanting to keep distance between us. "You wanted to talk, so talk," I insist, crossing my arms over my chest, growing impatient and uncomfortable.

Sage bites her lip. "So about last night..."

10

Sage

"You wanted to talk, so talk," Naomi says, her mouth set in a frown, the annoyance radiating off her.

When I first reached out to Naomi this morning, this wasn't what I expected. Embarrassment? Sure. Regret? Maybe. This degree of hostility? Never saw it coming.

I sigh, biting my lip. "So about last night..."

"What about it, Sage?"

"We need to talk about the kiss. You ran off before I could talk to you. And now, this morning? You seem annoyed with me."

Naomi sighs, dropping her shield a little bit as she goes and sits in the corner of her sectional. "No...I'm not annoyed with you. I'm just...really confused," she says, deflating.

This is exactly what I was afraid of. Naomi has limited romantic experiences to begin with, let alone with another woman. Add in her religious background, and she's probably spiraling.

I take a seat next to her on the couch, leaving a little space between us. I put my hands in my pockets, trying to prevent myself from reaching out to Naomi. "I'm sorry, Naomi..." I say, unsure of where to start.

She shakes her head. "It's not your fault, Sage. I'm just a mess."

"Want to talk about it? It might help. Working through your feelings with someone, I mean."

Naomi sighs, chewing on the inside of her cheek as she does when she gets nervous. "Well, I guess I'll start with the kiss."

"I'm sorry if I took it too far, I was just—"

She cuts me off. "Let me finish, please?" I nod, sitting back. "Sage, that kiss was...unexpected, to say the least. It was nice. Exciting even. It was a great kiss, even if I was three sheets to the wind."

I blush, rubbing the back of my neck. "You weren't so bad yourself, Naomi."

She gives me a small smile. "And I think that's a big reason why I'm confused. I've never had feelings for a woman. I've certainly never kissed a woman before. I've spent my whole life knowing that I was straight. Believing that that was the only way to love and spend your life.

Do I buy into the whole 'gays face eternal damnation and they are the devil incarnate'? I don't believe I do. But it's still jarring to consider that maybe I might share those feelings," she explains.

I stay quiet, mulling over Naomi's words. I would be lying if I said that hearing her moral conflict didn't hurt a bit, but I couldn't blame her. It was her upbringing. She grew up hearing that gays were bad and she couldn't possibly be gay. It's hard to reconcile your own feelings and emotions with what you think you should be.

"Your conflict isn't entirely unique. Sure, you have the added element of your religion, but I also struggled with my sexuality when I first came out."

Naomi's jaw drops. "You? I find it hard to believe *the* Sage Carpenter struggled with her sexuality," she says.

I laugh. "I wasn't always out and proud. That's come with time and finding a great support network that accepts me and my sexuality. But when I first came out, I was scared shitless.

I didn't always know that I was a lesbian. In fact, it took me a while to realize that I was emotionally, and later sexually, attracted to women. I did know from an early age that I wasn't interested in the male species. I've always found boys *icky*. Originally, I thought it was just age-related. I mean, after all, most girls find boys gross at one point or another.

For me, however, those feelings never went away. As I got older, I started to realize I wasn't interested in men at all. While my friends and classmates started chasing after boys and dating, that desire never came to me. It wasn't until I was well into high school that I started actually feeling attracted to women.

At first, I couldn't distinguish those feelings. I hadn't had a crush on anyone, so how could I differentiate between a strong friendship and a romantic connection? But then came along my first crush, Delilah Walker. I was hooked, fixated on her.

I couldn't get enough of her. I wanted to spend as much time as possible with her. I felt lighter when I was around her. Delilah made my days brighter. When I talked to an old foster sibling of mine, they helped me figure out what I was feeling was a romantic connection. Delilah and I dated for a brief moment, our relationship ending because I was unwilling to come out of the closet just yet.

Since I was in foster care, I feared coming out would have the worst outcome—that my foster parents would decide they didn't want a lesbian in the house, and I would get placed with a nightmare family or go back to the group home. Theia's parents were amazing, and in hindsight, I should've known they would be supportive. But I had finally found a family that accepted me. That wanted me, baggage and all. I wasn't ready to risk losing that yet."

"How did they find out that you were gay then?" Naomi interjects, her eyes wide as she follows along with my story.

I smile softly to myself, remembering the day vividly. "Because of my 'friend' Katie. Katie was the girl I started seeing after Delilah my junior year of high school. As I did with D, I spent a ton of time with Katie. Even more so this time around, and I brought her home, something I never did with Delilah.

I thought we were being very discreet. Keeping things strictly platonic when my parents were around. But my parents quickly put two and two together. Late night phone calls with the door closed; constantly going out just the two of us, to the mall, to the movies, out to eat; deciding to go to prom together, just as friends, but color coordinating our dresses. Nothing about our friendship was platonic.

So, about one week before prom, my parents sat me down and asked about Katie. I initially denied it, said she was just a friend. But they knew. They asked me what 'me and my girlfriend' planned to do after prom, and I just spilled everything. They were extremely supportive, even offered to get us a limo so we could have the 'proper prom experience.' One thing Melody, Theia's mom, said really stuck with me. 'When you find something that feeds your soul and brings you joy, love yourself enough to make room for it in your life.' I've tried to follow this every day since.

Katie and I broke up around graduation, but I've lived out and proud since the day I came out to my parents. They still tried to adopt me, and my worst fears of being rejected never came true. I've put my happiness first. That means pursuing what I want, dating who I please, and living life to the fullest."

Naomi sits back, chewing on her cheek, mulling over my words.

"I know you have the whole religious element to consider too, but you deserve to be happy, Naomi. You've already started down that path by leaving High Valley University and coming here. Alex told me about your ex. You might not have been fully interested in him because you might not be interested in men. Or maybe you are, but you're interested in women too. Sexuality is fluid.

I don't want you to feel any pressure, but I like you, Naomi, a lot. And it scares me, if I'm going to be honest." I sigh, squeezing my eyes shut. I debated whether or not to tell her. On one hand, I didn't want to influence her decisions as she worked through her emotions. On the other, I knew if I didn't say anything, she'd be unsure of what that moment meant, even if she did come to the conclusion she does have feelings for me. I was being vulnerable right now, telling her about my coming out story, might as well lay all the cards out on the table for her.

"Why does it scare you?" she says softly, leaning toward me to take my hand in hers.

My eyes open, meeting her soft brown ones. "I'm scared because I'm afraid of being rejected. It's easy to brush off someone declining a one night stand. But opening up my heart to someone, being vulnerable and hoping that they want me for me? I've been burned before. My birth mom left me, she decided I wasn't worth it. And then things ending with both Delilah and Katie, not that expected to live happily ever after with my first girlfriend, it all builds on each other."

I look down at our joined hands, her thumb stroking the back of my hand. "I guess I just want someone to choose me for once. To put themselves out there and say they want me, that they need me. So I'm not always getting left out in the cold when I put myself out there."

Naomi sighs, resting her head on my shoulder. We sit in silence for a few moments, the only sound the muffled music coming from behind

Alex's closed bedroom door. Her soothing strokes on the back of my hand, working magic on calming my nerves.

"I can't give you what you want, Sage, at least not right now." Her voice gentle, softening the blow. "I'm still trying to work through this mess of religion and what I want in my head, and it wouldn't be fair to drag you along for that, especially if I come out the other side and nothing's changed."

She sits up and lifts my chin with a finger before cupping my cheek. "What I can do though, is promise you that you are worth it. Whether my feelings are romantic or not, I am deeply connected to you. I choose you, Sage Carpenter, as a friend, as a partner, whatever it may be in the end. You're stuck with me, because I do need you. You're part of this little family that I've found here at Pinebrook, and y'all have shown me more love, compassion, and empathy than I could ever have asked for."

Even though it's not quite what I was hoping to hear, my heart feels a little lighter, the tension melting from my shoulders. It wasn't a profession of love, but it wasn't a rejection either, and this is next best thing. Naomi Williams is open to the possibility of me, of us. And that gives me more hope than I had when I walked into her apartment with.

"I'm stuck with you, huh? I don't think you realize what you've just signed yourself up for." I laugh, trying to lighten the moment.

Naomi gives me a little smirk of her own. "I know *exactly* what I'm getting into."

The lock on the front door turns, indicating Naomi's other roommate is back. We both jump up from the couch as the door opens, letting go of each other. "Hey, Sage," Maeve says with surprise, her eyes darting back and forth between us.

"Hey, Maeve."

"I'll walk you out?" Naomi says, looking up at me with uncertainty.

"Yeah, that'd be great. I have to catch up with Cora anyway. Last I heard she and soccer boy spent the night together."

"It's about time she gave that man a break," Maeve says with a laugh, heading down the hall. Once she's out of sight, Naomi takes my hand once again, leading me to the door. "I'm sorry for cutting things short, I just didn't want—"

"Hey, it's okay, Naomi, I get it. You didn't want Maeve to turn this into something it's not when you're still figuring it out," I say softly, tucking a stray curl behind her ear. "I completely understand, plus I wasn't lying. I do have to catch up with my roommate and find out how her night went."

"I'll see you later?" Naomi looks up at me expectantly, still holding my hand.

I give her hand a gentle squeeze, smiling wide. "Definitely." I press my lips to her forehead, lingering for a bit before pulling away completely. "Bye, Naomi."

I close the door behind me, heading into my apartment, my attention focused on my phone.

"So...how did it go?"

I jump, startled by the voice. "Jesus, you scared me, Cora." Both she and Gabby are sitting in the living room of our apartment, seemingly waiting for my return.

"I'll echo Cora. So how did it go?" Gabby asks me, patting the couch next to her.

I roll my eyes, coming into the apartment and taking a seat in my favorite armchair. "It was...interesting," I say, kicking my shoes off and getting comfortable in the chair.

"What's that supposed to mean?" Gabby laughs.

"I mean, it didn't go exactly the way I planned, but we're on good terms, so I guess that's better than the alternative."

"Sage, babes, I'm going to need you to give us a few more details." Cora raises an eyebrow, watching me expectantly.

"Well, to start, she said it was a great kiss."

Gabby rolls her eyes. "Like you need another boost to your ego. What else did she say?"

"That she's confused, she doesn't know what the kiss means to her or how she really feels about me."

"I'm sorry, Sage, I know how much you liked Naomi." Cora rests a hand on my arm in an attempt to be sympathetic.

I smile, shaking my head. "It wasn't an outright rejection. She seemed to be open to the possibility of us in a relationship together, just has to figure out her own emotions first."

"Are you sure? We just don't want you to get your hopes up and then get hurt in the end," Gabby says, being uncharacteristically gentle.

"I'm positive you guys. We had a heart-to-heart. I told Naomi about my coming-out story, and she told me she felt deeply connected to me. We held hands, she let me kiss her on the forehead, and she wants to meet up later in week, just us two," I say smugly.

"Look at her, excited over a forehead kiss." Cora laughs, nudging Gabby.

"Who are you and what have you done with Sage the Heartbreaker?"

I laugh. "I'm serious, I'm optimistic about how things will end up. I have a deep connection with her and even if it's just friendship, there is something there."

"Well, if you're happy, I guess we're happy for you," Cora says softly.

"Speaking of happy, what's up with you and lover boy?" She rolls her eyes. "You two looked pretty happy when you left the party last night. Together, I might add," I say, raising a brow.

"Anthony and I had a great night." Now, it's Cora's turn to be tight-lipped.

"Anthony? I thought his name was Dave."

Cora laughs. "His name is Anthony Davidson, but most of his teammates call him by his last name. All his friends call him Tony. I think I might be the only one who calls him Anthony besides his family."

"Aren't you special... What's the deal with you two anyway? He's been chasing after you since we were freshmen! I thought he would've given up by now," Gabby says, tilting her head and sizing Cora up.

She blushes. "Actually, he's been chasing me for longer than that."

"What do you mean?"

Cora sighs. "Anthony and I grew up together. Our moms were college roommates. We've been friends for years," she explains.

"Oh, this is juicier than I expected..." Gabby shifts on the couch, getting more comfortable as she leans in eagerly.

"Anthony and I also dated when we were thirteen. Not for very long though, he was a bit of a jerk at the time. So we grew apart. And then when my mom died, we grew apart even further, since my dad and I moved to live near my aunt in Chicago. I probably should've known he'd go to Pinebrook too, after all, it's where our moms met."

My jaw drops in surprise. "So you're the one that got away?"

She shrugs. "I guess? I mean, I've never thought of it that way because our distancing seemed to be mutual."

"So how'd you guys end up reconnecting?" Gabby asks, equally as invested in this story as I am.

"Remember that freshmen mixer that the Student Activities center threw? I know you guys missed it because of a rush event running over, but Anthony and I bumped into each other there. He saw me there alone and sat with me. We caught up, talked about how our high school years went, exchanged numbers, and went our separate ways. And then we kept bumping into each other. Econ 101, Student Government, Clash of Clubs, the Business Department's Annual Golf Tournament, parties here and there, Anthony kept finding his way into my life."

"So...? Do you have feelings for him?" I ask. "He's head over heels for you."

"I don't know. He's much more attractive now than he was at thirteen. I don't know if he's changed. He probably did, after all, that was almost ten years ago, but Anthony left my life right when I needed him the most, and it still hurts. That's why I haven't accepted any of his invitations to go on a date, because I don't know if I want to, or if I'm ready to, reopen those old wounds."

"Well, I think you two would be great together. I understand why you're hesitant, but that man adores you, Cora, and I think you deserve to have someone that puts you first the way he does. Maybe he didn't then, but he's definitely trying to make up for it now," I say, giving her a small smile.

Gabby nods her head, pointing to our full bookshelf. "Sage is right, haven't almost all your books come from him? He drops one off every time he comes across a new book he thinks you'll love. If that isn't love, I don't know what is."

"Or when he brought her coffee and walked her to class every day for a whole semester."

"How about when he cashed in a favor with his friend that worked at the golf course so that she could get private lessons leading up to the Business Department's tournament?"

Cora laughs. "Ha, ha, very funny. I get it, he's a real-life book boyfriend."

"That man is down bad for you, Cora, all you have to do is say yes," Gabby says, getting up from the couch, heading to the kitchen.

"I, unlike aggressive, hopeless romantic Gabby, support whatever decision you make. While I think you guys make a good-looking couple, and he seems to make you happy, I can completely understand your hesitations. We both know I have similar hangups."

Cora leans over to give me a hug, letting out a deep sigh. "Man, do we have a lot of baggage."

"That we do, Cor, that we do."

11

Sage

Today's Thursday, my favorite day of the week. *Toasty Thursdays,* as me and a few friends, including a couple of the KTA sisters, call it. Raven, Aleka, Stephanie, Davidson's buddy Chase, Noah, and I all get together on Thursdays while the weather's still nice and hang out in the clearing in the woods right at the edge of campus. There's a stream right there, nice and cold, perfect for dipping your feet in on a hot day. We found this spot late in my sophomore year, and we've been coming here since. It was our little stoner hideaway on campus.

While weed is legal in New York state, it's not permitted on campus, same with alcohol, technically. And since all of our apartments had no smoking policy, we had to find our own spot to light up. The biology program used to come to this spot to do an ecosystem lab in one of their introductory-level classes, which is how I found the place. The professor who taught the lab retired right before my sophomore year, and none of the other professors in the department picked up the experiment. So now the spot remains wholly undisturbed and under the radar, which is why it's perfect for a smoke session.

We all plan our class schedules so that we have only morning classes or no classes at all on Thursdays. Then, we come out here in the afternoon to smoke, catch up, and relax. Usually, someone brings lunch. Thursdays are always a great day for me because they allow me to turn off my brain completely. ADHD and Anxiety are a beast of a combination. The constant stream of thoughts in my head never stops.

Yes, meds help, but they come with some nasty side effects. I was already on Zoloft for the anxiety, but Adderall made me more anxious and irritable, Vyvanse made me nauseous, and Ritalin gave me migraines. Sure, I could keep trying different combinations of drugs until I found the right fit, but to be honest, I gave up trying. I make do academically, I've created my own workarounds and developed coping mechanisms to help me perform. But the thoughts, they just don't stop. I hyper-fixate on things—hobbies, facts, lyrics of a song I listened to three days ago, etc. Sometimes, the target of my fixation was my anxiety.

The nice thing about weed is that it silences everything: the hyper-fixations, the anxious thoughts, even my own internal monologue. My therapist actually supported my usage. She knows how much I've struggled with finding the right mix of medications and the way she saw it, as long as my marijuana usage didn't get in the way of my day-to-day responsibilities. She didn't feel like I was becoming dependent on weed; she saw no harm in me using it for this purpose.

She requires I journal my consumption—dates, times, method of consumption, dosage, you name it. But I do it. I've been required to do it since I had my medical marijuana card, and even though I've been getting it recreationally in recent years, the habit was already there. Plus, it keeps me accountable.

The weather so far this fall has been unusually mild, still having sunny, warm days in late October, early November. So, we were still meeting up on a weekly basis. This week was my turn to bring the food, so naturally, I bought my go-to munchie food—Taco Bell. I ordered two supreme taco party packs, six large Baja Blasts, and a crap ton of hot sauce. As I wait for the order to be filled, my phone pings with a text.

Naomi

> **Hi Sage!**

> **What are you up to today? I just got out of class and I was wondering if you wanted to hang out.**

I definitely wanted to spend time with Naomi, don't get me wrong, but these smoke sessions were part of my routine, and knowing her limited exposure to any kind of substance, I don't know how she'd feel about joining us.

Sage

> **Hey Naomi! I was actually getting ready to meet up with Alex and a few friends to smoke.**

> **You can join us if you'd like, otherwise, maybe we can do something tomorrow night instead?**

A Friday night hang out might be too date-adjacent, but I'm in class for most of the day, and I'd be lying if I said I didn't want to take her out on a date anyway. My phone pinged again.

Naomi

Smoke? As in *leaf emoji* smoking? Aleka's tried to get me join her a couple times.

I don't know if I'll join in, but I'll still hang out, if that's okay with you.

Sage

Absolutely, the more the merrier. I'll pick you up on my way back from grabbing food. I'm leaving Taco Bell now.

Alright, I'll see you in a little bit. *smiley face emoji*

My name's called out, signaling that my order was ready. With the help of one of the employees, I carry the order out to my car, putting everything down on the floor of the backseat. I start the drive back to campus, stopping at Naomi's apartment building first and texting her that I'm downstairs.

After a few minutes, she comes downstairs, smiling when she sees my car. She is wearing a flowy romper, a pink top, white floral shorts, and a blue denim button-up shirt. She has a brown leather crossbody bag slung across her chest, and she is wearing white Converse with her outfit. Her hair is braided back into two Dutch braids, tucked into a low bun.

"Hi, Sage!" she says excitedly, getting into the car. "Hey, look at you wearing shorts!" I say, poking fun at her as I pull out of her complex's parking lot. "I know, right? It's almost as if I can wear what I want, and the ground *isn't* going to open up and swallow me whole."

She grins, throwing on a pair of brown sunglasses. "So we're going to go smoke with some friends?"

"No, *I'm* going to smoke with some friends. You're hanging out with us as a sober buddy."

"What if I want to smoke with you guys too?"

I glance over at Naomi, trying to keep my focus largely on the road. "You're joking, right?"

She doesn't respond, fidgeting with a stray curl that escaped her updo. "Oh, you're not kidding..." I say, pulling into the commuter lot on the far side of campus.

She shrugs, picking at her cuticles. "Maybe... I haven't decided if I want to. But I haven't ruled it out either."

I turn the car off, turning toward Naomi. "Well, if you do decide to 'partake,' let me know. I brought a mix of products, so you'll be able to try a variety."

She nods, looking around. "What are we doing all the way out here?"

"You'll see," I say with a wink, getting out of the car. "Help me with this food, will you?"

We make a short trek through the woods, following the smell of weed. The scent is nearly indetectable from the parking lot, but it grows stronger with every step we take further into the woods. We approach the clearing to see that the crew has already set up. They laid two queen-sized quilts out in the grass, separating us from the stream.

Raven and Chase were stretched out on one of the blankets, Raven sitting with her legs stretched out in front of her, leaning back on her hands, and Chase laying on his back with his head in her lap. Those two are like an old married couple already. They met during freshman orientation and haven't been apart since. They just fit so well together, and they're so happy with each other.

Alex, Stephanie, and Noah were sitting on the other blanket, passing a blunt between them, each one taking a hit when it was their turn. "Hey, look what the cat dragged in," Raven says, looking in my direction.

Alex looks up to see me coming into the clearing. "Hey, it's Sage, and she brought my roommate with her. Hey, Naomi."

"And food!" Stephanie chimes in, reaching out for the boxes of tacos in our hands. I laugh, placing one of the boxes and trays of drinks in front of them and placing the other box and tray next to Raven and Chase. "You guys couldn't even wait. You got started without me."

"You were taking too long. But now I see why. You had to stop to pick up your girlfriend," Chase says jokingly, sitting up to grab a drink and passing it to Raven. She shushes him. "You're not supposed to know about that."

"Guys! They're not together," Alex says, grabbing a taco.

"Not yet anyway," she mutters under her breath to Stephanie, the two laughing maniacally.

I roll my eyes, knowing that they're just poking fun at us. "Ha, ha, you two are grade-A comedians." I lay down on the blanket with Raven and Chase, rolling onto my side. "Come sit, Naomi," I say, digging through my purse until I find my goods—a preroll, my pen, and a small baggie of peach ring edibles—laying them out on the blanket next to me. "You said you were considering trying it out? Take your pick. I'd recommend the gummies though, for you."

Naomi kneels on the blanket next to me, surveying my spread. She grabs the peach rings, sizing them up. "Peach rings, huh?" she says with a smile, taking one of the rings and popping it in her mouth.

"Of course, peach rings for my Georgia Peach," I say with a wink. "They just happen to be my favorite candy." She blushes, chewing the candy. "So, how many of these am I supposed to take?" she asks, popping another into her mouth. I take the bag from her. "Whoa, slow down. Let's just see how you feel in a few minutes, okay?"

She shrugs. "Okay." Naomi grabs a soft taco from the box, unwrapping it and putting a little fire sauce on it. I take my pre-roll and put the filtered end between my lips, holding a hand out toward Raven.

"When will you bring your own lighter, Sage?" she asks, handing it to me.

"When you stop letting me borrow yours." I light the joint, taking a hit and holding it in for a few seconds before exhaling and tossing the lighter back to her.

After some time and quite a few more hits, I finished my joint, and the high had fully set in. Naomi took another peach gummy and she was fully feeling her high as well. We were laying on our backs on the blanket, our shoulders pressed against each other. Raven and Naomi were going back and forth about their Global Strategy professor, cracking jokes about his awful hair piece and laughing up a storm.

"How ya feeling over there, Naomi?" Alex asks. She stopped smoking a little bit ago. While she did have a work shift tonight, she likely stopped because she wanted to make sure that her roommate was okay.

"I feel like I'm floating, but my arms and legs feel so heavy," Naomi answers slowly, carefully choosing her words.

I chuckle, rolling my head over to look at Naomi. "She's high as a kite."

Naomi looks over at me, grinning wide. "I should have tried this stuff ages ago," she says, scooting a little closer to me. Her arm extends out, pinky brushing against mine. I return the gesture before looking back up at the sky, spacing out and fully relaxing. A hand grabs mine, interlacing their fingers with mine. It brings my attention back to the present, and I look down to see that it is Naomi's hand holding mine. "Yeah?" I say, looking over to see her staring at me. She nods, biting her lip and scooting even closer to me.

I gave Naomi's hand a squeeze, pulling her right against my side. She rolls over onto her side, resting her head on my shoulder, nuzzling in close. "So you're a cuddler when you're high? Good to know," I say softly, burying my nose in her hair. *God, I love that scent.*

"Thanks. It's my curl cream." Naomi giggles. *Whoops,* didn't realize I said that one out loud. I move my arm, releasing Naomi's hand so I can wrap my arm around her back. She wraps her arms around my middle, throwing a leg over mine.

"Aww, don't you two look cozy." Stephanie stands over us, snapping a photo with her phone. Naomi buries her face in my shoulder, blushing profusely from embarrassment. "You're going to thank me for this later. Down the line, when you guys get married, you'll have a photo from the very beginning," she says, typing a few things on her phone.

My phone and Naomi's ping at the same time, indicating a text, and I pull out my phone with my free hand to check it. Stephanie sent the photo she took to both of us. *I love it.* I have my hand up, shielding my squinted eyes and grinning, and my other splays across Naomi's lower back. Her body is completely curled into mine, a wide, lazy smile across her face as she looks up at me.

It's a perfect photo. One that shows us effortlessly happy together. Sure, it's fueled by marijuana, but it's raw, and I want to bottle these feelings to save for later. I set the photo as my lock screen background before putting my phone away again.

Stephanie, Alex, and Noah gathered their things. "You guys are leaving?" Raven asks.

"Yeah, Alex has work, Noah has a workout, and they're my ride back to the sorority house, and I have homework to do for my nine AM," Stephanie responds, grabbing some of the leftover tacos. "Brain fuel."

Alex waves at us as she heads back toward the parking lot. "Don't stay out too late, you lovebirds. I'll see you back at the apartment, Naomi." She waves back lazily, not moving from her position draped on top of me.

Raven checks her watch. "Shoot, Chase, we have to get going too. We have that study group for econ in an hour," she says, tapping him on the shoulder to wake him up. He had fallen asleep maybe an hour ago, napping in his girlfriend's lap peacefully.

Chase takes the signal, sitting up and rubbing his eyes. "What? Is it time to go?"

"Yeah, we have work to do, dude." Raven stands, collecting her garbage and belongings, leaving the blanket with us. "You two going to be okay out here by yourselves?"

"Yeah, we'll be fine. See you guys later," I say as they take off, leaving Naomi and me alone in the clearing. It's five in the afternoon, so we have some daylight for an hour or two more. "Do you want to leave too?"

Naomi shakes her head, propping herself on her elbow. "Not yet. I like it out here. And with you," she says softly, giving me a smile.

One-on-one time with Naomi, and she's not itching to leave right away? I'll take it.

12

Naomi

*W*eed is one heck of a drug.

When I texted Sage and she told me she was going to smoke with some friends, I had no intention of smoking with her. In fact, my first instinct was to just take her offer to reschedule and go out with her tomorrow. But I wanted to see Sage so badly today. Since our kiss the other weekend, I've had the strongest urge to spend any time with her I can.

Dropping by her classes with coffee or her favorite matcha latte from Happy Sprout, spending a late-night studying at the sorority house with Sage, and bailing on Taco Night with my roommates. I think I've spent more waking hours with her in the last week and change than I have spent at home.

This led to me getting high with Sage in the woods. I don't know what compelled me to try her weed. I planned on just being a sober companion, Sage's designated driver. But the more I thought about it, the more I wanted to see what the fuss was about. Alex has been trying to get me to smoke with her for a few weeks now, so now that I knew that someone else close to me smoked, I figured, *why not?*

Nothing could have prepared me for the actual sensation of being high. It felt like an out-of-body experience in the best way possible. My body was lighter yet grounded. My inhibitions lowered, almost non-existent. My mind was completely clear, and I felt the most at ease I had in a while.

Which is why I'm currently draped across Sage, clinging to her like a koala. For once, my brain was incapable of second-guessing my actions, and I fully embraced this feeling. I propped up my head with my elbow, my free hand running up and down Sage's heavily inked arm, tracing her tattoos. I was fascinated by the work; so intricate and yet edgy at the same time. They fit her perfectly, adding to her non-conformity and still looking so feminine.

"How many tattoos do you have?"

Sage laughs. "I stopped counting a while ago. I have eight large projects, but I think I sat through twenty or so sessions to get the work done. It's roughly thirty or so hours of work. And then seven different piercing appointments for all the hardware."

I examine her arms, face, and ears, trying to count all her tattoos and piercings but coming up short. "You have some that aren't visible."

She nods, sitting up to pull off her hoodie and rolling up the band of her sports bra ever so slightly.

"There's this rose." She points to the small, slightly faded rose tattooed under her left breast.

"And then my thigh tattoo." Sage rolls the right leg of her bike shorts up, showing off the clock tattoo piece on her thigh.

"There's also my anklet tattoo. And the 'hidden piercing,' besides my nipple piercings that you already know about, is my belly button ring." She flips down the high waist of her shorts to show off the dangling bejeweled bar before fixing her shorts.

"Is there a story behind your tattoos?" I ask, sitting up as well, leaning in close to Sage. She gives me a sad smile.

"Some of them do. Most were just designs that I like. And some, the meaning is in the placement, not the design itself."

"What do you mean by that?" I reach out to trace the intricate design on her thigh when she grabs my wrist, holding me in place.

"Like the one you were just about to touch, for example." She guides my hand along her thigh, brushing over the slightly raised, horizontal bumps.

"You feel that?" I nod, assuming she's talking about the ridges. "Those are scars. Old self-harm scars, to be exact."

My heart breaks just a little, hearing the strain in her voice even now as she talks about them. "Oh, Sage, I'm so sorry for prying," I say, trying to pull my hand away. But she holds it in place, keeping my hand firmly planted on the top of her upper thigh.

"No, it's okay. It's hard sometimes, but my therapist says that I need to talk about it more, mainly to her, in order to heal.

When I was a pre-teen, things were tough at home. And then, when I ended up in foster care, I struggled a lot. At least until I ended up with the Davises. I was depressed and extremely anxious, and I hadn't yet been diagnosed with ADHD, so to most of my first foster families, I was just a problem child.

I didn't get bullied for being in foster care, thankfully, but I was originally bullied when I started questioning my sexuality. Everything just compounded on each other and I started self-harming to escape the pain that I was facing on a daily basis.

It started with snapping a rubber band on my wrist, and then, when that wasn't enough, I started pulling my hair out. That wasn't enough either, and that's when I began cutting. Mainly on the top and inside of my things, but I have some scars on the tops of my forearms too."

I reach out with my free hand to wipe the tears that began to fall. "And that's why you have large tattoos on your forearms too."

She nods, reaching up to dry her eyes with the sleeve of her sweatshirt. "Half sleeves, yes. When Theia's family took me in, things changed so much. They got me the help I so desperately needed. They provided me with a loving home I hadn't had in a long time.

Things got better. I got an ADHD diagnosis, I started on meds for my depression and anxiety, I was seeing a therapist on a regular basis, and I stopped self-harming. They were even able to have me transfer schools from my old public junior high school to a charter school in their area.

But the scars were still there, and they were an ugly reminder of the worst time of my life. I wanted them gone. I talked to my doctor about them. He said they would heal and fade over time, but it could take a while and they might not fade completely.

He mentioned all kinds of procedures and medications that they use for keloid patients or burn victims with scarring, but the healing process and medication side effects were terrifying."

"Is that how you ended up getting your tattoos?" I ask, my thumb massaging soft circles into the clock face on her thigh.

"Yeah, I started doing my own research on scar removals, and I came across a tattoo artist in New Jersey that specialized in cover-up tattoos. The day I turned sixteen, Melody, Theia's mom, took me to get my first tattoo," she says, pointing to the floral mandala tattoo on her right arm.

"After that, I just kept getting more and more. I didn't get my thigh tattoo until I was eighteen or nineteen. I think this one is my favorite. It was inspired by something that my therapist told me in a session.

She said, 'remember, today is the tomorrow you worried about yesterday.' It was a quote by Dale Carnegie and it stuck with me. So I got the clock tattoo as a reminder that time is fleeting, but it does go on."

"And the flowers?"

Sage laughs. "Everyone asks if there's a meaning behind the flowers. Or if my flower choice was symbolic. I just love the look of floral tattoos, and Ryan, the woman that does my tattoos, specializes in florals. I usually just go in for my appointments with an idea of the central element, so the clock or the woman's face, and then give her complete creative control over the surrounding elements."

I scoot closer to Sage, wrapping my arms around her in a hug. I felt sorry for her. I didn't pity her; Sage is such a strong woman. I don't think many people could've gone through what she did and have come out the way she did.

But I empathize with the pain and loneliness that she endured. It's hard to reconcile that the happy-go-lucky, wears her heart on her sleeve version of Sage I know was once a scared, lonely, broken-down kid.

"Sage...?" I start, unsure if the question I'm about to ask is one that should even be brought up.

"Yeah, Naomi?"

"How did you end up in foster care in the first place? You don't have to answer if you don't want to, I know talking about your tattoos with me was hard. I don't want to push you if it's too much."

She winces slightly, as if pained by the memory, and I immediately regret asking. She buries her face in the crook of my neck, holding onto me tight as she takes a few calming breaths.

I'm about to tell her to forget I even said anything when she speaks up. "My mom didn't want me anymore," she says in a small voice, barely above a whisper.

"My dad was in the army. While my mom was pregnant with me, he was deployed to Afghanistan. Shortly before I was born, he was killed in action. An IED took out him and couple of the other soldiers in his unit.

When I was born, my mom and I moved back in with my grandpa. My grandma had passed from breast cancer long before I was born, so it was just the three of us.

And for a while, things were good. Grandpa stayed home with me while my mom worked. He'd take me to the park, playdates, you name it. But then he passed away when I was six years old. Heart attack.

Then it was just me and Mom. I think the thought of being a single mom was too much for her. Especially now that she no longer had family to support her. She started drinking. A lot."

Sage's voice cracks as she retells her story, and I feel a tear of my own escape, falling down my cheek.

"We managed for a little. I had some friends whose parents would let me stay with them when my mom went on a bender. But she would clean things up, be back at work on a Monday with an apology to her boss, and things would be okay for a couple weeks.

But the problem with cycles is that they come back around again eventually. And after a few unexcused absences, my mom lost her job. We could've been fine. Between my mom's inheritance from her parents and the death gratuity she received from the military, we had enough to get by for some time.

But when you factor in my mom's excessive drinking, that money disappeared quickly. Then she started bringing home boyfriends, if you can even call them that.

They were guys that were also regulars at the bar she frequented. None of them signed up for a kid, especially not one that had the behavioral issues I did at the time. They'd put up with it only for so long, and then that's when the verbal abuse started," Sage says, her body trembling, her tears soaking my shirt. The memories still brought her so much hurt today, and I feel awful for bringing it up.

"After a little while, my mom would catch on to how they were treating me and kick them to the curb. But after boyfriend four, I think she just stopped caring herself.

Boyfriend number five was the first and only one that stayed around long enough to hit me. My mom didn't do anything about it. No, mother dear scolded me for pissing him off.

So I ran away. I tried to crash with one of my friends I stayed with before. Her mom saw the discoloration on my cheek and finally called DCF, the department of children and families, to report the abuse and neglect.

They didn't investigate for very long. We were overdue on all our utility bills, the bank was in the process of foreclosing on our house, and my mom was never around for the home visits. Add to that the reported abuse, they put me in foster care. And she never contested it either.

I bounced from home to home for a couple years before I ended up with Theia and her parents at fourteen. I had been with them for about eighteen months when they decided they wanted to adopt me."

Sage sits up, wiping her now red eyes, the mascara streaked down her cheeks. I rub her back in soothing circles, wiping my own eyes with my free hand, and giving her a small smile. "Well that's good, right? You were adopted into a loving family."

She shakes her head. "I wish it had been that easy. When I was originally put into foster care, after six months, if my mom hadn't gotten her act together or didn't try to claim me, my case worker was supposed to file to have her parental rights severed, allowing me to be adopted.

That never happened. And we didn't know that until the Davises tried to adopt me four years after I went into the foster system. After all this time, she was still legally my mom. So the courts tried to track her down, to give her the opportunity to voluntarily relinquish her parental rights or reunify with me.

But it was as if she dropped off the face of the earth. No one could track her down, and there was no record of her death either. Not only was it costly for Melody and Ken to fight this in court, it took forever too. By the time the judge finally agreed to terminate her rights in her absence, I had aged out of the foster system.

The Davises never treated me differently though. They always saw me as their daughter, regardless of my foster status. I'm named right alongside Theia in all their legal documents, even their wills." Sage sits next to me, leaning into my side, playing with the ring on her middle finger.

"Is that ring from the Davises?" I ask. Sage wears that class ring on a daily basis, it's clearly weathered and discolored, so I knew it wasn't hers. Hearing how important the Davises are to her, I assume it's one of theirs.

She shakes her head. "Actually, it was my dad's. When I was removed from my mom's care, I took it, along with a few photos and his dog tags. I was surprised she hadn't pawned it yet, like she did her wedding rings, so I took with me before she could.

Melody and Ken got it resized for me for my eighteenth birthday so I could actually wear it instead of just keeping it on the chain with my dad's dog tags. I never got to meet him, so this is my way of keeping him close."

I give her another tight hug, pressing my lips to the top of her head. "I'm so sorry that you've gone through all this, Sage."

She gives me a soft smile and a small shrug. "Now you know why Kappa Theta Alpha means the world to me. These girls, *my sisters*, they're the family I always wanted."

Noticing that the sun's begun to set, I pull away from Sage, relieving some of the tension of the moment. "I think we should probably head back to the car. Before we get stuck out here in the dark."

She nods, standing up to help me clean up our mess and blanket. We head back to the car in silence, walking hand in hand. Sage offers to drive me back home but I decline, telling her I'll just meet Alex at work.

"Thanks for listening to me, Naomi. It was...cathartic," she says softly, leaning back and leaning against the driver's door of her car.

I give her hand a light squeeze, smiling up at her. "I'm glad I got a chance to know the real you."

Sage looks down at my face, at my lips, and I feel a sudden surge, the same one I felt the night of the Kappa Halloween party. Deciding to throw caution to the wind, I follow that urge, stepping close to press my lips to Sage's.

This kiss has none of the urgency of the last one and yet more passion. My lips part slightly and she takes that as invitation, deepening the kiss, pulling my body into hers. We mold together, breathing in sync, the outside world disappearing as we get lost in the emotion shared between us.

If I had any uncertainty before, it's gone now. I'm positive. I'm falling for Sage Carpenter and falling fast.

13

Naomi

"**M**aeve! I need your help!" I call out from my bedroom. I was supposed to be going on a second date with Elijah tonight, but if I can't figure out what to wear, I'm never going to make it out of the house. I have been standing in front of my closet for the last thirty minutes or so, and the reject pile is close to having more clothes than my closet. I might be overthinking this date, but he's cute, and he's planning to take me to a nice restaurant a little bit away from campus. Much less casual than our first date.

Maeve pokes her head into the room. "You're still not dressed yet? Isn't he going to be here in...fifteen minutes?" she asks, checking her watch.

I nod, turning toward her and gesturing to the growing pile of clothing on my bed. "And now you see my dilemma. I can't figure out what to wear.

This place is nice. Like really nice. And it's chilly tonight. I can't just wear a sundress and call it a day."

Entering the room, Maeve signals for me to move from the closet before she starts rifling through my closet. "Do you have nice pants?"

I shake my head. "Not that I can think of. I only have that pair of floral pants that I wore for my pinning and then the leather pants Alex convinced me to buy for the drag show. I don't know if leather pants are appropriate for fine dining."

She hums, trying to come up with an idea. "Do you have dark tights?"

"Yes? I have pantyhose, sheer black tights, and a pair of opaque black tights."

Maeve reaches into my closet, pulling out a black satin wrap skirt of mine and a pale pink, off-the-shoulder sweater. "Wear these. French tuck the sweater into the waistband of your skirt and you can borrow my black leather booties," she says, handing me the outfit.

"Maeve, you're absolutely a lifesaver. Thank you!" I say, hugging her tight.

She waves me off. "Yeah, yeah. Go get dressed. Eli will be here any minute for you. I'll have the boots for you in the front hallway," she says, leaving my room. I change into the outfit, taking my hair out of its bun, and fluffing my curls up. I touch up my lip gloss before grabbing my small black purse and leaving my bedroom.

I head into the living room to see Maeve chatting with Elijah. She must've buzzed him in because I forgot my phone in the kitchen. I grab the device off the counter, tucking it into my purse, before taking the shoes from Maeve. "Hi, Elijah, sorry I was having a bit of a wardrobe emergency."

He gives me one of his signature grins. "It's okay, Naomi. It was well worth the wait, you look amazing." He holds out an arm to stabilize me as I put the booties on.

"Thank you. For the compliment and for the assistance with these boots." I stand, finally taking Elijah in. *This man is so handsome.* Elijah was dressed in dark jeans, a white button-down with the top couple buttons undone, a black suit jacket and dark grey boat shoes. His blond hair was styled, slicked, back on the sides, loose and wavy on top. He looks just like an Abercrombie model in the best way possible.

He smirks, catching me checking him out. "Like what you see?"

I push his shoulder, blushing and rolling my eyes. "Come on, we need to go. Don't want to miss our dinner reservation."

He takes my hand, leading me out the door. "I wouldn't worry too much about that…"

After driving to the nearest small city, thirty minutes from campus, we pull up in front of a darkened building. "Did we miss our reservation? This restaurant looks closed." I check the time to make sure we weren't too late. We were twenty minutes over, but the restaurant doesn't close until nine PM, and it wasn't even eight PM yet.

Elijah just smiles. "You still haven't figured it out yet? Come on, Naomi." He gets out of the car, coming around to open my door. He takes my hand, walking me to the front door of the closed restaurant. Elijah pulls a set of keys out of his pocket, using them to unlock the front door and holding it open for me. "After you."

"How did you? Why do you? Huh?" I sputter out, confused.

"Just go inside, Naomi," he says, slightly exasperated. He follows me into the restaurant. It was dark, one table in the middle of the restaurant set for two, tea candles lit to provide ambiance and some gentle light. The only other light in the restaurant coming from the door to the kitchen. There was a bouquet of roses sitting on of the restaurant chairs.

"The restaurant was closed for a private event earlier today, but I got the chef to come in to make dinner for us. My dad may or may not own the place," he says, walking over to the table pulling out my chair and picking up the bouquet. "These are for you."

I take the roses, sniffing them. "These flowers are beautiful. Thank you." I sit at the table, Elijah going to sit across from me. He drapes his suit jacket over the back of his chair, grabbing the bottle of wine from the bucket next to us. "Wine?"

"Yes, please."

He grabs two glasses, pouring the white wine for both of us, sliding a glass across the table to me. "So your dad owns this place?"

"And a few other buildings and businesses downtown. And the athletic center on campus," he says simply, taking a sip from his glass.

"Wait, your last name is Holton? Elijah Holton, as in the Holton family trust that's behind Telecor? We've talked about some of your family's business dealings in my Strategic Management class."

He nods. "Yep, that's my family."

"So is this your idea of a simple first date then? A private dinner at your dad's restaurant?" I poke fun at Elijah.

"Just the women I'm interested in taking things further with."

"I mean, it's only a first date. I think it's a bit soon to ask me to be your girlfriend."

He cocks his head, studying me curiously. "Is that what you think this is? Me asking you to be my girlfriend?"

I nod. "What else would it be?"

He chuckles. "I'm not looking for anything serious, Naomi. Maybe some casual sex, go on a few dates here and there. No-strings-attached fun."

I nearly spit out the wine I was sipping. "That's a good one."

"It wasn't a joke."

"You think that just because you did all this, I'm going to sleep with you?"

He shrugs. "That's usually how this works. I wine and dine the woman I'm seeing, sleep with her, spoil her for a little bit, and then we go our separate ways when I'm ready to move on."

I thought Elijah was a nice guy, sweet even. But deep down, he's a disgusting pig. "You're disgusting. I had no intention of sleeping with you, regardless of how this night went, and I certainly won't be doing it now."

"Come on, Naomi, don't be like that. I'm not trying to find my wife, it's just dating. I have no interest in continuing anything beyond school."

"If you had listened to anything I said during our first date, you should've known I'd never say yes, Elijah."

"Well, you're a fool if you think a man would do all this without the promise of sex afterward."

"Then maybe I shouldn't be dating men!" I say, my voice raised as I grab my purse.

"And there it is. I knew there was something going on between you and that dyke Sage," he says, looking at me with disgust, never once rising from his seat at the table.

I gasp, surprised by his cruelty and blatant homophobia. Clearly, I had him all wrong. "You know what, Elijah? Fuck you. You can rot in hell."

He raises an eyebrow, at least a little surprised at my profane outburst. "And you can find your own way back to campus."

I flip him off, feeling emboldened, and storm out of the restaurant. I walk for a couple blocks, still fuming before coming across a twenty-four-hour McDonald's. I duck into the fast food place, taking a seat to text my roommates.

Naomi

> **SOS. I need a ride back to campus.**

Alex

> **???????????????**

Maeve

> **What happened? Are you okay?**

> **Turns out Elijah is a giant douche-canoe.**

Alex

> **Oh shit.**

Maeve

> **Must be really bad if Naomi's calling him a douche.**

Alex

> **Drop us a pin with your location. We're on our way.**

"Wait, wait. So let me get this straight. He thought that reserving a whole restaurant would be enough to get in your pants? Does he even know you?"

"Apparently not," I say, stuffing fries in my mouth. When Alex and Maeve showed up to my rescue, we decided to stay and order some McDonald's so I could recap the night for them. "Elijah said I was stupid if I thought that a man would do this for me without sex. So I said, maybe I shouldn't be dating men. Then he accused me of hooking up with Sage. Said some nasty things about her sexuality too."

"So that's when you left?"

I nod. "To be specific, I said, 'fuck you, you can rot in hell.' Then I flipped him off and stormed out."

Maeve and Alex both stare at me in shock with their jaws dropped. "You cursed him out?" Maeve asks.

Alex holds her hand up for a high-five. "Hell yeah, Naomi, you tell him."

I slap my hand against hers with a smile. "You guys are rubbing off on me."

"Apparently so. Especially if you're actually considering dating a woman. Or was that something you just said in the moment?" Maeve asks.

I shrug. "I think I just said it in the moment. But I definitely have feelings for Sage. I've accepted that much. I can't deny there's something there, but I also don't know if I'm ready to act on those emotions, either. I'm still so stuck in my head over the idea of dating a woman," I say.

"It's about time you admitted it!" Alex says excitedly. "Now you need to go on a date with her. Just to get out of your head once and for all."

I think about it for a little while. "Maybe. I can't think about going on another date right now though. I'm still reeling from this disaster of a date with Elijah."

Maeve gives me a sympathetic smile. "Well, just some food for thought. And in the meantime, I propose a toast to you, Naomi. Boys are icky, and you put Elijah in his place. Good for you." She holds up her cup, Alex and I laughing and tapping our cups against hers.

I'm grateful for my roommates. They turned this disaster of a night into a good one and were ready to come to my rescue. I couldn't ask for more.

14

Sage

N ow that the weather's begun to change, going for a morning run absolutely sucks ass. I'm currently two miles in, and it's freezing cold outside. We had our first frost warning this week, so I can see my breath coming out in short puffs as I run. I have a jacket on and long pants, but it just feels so restrictive. I guess I could just hit the gym on campus and run on a treadmill, but it's not the same. I love the fresh air and the quiet of jogging on the hiking trails near campus. I go running most mornings, but I like to come out here and do my long runs once a week.

I ran track in high school and played soccer for a little bit. Once I started at my charter school, the coaches tried hard to recruit me to their teams. Trenton Prep was not known for their athletic success. I think they saw me, a 5'10" fourteen-year-old, and just hoped I had amazing athletic abilities. News Flash, I didn't. They tried to get me to play volleyball, but my hand-eye coordination was off, so I could never connect with the ball on my hitting or blocking attempts. They tried to get me to play basketball, and I could not shoot a basket to save my life. Even my free throws were all over the place. Softball was completely off the table, I'd flinch and back away from the plate every time the ball was pitched to me.

Soccer was a complete fluke. I was a midfielder, and I think because of my long legs, I was able to sprint up and down the field easily. That's actually how I ended up doing track. Playing midfield, I could move the ball down the field quickly, but I was horrible at defending myself. If they could catch up with me, that ball would be gone. But clearly, I had speed, so they suggested I try track, and I fell in love with it. I primarily competed in the 1500m race and the 4 x 4 relay, but I've trained and ran in a few 5k runs, 10k runs, two half-marathons, and then one full marathon.

I just love pushing myself and seeing what I can do. Which is why I still come out here every morning to try and run at least ten miles a few times a week. Not nearly as intense as when I was actively training for races, but it still keeps me in good shape should I decide to run in another half or full marathon in the future. I make it to the eight-mile mark on this twelve-and-a-half-mile trail when my phone rings. I answer the call from my watch as I gradually slow to a stop. "Hello?" I ask, my breathing a bit labored.

"Sage, are you running a marathon?" The familiar Southern accent comes through my earbuds, and I smile.

"Something like that. What's up, Naomi?"

"Remember how you offered to connect me with the person who does your tattoos and piercings if I ever wanted to get one?"

"Yeah…" I drag out, curious to see where Naomi is going to take this.

"It's time," she says.

"What do you mean?"

"I mean, it's time! I want to get my nose pierced, Sage."

"No fucking way."

"Yes! Can we do it today? Before I chicken out," she says with a laugh.

"I mean, they're open on Saturdays, so probably. Let me finish my run and I'll reach out to them and see how packed their schedule is for today. I'll get back to you in like an hour."

"Wait, you're on a run? For fun?"

I laugh loudly, a small snort escaping. "Yes, Naomi, I am running for fun. I go out on the trails near campus every weekend."

"Ew. Well, do they have an easy trail? Maybe I can join you for a *walk* one weekend," she says, emphasizing walk. I get it. A lot of people hate running.

"Yeah, that'd be nice."

"Okay, well, I'll let you get back to it, Flo Jo," she says teasingly.

I roll my eyes, knowing Naomi can't see me. "I talk to you later." I end the call, slowly getting back into my run.

Once I make it back to my apartment, I call the tattoo and piercing shop I go to, Wild Thorn Ink in my hometown, to see if James is in today, which he is. He let me know his schedule is pretty wide open today, so we could just drop in whenever we are ready. So, I text Naomi that I'll come pick her up in thirty minutes after I shower.

James was the Wild Thorn piercer who did most of my piercings. He was probably the best piercer in Trenton or at least the one I trust the most. He makes the process as quick and painless as he can, and I've never had any issues with the healing of any of my piercings. I figured he was the perfect person to do Naomi's first piercing.

I throw on a long-sleeved shirt and sweatpants, grabbing a zip-up sweatshirt and putting on my sneakers. I text Naomi, letting her know I'm on my way before I head out of my apartment.

I pull up outside her apartment, honking my horn to let her know I'm here. Naomi comes running down the steps, looking around embarrassed. "You couldn't have just texted me to let me know you were here?"

"Nope!" I say, grinning from ear to ear, leaning toward her side of the car. She gets in, turning toward me and pressing her lips against mine gently in a quick kiss before pulling away. "Hey, you."

"Hey?" I raise an eyebrow, surprised by Naomi's kiss. We'd been heavily flirting through text and a bit touchy-feely when together since our smoke session a couple weeks ago, but this was the first time that Naomi's even remotely tried to kiss me since then.

Her smile drops, sensing my apprehension. "Was that okay? Sorry, I just thought—I should have asked you if you even wanted to kiss me. I just thought that since we'd been flirting—"

"It's okay, Naomi," I interject, taking her hand and trying to stop her impending spiral, "you just caught me off guard, that's all. I absolutely do want to kiss you."

She smiles, looking at our joined hands on the center console. "Want to do it again?"

I laugh out loud, tipping her chin up with my free hand and pressing my lips to hers again. She reaches out, cupping my cheek as she kisses me back, this time with more urgency. I part my lips and she matches my movements, parting hers as well, leaning further into me as best as she can across the center console of the car.

I pull away, smiling wide at Naomi. "So, is this going to be a thing now?"

She blushes, biting her lip. "I don't know, is it?"

I drive off to the piercing shop, our hands still joined on the center console. "The ball's in your court, Church Girl," I say playfully.

It was a two-hour drive to the shop. Sure, we probably could have gone to a shop near campus, but I was personally familiar with this shop. Plus, I was excited to show Naomi my hometown.

Truth be told, I texted my parents to let them know we'd be in the area today. I was just going to swing by real quick, say hi, and grab some warmer clothing while I was in the area, but my mom wants me to bring Naomi by for dinner. Apparently, Theia told them about her, so they were excited to meet my 'almost girlfriend.'

"Hey, I'm not sure how long this appointment will end up taking, but while we're in the area, my mom wants us to stop by. Is that okay with you?"

"Your mom wants to meet me?" Naomi asks in disbelief.

"Yep. I let her know I would be in town and why, and I guess Theia's mentioned you in conversation with them because they're eager to meet you."

"Oh gosh, what did she say?" Naomi asks, beginning to get nervous. I could feel the hand holding mine beginning to sweat, her pulse starting to race.

I give Naomi's hand a gentle squeeze. "Hey... It's nothing major. I'm sure Theia didn't say anything bad. If it's too much, we don't have to go. I can visit my parents another weekend."

She gives me a small smile, shaking her head. "No, I'll be fine. Let's go after we're done."

"Nervous?" I ask as we near the shop.

"Very. But I want to do it." Naomi looks out the window at the shop. The tattoo and piercing shop was in a larger space. The owner, Michael, bought an old car garage fifteen years ago and converted it into a tattoo shop. The whole space had an edgy, industrial feel, especially with the matte black garage door, painted with the shop's logo. When they first opened, they only occupied about half the space, renting out the other half to a local boutique.

But they eventually grew so big that they bought the boutique out and now use the full space. The tattoo shop is on one side, and the piercing parlor is on the other side. They updated the waiting room from the original building layout. Now there was a full snack bar set up with a variety of mess-free snacks, candies, and then some waters and sodas in a mini-fridge under the counter. They've turned the shop into such a welcoming space, and I honestly hung out here a lot my senior of high school. To the point where they hired me as a receptionist because I was practically doing the job already.

Now it's been four years, and I still work here during the summer and a few shifts while home on breaks. I've been upgraded though, because James and Ryan have started to train me on tattooing and piercing. Now, sometimes, when I want a new piercing, they'll let me do it myself, under their supervision, of course. It's not something I want to pursue, but it's a neat little skill to have tucked away.

I head into the shop, Naomi's hand in mine, pulling her along with me. "Honey, I'm home!" I call out, not seeing anyone at the check-in desk. Ryan comes out of her office, grinning when she sees me.

"Sage! I didn't know you were coming by today," she says, rounding the counter to give me a big hug. I lean down to hug her back, giving her a tight squeeze.

"James didn't tell you? I called this morning."

"You know that man has the attention span of a gnat. He probably forgot by the time he got off the phone with you." She laughs, pulling away from me and turning her attention to Naomi. "And who is this gorgeous lady?"

"This is my...friend, Naomi. Naomi, this is Ryan, she's the tattoo artist I was telling you about."

Naomi holds her hand out to shake. "Nice to meet you, ma'am."

"Aren't you the cutest? Come here, I'm a hugger." Ryan throws her arms around Naomi for a hug. "It's so nice to meet a *friend* of Sage's," she says, giving me a pointed look over Naomi's shoulder, and I roll my eyes in response.

"Sega Genesis is in the house!" calls from behind me, I turn to see James coming from the hallway to the piercing side of the shop.

"You know you're making yourself sound old every time you call me that," I say, giving him a fist bump. I had just started taking meds for my ADHD when I first started coming by the shop. I had so much restless energy and could barely stay still, James used to call me a video game character, hence the nickname.

"What does it say about you since you get the reference?" he asks with a wink, laughing as I attempt, poorly, to shove him.

Ryan was the younger sister of the shop owner, and James was her husband. She originally started as just a business partner in the shop, but after she and James started dating, she got into piercing and tattooing. Now they all run the shop together. Ryan and James are the cutest and polar opposites in every way. Ryan's a tiny, little pixie of a human, and James is basically a heavily tattooed, Paul Bunyan. They're both amazing people, and they complement each other well.

"So, is this the friend that wants to get her nose pierced?" He points to Naomi.

I nod. "Yep. This is her first piercing too, so be gentle."

He gives Naomi a friendly smile. "Ready to do this kid?"

Naomi turns to me, her nerves kicking in again. "Can Sage come back with me?'

"Of course. Hell, you can even have her do your nose piercing if you want." James laughs, patting me on the back.

I shake my head. "Let's not do that. But I'll be right there with you, Naomi," I say, taking her hand once again and giving it a squeeze.

She smiles at me before turning to James. "Alright, I'm ready as I'll ever be."

We head back to one of the rooms, and Naomi takes a seat on the table along the far wall. I stand in between her legs, running my hands up and down her thighs in a soothing motion. "Breathe, Church Girl, breathe," I say, coaching her through some deep breathing. Her heart rate begins to even out as she matches me, breath for breath. "Good, that's my girl."

She grins ear to ear at the praise, her arms draped around my neck. "I'm still nervous."

I shrug. "That's completely normal. I'd be more concerned if you weren't."

James comes over to us, holding a tray of piercing utensils. "To the side, Sage."

"Yes, sir." I drop Naomi's hand, stepping out of the way.

"Okay, Naomi, which side?" James asks, setting his tray down and grabbing a fresh pair of gloves.

"I'm sorry?" she asks, tilting her head a bit, confused by his question. She looks over to me for assistance.

"Which side of your nose do you want pierced?" I clarify.

"Oh! Right," she says, looking back over at me. "I like how yours looks."

James switches his tray and supplies over to her right side, shifting to that side, and I take a spot over on Naomi's left. She takes my right hand in both of hers, squeezing tight. "Easy. He hasn't even started yet."

James chuckles, disinfecting Naomi's nose, concentrating on the right side. He marks the placement of the piercing, letting her check it out and approve it. When she gives him the okay, he clamps her nostril, grabbing the piercing needle. "Okay, take a deep breath in. And breathe out through your mouth," he says, counting down before piercing her nose.

Naomi squeezes my hand tight as the needle pierces her nose, tensing up. I use my free hand to rub small circles into her thigh. "Hey, the hard part is already over."

James changes the needle out, leaving the stud in place. "All done!" he says, using a cotton swab to clean up any blood around the fresh piercing.

"That's it?" Naomi asks, using her right hand to wipe the couple tears that had formed.

"That's it. Here's a mirror if you want to check out how it looks."

She takes the hand-held mirror, examining her new piercing. "I love it!"

James takes a small gift bag from one of the cabinets and hands it to Naomi, walking her through after-care instructions. One of the things I love about the shop is they send every client home with after-care instructions *and* the supplies you need to take care of your new mod, whether you got a piercing or a tattoo. This way, you have everything you need, and there's no confusion on the client's part.

I hand Naomi a strawberry lollipop that I swiped from the snack bar. "Eat it before you get up from the table."

She pops the candy into her mouth and salutes me, mocking me. "Yes, ma'am." Now's my turn to blush.

James turns to me as he cleans up the room. "You not going to get one, Sage?"

"Nah, not today. We have to make a pit stop over to the parents' before we head back to campus."

"A meet the parents? Already? Wow, seems pretty serious," he says in a low voice.

"It's not like that. It's... It's complicated," I murmur, glancing over at Naomi, who's eating her lollipop and checking out her new piercing in the mirror.

"Regardless, you seem happy kid. She makes you happy."

I let out a sigh, still watching Naomi. "Yeah. Yeah, she does."

James pats me on the back. "Don't screw it up," he says before walking over to Naomi. "Let me help you down."

Naomi hops down from the table with his help, stabilizing herself.

"Feeling okay?" I ask, trying to make sure she's not feeling light-headed or faint in any way. She nods.

"I'll walk you guys out." James heads out of the room with us following, heading back to the reception desk at the front of the shop.

"How much do I owe you?" Naomi asks, reaching for her wallet in her purse.

"Oh, she didn't tell you? Sage prepaid for the appointment. You're all set to go."

She whips around, turning to me. "Sage! You didn't have to do that."

"Eh, it was my treat. Think of it as my welcome present into the rebel club," I say with a wink.

She takes out a ten-dollar bill, sliding it across the counter to James. "Well, here's a tip. And if she pre-tipped, I don't care, take it anyway."

He laughs, taking the bill and tucking it away into the register drawer. "You are welcome back any time you want, Naomi. Maybe next time you'll get a tattoo."

She grins, taking my hand. "Maybe! Thanks again,"

Naomi and I go back outside to the car, driving off to my parents' house. "I can't believe I just did that!"

I laugh. "Yeah, you did! I'm proud of you."

"For what?" Naomi asks with a laugh, looking over at me.

"For being brave. I know how tough this was for you, but you ignored other people's thoughts and did what you wanted to do."

"Well, I have you to thank for that. And Maeve and Alex. Y'all have been so encouraging and supportive of me. It's given me the courage I needed to step outside my bubble."

"Always, Church Girl. You're stuck with me, remember?" I ask, grinning at Naomi.

"Forever and always."

15

Sage

I pull up to my parents' house, parking in the driveway behind my mom's car. I go to get out of the car, but Naomi stops me. "Wait."

I pause, letting the car door close slightly. "Yes, Naomi?"

"What if your mom doesn't like me? I'm not even dressed up. I look like I just rolled out of bed."

I playfully roll my eyes. "Naomi, even when you roll out of bed, you look beautiful. Either way, my mom doesn't care. Plus, I know she's going to love you."

"How can you be so sure?"

"Because you're extremely important to me. So, by association, she'll love you. Now come on, I say, giving her a quick peck on the cheek before getting out of the car. We head to the front door and I let us in, kicking my shoes off in the front hallway before making my way to the kitchen. "I'm home!" I call out, rounding the corner to see both my parents standing in the kitchen, my dad cooking and my mom sitting at the kitchen island, pouring herself a glass of wine.

Melody gets up from the bar stool she was sitting on, walking over to me with open arms. "Sage! It's so good to see you, honey," she says, pulling me down for a tight hug. I'm 5'10," but Melody is 5'3" on a good day. Our height difference is comical at times, especially since she always insists on pulling me down to her level to hug me. But this woman gives the best hugs.

"Hi, Mom, I missed you. I'm glad you guys were home today."

I finally started calling them Mom and Dad, when I was eighteen. It was a tough adjustment at first, but they truly are my mom and dad. They've cared for me in a way no one else has. They chose to be my parents and have lived up to the task every day since.

She releases me, turning to Naomi. "Oh my goodness, you're even prettier in person! You must be Naomi. Sage has told me so much about you," she says, pulling Naomi in for one of her famous hugs as well.

I blush, a little embarrassed that my mom revealed I've been telling her about Naomi. "Mom! You weren't supposed to say that."

Naomi gives me a smile before turning her attention back to Melody. "I hope it was all good things?"

"Don't worry, I don't think Sage could say a bad thing about you, even if she tried." Melody gives me a wink before steering Naomi into the living room to sit.

"You're going to have to watch out, I think your mom's attached to Naomi," Ken calls out from the stove. "You know how she gets when she likes a girlfriend of yours."

I roll my eyes, walking over to him. "Naomi is *not* my girlfriend. But I remember how she was with Katie. You would have thought she went through the break up, not me."

I give him a peck on the cheek, leaning in to smell what he's cooking. "Are you making short ribs?" I ask in disbelief. "What's the occasion?"

Braised short ribs and crawfish etouffee are my dad's two best dishes. They're also reserved for special celebrations only because of how labor-intensive they are. So to see him cooking short ribs just because I decided to drop home while in town for an appointment at Wild Thorn caught me off guard.

"Naomi coming home with you." He holds his hands up in surrender when I narrow my eyes at him. "I didn't choose to make this, your mother insisted."

"Of course she did."

"I know you said you two weren't together, but for what it's worth, I don't think I've seen you this happy with anyone since Katie."

"James and Ryan basically said the same thing while we were there."

"So what's the deal then? Why aren't you two together?"

I sigh, taking my mom's spot at the kitchen island. "Because of Naomi."

He raises an eyebrow. "You're trying to tell me that woman isn't into you?"

"I think she is? It's complicated. She's very religious. Or I guess *was* very religious. She told me she has some kind of feelings for me, but whether or not she'll act on it? I have no idea."

Ken puts the lid on the pot, leaving it to simmer before walking over and pulling me in for a hug. "I have faith that everything will work out, Sage." He kisses the top of my head, rubbing my back.

"Thanks, Dad."

A loud laugh echoes from the living room. "You should probably go check on those two, thick as thieves already. I'll call you guys when the food is ready."

I give him a smile before climbing down from the bar stool and heading into the living room. Naomi and Mel were sitting on the couch, going through photos on her laptop, which was placed on the coffee table. The bottle of wine they brought in with them was already empty. "You guys are having a blast."

Naomi looks up at me, wiping the tears from her eyes from laughing so hard. "Sage, teenage you is a riot."

"Oh god, Mom, what did you show her?"

"The lip-sync videos you and Delilah made in your mullet era."

When I was fourteen or fifteen, I went through a pop-punk phase. I was convinced I was going to be the next Avril Lavigne. So I attempted to cut my own hair similar to hers. I failed and ended up with something closer to a mullet, and then I dyed it with blue, pink, and black streaks. The blue ended up turning green in my hair, and the black bled a lot. It looked awful, but for some reason, teen me loved it.

Delilah, a couple of our friends, and I made mock music videos with instruments we borrowed from the school at the time. I think she was the only person with actual musical talent. The rest of us were awful, hence the lip-sync videos.

Mel insisted on keeping photos and videos from that era because she said, "One day, you'll look back on this and be utterly horrified by what you wanted to do as a kid," and she was absolutely right. Now in retrospect, I'm completely embarrassed that it happened.

"Yeah I've definitely made some better decisions," I say, taking a seat next to Naomi and slinging my arm across the back of the couch behind her. She leans into me a little, her back resting against my side.

"So, how long have you guys been together?" Mel asks, watching us closely.

Naomi sits back up quickly, and I pull my arm down from the back of the couch. "Oh, we're not—it's not like that," she stutters, getting a bit flustered.

My mom rests her hand on Naomi's knee. "Sweetie, I see how the two of you look at each other. There's a lot more than just friends there."

"Why does everyone keep saying that?" she mumbles under her breath.

"Because you both are horrible at hiding your feelings. And if I'm going to be honest, Naomi, if you're not out yet, that closet door is made out of glass."

"Mom!" I say, giving her a pointed look. "*Stop,*" I mouth.

"It's okay, Sage. She's not wrong. Or at least not entirely. I mean, we've talked about it. I do like you, which means I must not be entirely straight. I'm just not sure where exactly I fall. Still trying to figure this all out," she rushes out, tension visibly melting from her shoulders.

Mel gives her a smile. "Well, whatever you decide, know you have plenty of support from us."

I can see tears begin to well up in Naomi's eyes, but she blinks them away quickly. "Thank you, Mel, that means more than you know

After a full and hearty dinner, Naomi and I make the drive back to campus. My mom sent us on our way with my warm clothes, some wine, and an insulated bag full of leftovers from tonight's dinner and dinner from the day before. She was snoring softly from the passenger seat, having fallen asleep shortly after we got into the car.

It was pretty late. After dinner, my mom insisted that we stay for dessert, which turned into more storytelling about my youth. When my dad decided to call it a night, we took that opportunity to make our escape, promising Mel we would come back and visit again soon.

I pull up to Naomi's apartment building, putting the car into park. I turn to her, shaking her gently. "Hey, Georgia, we made it back," I say softly, rustling her out of her sleep.

Her eyes flutter open as she stretches out in the seat. "Hmm, the ride back went a lot quicker than the ride there."

I laugh softly. "Well, maybe that's because you slept the whole ride."

Naomi grabs her purse and after-care goodie bag from the floor. "Thank you for today, Sage. For supporting me with this little act of rebellion. For introducing me to your parents. It was such an amazing day."

I smile, leaning in to press my lips to hers, lingering for a moment before pulling back. "I'll gladly do it again with you. I'm pretty sure my mom's ready to adopt you too, so you're always welcome back there."

Naomi turns to exit the car, pausing with her hand on the door handle. "Sage? Do you want to come upstairs?" she asks, biting her lip nervously.

"It's late, Naomi, I should probably get going."

"You could always just spend the night?" she asks hopefully. "Alex is spending the weekend at her boyfriend's place, and I don't remember Maeve saying she was going anywhere, but her car's not in the lot."

I look at Naomi in disbelief. If she was implying what I thought she was, this would be a huge step in whatever you would call our situationship. "Are you sure?"

She nods. "Positive, Sage." *Well, I'll be damned.*

I grin wide. "Let me park my car, and I'll come upstairs."

Naomi sits back, directing me to the overnight guest parking for the complex. I park my car and head up to her apartment, walking hand in hand with Naomi. Once inside, I hover in the kitchen, not sure where to stand or where to sit. I don't want to push Naomi into more than she's comfortable with, so I'm willing to let her set the pace.

She lingers in the hallway once the door is closed.

"We don't have to do anything, Naomi, if you're too nervous. We can just hang out and watch a movie if you'd feel more comfortable with that," I call out from the kitchen.

After a few moments, Naomi rounds the corner, looking nervous as hell. "Sorry, I had to take a moment and collect myself. This is a big step for me."

I hold my hand out to her, and she takes it. I pull Naomi into me, our torsos pressed together, my hands on her hips. "You don't have to do anything you're not ready for just because you think I might want it. I'm willing to go at whatever pace you set. If that means waiting forever to move beyond kissing, then so be it. I like you, Naomi, a lot. And I'll do anything if it means that I get you in the end."

"Really?" she asks, throwing her arms around my neck.

"Really, you're it for me, Church Girl. You're unlike any woman I've ever known, and I mean that in the best way possible."

Naomi hesitates briefly before pressing her lips to mine. Unlike our previous kisses, this one is aggressive out of the gate. I feel her tongue running along the seam of my lips, seeking permission. I part my lips, letting her in. Our tongues battle for dominance, unable to get enough of each other. Her hands make their way into my hair, fingers tugging gently on the short strands, pulling my head back and exposing my throat.

Naomi peppers kisses along my jawline and down my neck, using her light grip on my roots to guide my head. A moan escapes my mouth as she kisses along my neck, my hands drifting down to cup her ass. "Is this okay?" I ask, making sure to check in with her. She nods, and I adjust my grip, picking Naomi up and wrapping her legs around my waist. I place her on the kitchen island, standing between her legs.

My lips part, welcoming her tongue as she kisses me deeply. She grabs at the hem of my shirt, tugging upwards. I separate from her long enough to discard my shirt, Naomi pulling hers off before diving back in. She reaches behind me to unhook my bra, tossing it to the side. She pulls back, scanning me from head to toe. "God, you are beautiful," she murmurs.

I blush a little. "Yeah?"

Naomi nods. "C-can I touch you?" she asks, a bit flustered.

"Absolutely."

She reaches out, cupping my breast. Her thumb brushes over one of my nipples and I shiver.

"Oh, I forgot. The piercings make them more sensitive," she says, trying to hide her smirk.

"You liar, you know exactly what you're doing," I say, pressing my lips back to hers. She continues to brush her thumb over my nipple until it hardens fully, coming to a stiff peak. The arousal shooting straight to my core, I let out a throaty moan.

"You like that?" Naomi asks, her voice thick with need as I feel the warmth of her breath in my ear.

"Here's a little tip for pleasuring me. I'm a T&A girl through and through."

"T&A?"

"Tits and ass. Doesn't matter if it's mine or someone else's. If you want to get me turned on in point-five seconds, playing with my nipples is the way to go. But if you have a full, round ass," I say, gripping Naomi's to emphasize my point, "or beautiful breasts, you can easily get me on my knees."

Naomi presses her lips to mine, nipping at my bottom lip. "I'd love to see that."

I raise an eyebrow, surprised at how forward Naomi is in this moment. "Yes, ma'am," I say, sinking to my knees, kissing a trail down Naomi's neck, chest, and stomach. I hook my fingers in the waistband of her sweats, looking up at her for approval. She gives me a nod, lifting up off the counter a bit so that I can tug her sweatpants and underwear down her legs, tossing them to the side.

I press soft kisses to her inner thighs, nearing her core, before switching to the other side. I nip gently at the soft supple skin of her upper thigh, licking the spots to soothe them, slowly working my way to the spot where she wants me the most. By the time I reach the apex of Naomi's thighs, I can smell her arousal. I look up at Naomi to see her chest heaving, her eyes hooded and filled with lust.

"Just say the word," I start, pressing a soft kiss to Naomi's lower abdomen, right above the soft patch of curls at the top of her mound. "Say the words, and I'll give you everything you desire right now."

Naomi's fingers run through my hair, tugging on the roots, pulling me closer to her. "Sage, I want you. I want this so bad."

I grin, gripping her thighs and pushing her legs open, exposing her glistening pussy to me. "God, I've wanted to do this for so long," I say, burying my nose in her center, deeply inhaling her scent. I press a kiss to the top of her slit before running my tongue through her folds.

Her grip tightens on my hair, holding me in place as I lap at her clit, my tongue brushing against it with long strokes. I gently suck it into my mouth before releasing it, my tongue running down to her entrance, dipping into her dripping pussy. "Oh, fuck yes," Naomi moans rather loudly, leaning back, her legs falling open further. "Sage, don't stop."

I grin, buried in her. *My girl is so vocal, I love it.* I insert a finger into her pussy, thrusting with slow deep strokes. I curl my finger against the front wall of her cunt, my lips latching onto her clit, sucking firmly. Naomi's head drops back, a loud moan escaping from her.

"Sage, I–I'm gonna," she stutters, unable to finish her thoughts as I feel her walls clench around my finger. I insert a second finger, sending her over the edge with my thrusts, my tongue circling her clit. Her thighs clench around my head, trapping me in place as she rides out her orgasm. I lap at her entrance, savoring her taste.

Naomi lets up on her grip, her muscles unclenching as she comes down from her orgasm. "Fuck," she says, leaning back, trying to catch her breath.

I stand up, grinning at her. "I didn't know you had a dirty mouth like that."

She laughs. "I didn't know I did either." Naomi reaches for me, pulling me close. "Sage, that was..." She trails off, searching for words.

"Amazing? Toe-curling? Best you ever had?" I smirk. One thing about me is that I love pleasing my partners. I get my pleasure from bringing them to orgasm, so going down on a woman is a skill I've honed carefully over the years. Call it cockiness, but I'm just very confident in what I can do.

Naomi shoves my shoulder. "You're so full of yourself, " she says teasingly.

"Am I wrong, though?"

"Not in the slightest," she says, with a grin, pressing her lips to mine. We kiss each other deeply, tongues brushing against each other. I'm sure Naomi can taste herself on my lips, on my tongue. Now that I've had a taste, I can't enough.

She pulls back slightly, kissing along my jaw, up to my ear. She takes my ear lobe between her teeth, tugging gently. "Let me return the favor," she says softly into my ear. I can sense her hesitation, her hands trembling ever so slightly.

I shake my head. "Baby steps, Church Girl. I'm not going anywhere. You have plenty of time to learn how to please me."

"Are you sure?"

I nod. "Positive," I say, pressing my lips to hers.

She hops down from the counter, grabbing her clothes from the floor. "Come to bed with me?" she asks, holding her hand out.

I grab my shirt, taking her hand. "Gladly."

I follow her to her bedroom, taking a seat on the edge of the bed. She takes her bra off, arms across her chest to cover her breasts, turning away from me, still a bit shy. She throws her T-shirt back on and gets into the bed. I pull off my sweatpants, getting under the covers with her.

Naomi looks over at me, a wide smile plastered on her face. "Thank you for today, Sage. For... everything."

I press my lips to hers gently. "I'll do anything and everything for you, Naomi." She snuggles close to me, resting her head on my chest, and I wrap my arms around her. After a little while, her breathing evens out, and I look down to see her fast asleep. I reach over, turning off the bedside lamp, trying not to disturb Naomi as the room goes dark.

"Love you, Georgia," I whisper, pressing my lips to the top of her head.

Naomi

I'm woken up from my sleep by knocking at my apartment door. I groan, turning over and reaching for my pillow to pull over my head when my arm hits something warm and soft.

"Oof."

I open my eyes, looking over to see Sage laying next to me, sleeping on her back. Our legs are entwined under the covers, our bodies pressed close to each other. In reaching over for my pillow, I had draped my arm across Sage's throat. "Oh, sorry," I say, pulling my arm back.

She opens a single eye, grinning when she sees me. "Morning, Church Girl."

I return her smile, propping myself up on my elbow to press my lips to hers. "Morning, Tarragon."

"Gabby's got you doing the nicknames too? I like it better when you call me Sage," she says with a slight whine to her voice.

I laugh, running my fingers through her hair. "I'm just messing with you."

Sage reaches out, grabbing my hip and pulling me close so I'm straddling her. "There's just something so sexy about hearing my name come out of your mouth," she murmurs, her hands stroking up and down my exposed thighs.

"Yeah?" I ask, bending down and pressing soft kisses to her exposed collar bones and neck.

Sage just lets out a breathy moan in response, her hands migrating to grab my butt, grinding my center into her.

There's another knock at the door, this one more urgent, and my phone rings simultaneously. I groan in annoyance, sitting back up to reach over and check my phone that was sitting on the side table. *Why is my father calling me?*

Our communication has been fairly limited since I moved to Pinebrook, sticking to short text exchanges. So for him to be calling me this early in the morning, for the first time in a couple months, was out of character. I send the call to voice mail, not in the mood to talk to him right now. I was about to turn my phone off when I saw an unread text message from my mother.

Mama

> **Hi baby, we were traveling for a conference and decided to stop by and visit before heading back to Georgia. We'll stop by your apartment after your father's live stream service.**

> **We're here sweetheart. Are you asleep? I'm disappointed that you weren't watching the service.**

> **Naomi, open the door honey. We want to see you before we get on the road.**

My eyes go wide, reading through my text messages. I scramble off of Sage, looking around my room for my pants. I grab my sweatpants, pulling them on before collecting Sage's clothes off the floor and throwing them at her.

"What's wrong, Naomi?"

"My parents are here!" I hiss. She jumps out of bed, stumbling a little bit as she tries to put on her shirt and pants.

I go look in the mirror and see I have a few faint hickeys scattered across my neck and collarbone, courtesy of Sage. I grab a hoodie, throwing it on and taking my bonnet off, shaking my hair out. Hopefully, between the curls and my hoodie, they're all covered.

Sage grabs her phone and pulls on her sneakers, heading into the living room. I follow her, heading to the door. "Mama, Daddy, hi. This was... unexpected." I let them into my apartment.

Mama does a quick scan of the room, her eyes settling on Sage. She gives her a once over, her lip curling ever so slightly. I can only begin to imagine all the rude and judgmental things she is saying in her head. "And you are...?"

Sage looks at me, hesitating slightly, before holding out her hand to my mother. "I'm Sage, one of Naomi's roommates. Nice to meet you, ma'am."

Mama just looks at her hand, giving her a tight-lipped smile before turning to me. "Sweetheart, why weren't you watching the service?"

Sage drops her hand to her side, letting out a small sigh. "I'm going to go on my run. I'll see you later, Georgia," she says softly, winking at me before heading out.

"Why did she call you Georgia? Are you having problems with your roommate?" my father asks, worry in his voice.

"Daddy, it's okay. It's just an inside joke. Things are fine with my roommates," I say, taking a seat on the couch, curling up in the far corner. I can already feel a headache coming on from this visit and my parents just got here. The way my mother was just so dismissive of Sage, likely because of her tattoos and piercings, has my blood boiling just a little bit.

"Sweetheart, we just worry about you since you moved all this way away from us," my mother says, taking a seat on the couch near me. I roll my eyes at how dramatic she's being.

"Naomi, don't be rude and roll your eyes at your mother. Have you already lost your manners?" my father scolds, taking a seat next to her.

I sigh, holding my head in my hands. "No, Daddy. My move up here had nothing to do with y'all, and you know it. This was the only school that would let me transfer so late in my degree, and still offer me scholarship money."

"Well, you could always return to High Valley University and pick up right where you left off," my mother counters.

"And there's the real reason for your visit," I say exasperatedly, sitting back. "I already told you guys multiple times, I'm not going back there. I don't agree with a lot of their policies *or* why I was kicked out."

"Don't be so dramatic, Naomi, they are just preparing you to follow in your path with Christ."

I scoff. "Christ isn't going to turn his back on me just because I wore shorts."

"No, but leading Godly men to temptation is a sin."

"Oh my God, are you even capable of realizing how ridiculous that sounds?"

"Naomi, language!" my mother scolds. "You know better than to take the Lord's name in vain."

I sit back, crossing my arms across my chest. "Fine. Sorry," I grumble.

"So tell me about this Sage girl," my mother starts, "she's... interesting looking."

"She's a degenerate, that's what she is. Did you see all those tattoos?" my father asks, his voice dripping with disdain.

My mom shakes her head in disapproval. "I don't understand how anyone can desecrate their bodies like that. It's not just the tattoos, it's the piercings, and the colored hair—so many signs of the devil's influence."

"I'll be sure to include her in the opening prayer of the next service. In fact, I'll include the whole younger generation. So many of them need saving."

I mentally tune out my parents. This is exactly why I left Georgia, why I wanted to get away from them. They constantly cast judgment on everyone. Everything is a sign of the devil's influence to them. Frankly, I was sick and tired of it. So when I had to move far away to finish my undergraduate degree, I was grateful to be able to put distance between me and them. It was a blessing in disguise, honestly.

"Naomi! Are you even listening to us?"

The shouting of my name catches my attention, bringing me back into the current conversation. "I'm sorry, Mama, I didn't quite catch that," I say softly, trying not to get any more on her bad side. I was hoping I could get through this conversation relatively unscathed without my parents noticing the new addition I'd made to my face.

"I asked you if that Sage girl was one of them."

"One of who, Mama?"

"The GLBTQI agenda, Naomi. The queers and the transsexuals," my father states.

I wince at his blatant bigotry. "Daddy, you can't say that. It's the LGBTQ community, and it's gay and transgender. Not queer and transsexual."

"Whatever they call themselves, they're sinners, every last one of them."

"They're just normal people that found love, just like you and Mama. Just because they found it with someone of the same gender doesn't mean that they're bad people. Sage is one of the kindest people I've ever met. I mean, she could give some of the parish leaders a run for their money. The way she's able to form a community and make everyone feel welcome? It's pretty remarkable."

"So she is one of them!" my mother confirms.

I groan. There was just no getting through to my parents. "Yes. Sage is a lesbian. She's also one of my best friends and the best person I've met here."

My father grins proudly. "That's my girl, leading the sinners to the Lord. That is our mission, after all."

"Daddy, that's not what this is. I'm not proselytizing Sage, we are just friends. I can have friends that aren't religious."

"Blasphemous!"

I jump up from the couch. "I can't take this anymore, I have a headache," I mutter, going into the kitchen to grab some Advil. I grab a water bottle from the fridge, taking a sip and knocking back the pills.

I close my eyes and rest my arms on the counter, resting my head on top of them, taking deep, calming breaths. When I open my eyes, I notice a bra tucked under the cabinets—Sage's bra. I start laughing to myself, first softly and then louder.

The hilarity of the situation wasn't lost on me. My crazy religious parents were sitting not more than twenty feet from me, and here I was, staring right at my lesbian lover's bra.

"Is everything okay over there, Naomi?" my mother asks, coming into the kitchen, gently rubbing my back. I stand upright, tucking Sage's bra further under the cabinets with my foot.

"Everything's fine," I say, turning toward my mother and giving her a small smile.

Her smile quickly turns to a frown as she scans my face. *Oh crap.* She grips my jaw, tilting my head. "Naomi! Don't tell me that's real," she scolds, looking at my new nose piercing.

I move out of her grip, taking a step back. "It's real, alright. Got it done yesterday."

"Jackson, come look at what your daughter's done to herself."

My father gets up from the couch, coming to join us in the kitchen. "What is it, Adora?"

"Naomi went and got her nose pierced! Yesterday!" she says incredulously.

I can already see the smoke billowing out of my father's ears. "You did what? I didn't give permission for this!"

"You didn't have to. I'm an adult, Daddy, I can make decisions for myself."

"Naomi, you cannot talk to your father like that. He is the leader of this household and you will treat him as such and obey."

I shake my head. "You know what? I'm not doing this anymore. Y'all are in my place, not the other way around. I am asking you to leave."

"Naomi!"

"Mama, I'm sorry. I love y'all, I really do, but I can't handle this today. So I'm asking you politely, please leave," I repeat, heading toward the front door and opening it, showing my parents out.

They both shake their heads but head out anyway. "I'm disappointed in you, Naomi," my mom says. My father can't even look at me as they both exit my apartment. I close the door behind them, collapsing against the door. *Thank God that's finally over.* I remain seated against the door for a few minutes, completely spacing out until I feel someone try to open the door.

"Oof."

"Naomi, is that you?"

I get up off the floor, letting Maeve in. "Sorry."

"Were you sitting against the door?" she asks, entering the apartment.

I nod. "My parents came to visit, and I just crashed once they left."

Maeve drops her bags in the kitchen, looking at me in disbelief. "Wait, what? Your parents were in New York and you had no idea?"

"Nope. I guess they were 'in the area' for a church conference, so they decided to drop by unannounced."

"How did that go?" she asks, moving to put the groceries she bought away. She stops, looking down at the floor before bending down and coming up with Sage's bra, dangling from a single finger. "Wait, who's is this?"

I blush deeply, embarrassed that Maeve found the bra before I could move it. "Sage's..." I say, hiding my face.

Her jaw drops, looking at the bra. "Shut up! Did you two hook up last night?"

"Maybe... I would disinfect the counters before you make anything in here."

She steps away from the counter that she was leaning against. "Naomi!"

I bite, my lip shrugging. "Sorry? We got a little carried away last night. I'll clean up though."

Maeve squeals excitedly. "I'm so happy for you, Naomi! I love you guys together, so I'm glad you guys are making some serious progress."

I smile. "It was so nice. And the lack of remorse that I feel for what we did, even when my parents showed up here, I think proves that what we have is right. Even though they definitely would *not* approve, I kind of don't care anymore."

Maeve gives me a big hug. "I'm so proud of you, Naomi! You've grown so much."

"You should've seen me. I stood my ground and told them to leave when things got out of hand. My dad scolding me for getting my nose pierced without his permission was the last straw."

Maeve pulls back to examine my face, checking out the piercing. "No way! That looks so good on you. When did you do that?"

I grin. "Yesterday. That's kind of what started it all. I called Sage in the morning and asked her to take me to her piercing shop. We drove all the way to Trenton, I got it done and then we had dinner with her parents. When we got back, I invited Sage up, things got a little hot and steamy, and we spent the night together."

"So wait, does that mean Sage had to do the walk of shame, bra-less, in front of your parents?"

I nod. "Yup. We told them she was one of my roommates and she was heading out for a run. We were literally about to try for a round two when they showed up."

Maeve laughs loudly. "No way, cock blocked by your parents. Or whatever the female equivalent is."

"Taco block-o?" I suggest, feeling proud of myself for coming up with that one.

"Clam jam?"

"Beaver dam?" Maeve and I exchange puns, breaking down into a fit of hysterical laughter.

We're still laughing when Alex returns home, finding us in tears in the kitchen. "What did I miss?" she asks, confused.

"Clams, tacos, and forgotten bras," I reply, finally coming up for air and wiping the tears from my eyes.

Alex continues to stare at us, the confusion even worse now. Maeve finally collects herself and fills Alex in on my last twenty-four hours. Alex sits at the breakfast bar in the kitchen, processing the information we gave her. "So wait, are you and Sage together now?"

I shrug, chewing on my bottom lip. "I don't know. That's not a conversation we've had yet."

"You know, you're going to have to be the one to initiate that conversation, right?" Maeve points out.

I nod. "Yeah, I know. Same as last night. Sage even said that. That at this point, she's just following my lead and letting me set the pace. So if I want to pursue something more with Sage, yeah, I'll have to put myself out there."

"I know it sounds scary, but at least you're going in knowing that Sage is head over heels in love with you."

"You really think so?" I ask, turning to Alex. "I know she likes me a lot, but loving me? You really think that's a strong possibility?"

"Absolutely. She's devoted to you. I mean, she took you to meet her parents last night. That's not something she does with every girl she's interested in. In fact, I don't think she's had her family meet any of her college girlfriends," Maeve states, "you would be the first and only."

It's a bit reassuring to hear that, honestly. I would be lying if I said Sage's reputation didn't contribute to my hesitation to pursue things further with her. I've heard the stories about her revolving door and endless roster of women. Not that it's something she should be ashamed of. She's just not a relationship person or at least her track record in college would show that she's not a relationship person.

At this point, I think I've made peace with my sexuality, at least where it concerns Sage. I like women, or at least I like her, and today just confirmed that I no longer care for my parents' approval. But I'm still looking for love, and I'm not interested in dating around, so Sage needs to be serious about me for me to open that door.

17

Sage

"So tell me about this Friendsgiving dinner?" Naomi asks me as she peels some sweet potatoes. She and I were busy in my kitchen, working on making some mac and cheese and candied yams to bring to the annual Kappa dinner. Ever since our hookup a couple weeks ago, we've been inseparable.

Outside of our classes, executive board meetings, or her pledge meetings, we've spent just about every moment together. After that night, it's clear our friendship morphed into something more, even if we haven't had a conversation to properly define it yet. We even take turns, sleeping at each other's apartments. I don't think we've spent a night apart since.

We can't keep our hands off of each other. Naomi's still getting used to being with a woman, or anyone, sexually. So, has she eaten me out? No.

Has she fingered me? No. But she's not shy about voicing her attraction and appreciation for me. *Boy, is she loud*, in the best way. I'm letting her get comfortable at her own pace, but now that I've gotten her off once before, I can't get enough. Which is why we've made very little progress in the hour we've been working on our dishes for tonight.

Naomi's trying to be a good girl and focus on making her grandma's candied yams recipe, but I can't help myself. I stand behind her, lips pressed to her neck. We were both still in our pajamas, Naomi in just a large, oversized T-shirt and me in a tank top and shorts. I leave soft, lazy kisses along her neck and shoulders, my hands snaking up the front of her shirt, cupping her breasts.

She lets out a soft gasp, moaning as my fingers graze her nipples, gently pinching and rolling them between my fingertips. "Sage, stop. I have to finish prepping these potatoes," she whines, leaning against me and arching her back, pressing further into my hands.

"You say that, but I don't think you really want me to. Your body's responding so well to my touch," I murmur into her ear, my teeth grazing against her ear lobe. "I bet your pussy's so wet for me right now."

She bites her lip, trying to hold back a moan as I continue to toy with her nipples. I was playing with fire, touching Naomi like this out in the open in the kitchen. While Cora spent the night at Anthony's last night, Gabby was still asleep in her room right down the hall. We woke up early, knowing that it would take us a while to get everything cooked. Gabby was smart, making her pernil yesterday, so it just needs to be reheated when we get to the Kappa house. Since we do have the apartment to ourselves, at least for the moment, I decided to take advantage of that and Naomi.

I nip at Naomi's neck, gently grazing my teeth over her skin as my left hand runs down her front, dipping below the waistband of her panties. My fingers dip between her legs, brushing over her clit and circling her entrance. *Just as I thought, soaked.* I grin against Naomi's neck when I hear the clang of the peeler dropping to the countertop.

"Oh fuck, Sage," she says breathlessly as she spreads her legs wider for me.

"Good girl," I say softly, my fingers circling her clit lazily, my body flush against her back, trapping her against the counter. I slowly increase the pressure and speed, rubbing Naomi's sensitive nub. Her heart rate picks up rapidly as her breath comes out in labored pants. I can feel her rapidly approaching the brink of her climax, her knuckles white as she grips the edge of the counter.

I insert a single finger into her warm, wet cunt, stroking her inner walls and sending her over the edge. I can feel her body shuddering as she climaxes, riding out her orgasm on my hand. I plant soft kisses along her neck as she comes down from her orgasm. "My legs feel like jello," she says shakily, still gripping the counter tight.

I grin, pulling my hand out of the front of Naomi's underwear and bringing my fingers to my mouth. I lock eyes with Naomi as I lick my fingers clean, savoring her taste. Her chest still heaves as she watches me, desire still written all over her face. A door opens from behind us, Gabby finally emerging from her bedroom.

"You guys aren't as quiet as you think—" she shouts out, stopping short when she finds us in the kitchen.

I just flash her a wink as Naomi blushes, tugging on the hem of her oversized T-shirt.

Gabby looks from me to Naomi, realizing what went down. "Come on, Sage. Seriously, in the kitchen? In front of the food?"

I laugh. "Sorry, I just can't help myself. She's irresistible," I say, looking over at Naomi.

She blushes even more, scanning me from head to toe, clearly checking me out.

Gabby rolls her eyes, a smile on her face. "Get a room, you two. Some-where private, not the kitchen."

"I'm going to go freshen up, but don't worry, I didn't touch anything that will be made available for public consumption. Just this one," I say, smacking Naomi on the ass as I walk by. I'm barely out of earshot when I hear Naomi and Gabby talking about me. I wash my hands in the bath-room, collecting myself, trying to tamper my arousal before heading back into the kitchen.

Gabby and Naomi are working together, finishing off the tray of candied yams and sticking them in the oven before moving on to making the mac and cheese. I decide to take a seat at the counter, staying out of their way because, clearly, I'm just a distraction at this point.

"So Naomi, what are your plans for Thanksgiving?" Gabby asks as she shreds some cheese.

Naomi pauses as she makes the noodles, contemplating her answer. "I'm not sure, actually. Usually, my whole family gets together at my Granny Mae's house for Thanksgiving dinner. I don't know if I want to see my par-ents, though. My grandmother bought me a round-trip flight to Atlanta, but she said it's up to me if I want to use it or cancel the flight and take the airline credit. If I don't go home, I don't know what I'm going to do though."

When she turns back toward the stove, Gabby glares at me.

What? I mouth, unsure what I did to be on the receiving end of one of her scathing looks.

She gestures in Naomi's direction. *Ask her to stay,* she mouths back.

I had considered inviting Naomi to spend Thanksgiving with my family, but I wasn't sure if it would be too much too soon. Especially since we still hadn't defined our relationship yet. It would be one thing if it were just me, Theia, and our parents, but it's not. Ken's side of the family usually comes to visit as well.

If we were to go to my house for Thanksgiving, given how touchy-feely and affectionate we've been in the last couple weeks, there would be a ton of questions regarding our relationship status—questions we're just not ready to answer yet. Not just from my parents but from the rest of the family as well. I don't want Naomi to have to deal with that pressure.

"Hey, Naomi! Sage has a question for you," Gabby calls out, drawing her attention.

"What's up, Sage?"

I let out a large sigh, narrowing my eyes at Gabby. "I was just wondering if you'd maybe like to join me and my family for Thanksgiving."

"That's sweet of you to offer, but I wouldn't want to impose," she says, misinterpreting my exasperation.

I shake my head. "I wasn't sighing because of you. I'd love to have you there. You know I would. I just wasn't sure if that was even something you were interested in, given that we're still very up in the air."

"I'm not sure I'm following..."

"Well, we act like we're in a relationship together, but we still haven't really talked about it or made it official. I know that's something you have to take your time with, so I'm not trying to pressure you into making a decision. My family's going to have a lot of questions though, especially if we're interacting with each other the way we normally do. I'm not sure if you even wanted to deal with that."

Naomi pauses, mulling over my words. "Well, I would love to spend time with you and your family. Maybe we can just keep things platonic on Thanksgiving when everyone is over, and then we can just be us the rest of the week. Unless you go home for the full week?"

"Depends on what Mel and Ken have planned. Since I just saw them a couple weeks ago, I was actually planning to just stay here for the first half of the week and then maybe just go home the morning of and stay overnight."

"Then I would love to go home with you for Thanksgiving, Sage—on one condition."

"What's that?"

"Can I stay with you the whole week? Maeve is going home for Thanksgiving and Alex is spending half the break with her boyfriend, half the break at home, so my apartment is going to be empty, and I don't want to be there by myself."

Gabby interjects. "Uh-uh, you guys can stay at her place. You know I stay here during Thanksgiving break."

I laugh. "Gabby's right. She's from New York City, so she usually just sticks around for breaks and just goes home for a couple days at most to celebrate the holidays. But I will gladly come stay at your apartment with you, Naomi."

She grins. "Then it's settled. We're going to spend Thanksgiving break together."

I smirk. "Mmm, having the place all to ourselves for a whole week? Can't wait," I say, giving Naomi a wink.

Gabby looks between the two of us. "Can't you guys tone down the flirting? At least a little bit?"

Naomi laughs. I look at her before shaking my head. "Not in the slightest, Gabby."

Later, we were all seated in the dining room of the Kappa Theta Alpha house, passing platters of food around the table as we served ourselves. Thankfully, the way this house was designed, the rooms are very large, and the main floor is an open concept. So we lined up a bunch of tables next to each other, from the dining room, into the kitchen, and in the hall a bit in order to fit everyone.

The Kappa Friendsgiving is a big annual celebration that we do every year, usually the weekend before the start of our fall Thanksgiving break. All the sisters sit down together for a potluck-style dinner and everyone's granted a plus one that they could invite. So we could have upwards of fifty or so people in the house, though usually only half the girls bring plus ones.

This year, not many sisters brought anyone. I invited Cora, and Gabby, forever the matchmaker, invited her boy toy, Anthony. Alex invited her boyfriend, I think his name is Matt, but something came up last minute. Raven brought Chase, and a couple of the pledges brought their significant others or their roommates. My sister Theia has a standing invitation, even as an alumni, but this year decided not to come. She said she had plans, but I can't imagine what she could have that would have taken priority over this?

I was seated between Naomi and Gabby at the table, across from Cora and Anthony, digging into my plate that had a little bit of everything. Or at least as much as I could fit. Not everyone brought food, but we still had about twenty dishes we were passing around. In hindsight, it probably would've been easier if we had just set up a buffet table with all the food and then just had people go up in groups to grab plates. But this always felt more intimate, like we were actually sitting down with family.

"So, Sage, how long have y'all been together?" Anthony asks, looking between me and Naomi. I raise an eyebrow, looking to Cora for the assist. She leans into him. "They're not—"

Naomi grabs my hand, interlacing her fingers with mine. "It's in the early stages," she says, interrupting Cora, "we're still figuring things out right now."

I stare at her in total confusion. Nothing she was saying was false, but at the same time, we haven't exactly been out and open with our feelings and pending relationship status with people outside of just our roommates. So for Naomi to be so outwardly affectionate with me at a dinner with all of our sorority sisters, especially when we still haven't talked about what we are? I was shocked.

As time goes on, I'm growing more and more impatient with Naomi, and it's completely selfish of me. I'm trying to be considerate of her feelings and emotions. I really am, but I'm getting antsy. She's gotten so comfortable being with me romantically but still hasn't defined it. And the less careful we are, the more questions we get, but I continue not to have any answers for them.

Sure, I probably could initiate the conversation myself. But I've already made my feelings clear to Naomi. I've loudly and proudly told her I'm falling for her. I've told our friends and my family how I feel. I just want her to claim me in the same way. To make me feel wanted and loved by her. And I haven't gotten that yet.

If I'm going to be honest, I think there's a part of me that's terrified that this is just a phase for Naomi. That this is just part of her big, secular exploration. One day, she's going to wake up and decide that she's done experimenting, done with me, and just move on. And in the end, the only person that's going to get hurt in that situation would be me. I've already bared so much of myself to her in a way I haven't with anyone else. At this point, I'm constantly on edge, waiting for her to shatter my heart into a million pieces.

The sensation of Naomi's fingertips stroking my palm brings my attention back to the present. "Hey, where'd you go?" she asks, cupping my cheek, eyes searching mine. I shut my eyes, leaning into her palm a bit. I pause, soaking in her concern and trying to push my insecurities to the back of my mind.

Opening my eyes, I see Naomi still watching me intently. "I'm fine, I just spaced out. I was trying to figure out what my sister was up to tonight."

The lie rolls off my tongue a little too easily, but I give Naomi a fake smile, hoping it's all convincing enough.

She doesn't press me any further, but I can tell she doesn't completely believe me. I redirect my attention, striking up a conversation with Cora as I resume eating my food. The rest of the night goes smoothly, sharing laughs, food, and drinks with my sorority sisters and our friends. It's nearly midnight by the time we all vacate the house, armed with take-home plates of leftovers because we made way too much food.

Gabby decides to hang out with Stephanie after Friendsgiving, so it's just Naomi and I alone on the ride home. We sit in an awkward silence, neither of us daring to bring up the moment we had earlier. When we get back to my apartment, I stick our take-home plates in the fridge before heading to my room. Naomi follows, watching me as I strip out of my clothes, changing into some pajamas. She rests a hand on my shoulder, coming to stand in between my legs. "Are you okay, Sage? You've been quiet since dinner."

I nod, giving her a small smile and pressing my lips to the back of the hand on my shoulder. "Yes, of course."

She tilts my chin up to look at her, her gaze disarming. I feel like she can see straight into my soul as she looks into my eyes. "Are we okay?"

I nod, reaching up a bit to press my lips to hers in a brief, gentle kiss. "Of course."

Naomi seems to accept that answer because she pulls away, reaching into the drawer of my dresser and pulling out one of my jumbo T-shirts to sleep in. She changes into the shirt before crawling into the bed with me, curling into me from behind. "Goodnight, Sage," she says softly, her lips pressed to the back of my neck.

"Goodnight, Naomi."

18

Naomi

There's been a shift in my relationship with Sage and not the good kind. Ever since Kappa Friendsgiving a few days ago, Sage has been... detached. We've been spending our Thanksgiving break together, staying at my apartment and continuing to share a bed, but she hasn't been very present.

Her smile doesn't quite reach her eyes. She's been keeping her hands to herself besides a sweet kiss, a hug, or cuddling at night, which is entirely unlike her. I've tried talking to her to find out what's wrong, but she just tells me everything is fine and not to worry.

It's just been the two of us in this apartment for the last three days, and I think I might go crazy. We're supposed to be going to her parents' house tomorrow for Thanksgiving dinner, but she hasn't been herself, and I don't even know how to get her to talk to me and open up. It's like she's shut down and closed herself off to me.

I roll over in bed to check the time on my phone. Sage left a while ago to grab us some breakfast, but she still hasn't been back yet. I would call her, but I was staring at her phone on the nightstand next to me. I grabbed hers by mistake and I was staring at her lock screen.

It was the photo Stephanie had taken of the two of us the day I smoked with them. We were both high, but we looked so madly in love in that photo. I had no idea Sage had been looking at that photo this whole time. Maybe I had underestimated how much she really liked me? I've been worried this whole time that I was just Sage's latest flavor of the week, but if she's been holding onto this photo for this long, maybe she's in it for the long haul too.

Her phone lights up, buzzing on the nightstand, Gabby's name rolling across the screen. I answer it since Sage was still at the store, putting it on speaker.

"Hey! How's it going? Have you had the talk yet?" Gabby asks, her voice echoing. It sounded like she was in a car, a lot of background noises.

"Hey Gabs, it's me, Naomi. Sage went out to grab us breakfast and left her phone."

She's silent on the other line for a little bit. "Oh my bad, just have her call me later when she gets back."

"Wait! What do you mean 'the talk'?"

"Naomi…" she starts and I can hear the sympathy in her voice.

My heart begins to race, my chest feeling tight. My mind starts spiraling, worried that my fears were coming true. "Gabby, I just need to know. What talk were we supposed to be having? Was she going to end things with me?"

"What? No! Why would you think that?"

"Because she's not a relationship person! She has a reputation for casual hookups and one-night stands, and that's not me. That's not what I want."

"That's not what she wants either. At least not with you. Sage is so down bad for you, Naomi. She has been since Rush."

My mind begins reeling at the realization that she's had feelings for me this whole time. "Really? I had no idea."

"Yup. I mean, your roommates definitely wanted you to join us. But once Sage made her feelings clear, your membership was never in question. You were the only definite from day one."

"Then why has she been so distant since Friendsgiving?" I blurt out, so extremely confused.

"That's something you're going to have to ask her," Gabby answers softly.

"Well, I guess we're going to have this conversation today after all."

I turn to see Sage standing in the doorway, a tray of drinks in one hand.

"And that's my cue," Gabby states, ending the call.

There's thick tension in the room as Sage remains in the doorway, not stepping into the room. I try to form words, but my mouth has gone dry. A few beats of awkward silence pass between us before she speaks up again. "I left my phone behind."

"I saw," I say softly, holding up her phone that was in my hand.

"Sorry I took so long. All the places by campus are already closed for the weekend because of the holiday, so I had to drive out of town for food if I wanted something made to order."

"It's okay."

More moments of awkward silence pass. "The food is in the kitchen," she states plainly before turning and walking away. I take a few calming breaths, pausing for a moment to collect myself before throwing on a pair of sweats and following after Sage. We sit at the counter in the kitchen, eating our food in silence.

"Is that really what you think of me?" Sage says so quietly that I almost missed it.

"What?" I ask, turning to her.

She takes a deep breath and looks up from her food to meet my gaze. Her eyes were rimmed red, shining with unshed tears. "Is that what you really think of me?" she repeats, a little louder this time. "Do you really think I'm unable to have a relationship? That I'm just using you until I get bored?"

I swallow the lump that formed in my throat. "You heard all that?"

Sage nods. "Every last word."

I let out a sigh. "Yes. No. Maybe? Honestly, I wasn't sure. I was hoping this was different, that I was different, but there's been a nagging voice in the back of my head telling me I was just another notch on your bedpost and I would just get hurt."

Sage winces at my confession. "Ouch. I knew my reputation was... questionable, but I didn't know it was that bad. Especially if that's the impression that you have of me, and you just got here."

"Well, what am I supposed to believe?"

"I thought my actions would speak for themselves," she says in a small voice.

"It's only been you, Naomi. I've told you how I've felt about you. I've opened up to you. I've shared things about me, about my past, that I haven't told anyone. I haven't hooked up with anyone else, kissed anyone else, I haven't even looked in another woman's direction since I met you. But I guess this was the out you were looking for, so there you go," she says, the frustration evident in her voice as she gets up, cleaning up her garbage.

"What are you talking about?"

She turns on her heels, looking at me. "I've been waiting for you, Naomi. I've been really damn patient, allowing you to set the pace and tone of whatever we have going on. But I can't shake the feeling that this is just a phase for you.

That I'm the first woman you've been with, the first person you've been with, and you will just move on from me. Whether that's moving on to a man or even another woman. I've given you everything I've had, and I've just been waiting for you to destroy it all."

That felt like a punch to the gut. I didn't realize how hurt Sage was, but having her standing in front of me, laying it all bare for me, I could see the pain in her eyes, hear it in her voice. It was all beginning to make sense now.

I get up from the counter, crossing the kitchen to stand in front of Sage. "Is this why you've been distant since Friendsgiving? Because I told Anthony and Cora that we were still figuring things out?"

She averts her gaze, unable to meet my eyes, but nods. "I started spiraling, second-guessing our connection. I was worried that if you were still 'trying to figure things out' at this point, you might not ever figure it out. That things will end between us, and it'll just be me getting hurt."

My heart breaks a little to hear how vulnerable she was. She had a point though. I have been the one in the driver's seat of our relationship, and I think this has been a long enough detour.

I reach out for Sage, taking her hand in mine and intertwining our fingers. I reach up, gripping her jaw lightly, turning her head to force her to make eye contact with me. I've never seen Sage so upset. Her usual spark has just vanished completely. "I'm so, so sorry, Sage," I say softly, pressing my lips to hers gently. I plant soft kisses to her left cheek, then her right. Her forehead, then her jawline. I can feel the tension still radiating off of her. She doesn't say a word, as if she's bracing herself for impact.

"Sage, I'm sorry that I've hurt you. This wasn't my intention at all. I was just so afraid, so hesitant, to fully accept what this is between us. Not because I don't care for you, not because I'm not falling for you, but because this is all so new to me. Being in a relationship where feelings are actually involved. Being in a relationship with a woman.

Yes, you were right. I am exploring things with you. But not so I can move on to someone else, but because I want to do things right *with you*. I want this to work out between us, so I wanted to make sure I had no hesitations. I needed to be a hundred percent sure about us, about how I felt, before diving in fully."

"So are you?" Sage asks, finally meeting my gaze.

"Am I what?"

"Are you a hundred percent sure about us and how you feel now?"

I give her a small smile, staring deep into her eyes. "Absolutely. I want you, Sage. I want to be with you. Officially."

A smile begins to spread slowly across her face, her normal joy and playfulness returning to her eyes. "Officially?"

I match her grin. "Yep, officially. Sage, you wanna be my girl?"

She laughs, wrapping her arms around my waist. "Oh, so romantic," she teases.

I shrug, draping my arms around her neck. "I just thought, what would Sage do?"

Sage shakes her head. "I do not talk like that."

"So, is that a yes?"

"A yes to what?" she asks slyly.

I playfully roll my eyes, realizing Sage just wants me to repeat myself.

"Sage, will you be my girlfriend?" I ask again, one hand reaching up to cup her cheek.

She nods, pressing her lips to mine. "I've been waiting a long time for you to ask me, Church Girl. Absolutely."

I deepen the kiss, pressing my body into Sage's. I was finally ready to give myself to her fully, and I wanted to savor this moment. She parts her lips, her tongue brushing over mine as her hands drift down my back, grabbing two handfuls of my butt. "God, I love your body," she murmurs, spanking me on one side and then the other, relishing in how my flesh rebounds in her hands.

I pull away, giving Sage a playful smirk as I grab the hem of my T-shirt, pulling it up over my head. In all of the intimate moments Sage and I have shared so far, she's never seen me completely naked. It's something I've been afraid to do, exposing myself like that, but if Sage can be completely emotionally vulnerable with me, I can return the favor by being physically vulnerable with her.

I can see her green eyes widen, her pupils dilate as she watches me strip, her pulse thrumming in her neck, chest heaving as she watches me intensely. I hook my thumbs into the waistband of my sweats, tugging them down my legs, taking my panties with them. I step out of the pants, standing completely naked in front of Sage in the middle of the kitchen.

The look on her face was ravenous. She was gripping the edge of the counter, clinging to the last thread of self-control she had. I cross the kitchen back to Sage, pressing my body flush against hers. My bare, ample breasts were pressed into hers and I could see her eyes flitting between my chest and my eyes.

"Are you going to join me, baby?" I murmur softly, looking up at her through my lashes. Sage practically melts in my touch.

"God, I love when you call me that. Don't get me wrong, I love hearing my name come out of this pretty little mouth of yours," she says, running her thumb along my bottom lip, "but baby? Sounds even better."

I smile, taking her thumb into my mouth, gently sucking on it before releasing it from my mouth. Sage groans, gripping my butt with her free hand, pulling me further into her. "You are going to be the death of me, Church Girl."

"Then come on, baby, join me," I say, nipping at her jawline gently, pulling away from Sage's reach this time. I throw a wink toward her over my shoulder before heading off to my bedroom. I can hear Sage's footsteps behind me as I enter my bedroom. Her arms snake around my waist, pulling me into her. She must have stripped on her way because I feel her bare body pressed into my back, the barbells in her nipple piercings cold against my skin.

I feel Sage everywhere, her lips on my neck, her hands reaching up and cupping my breasts, body molding into mine. We fit so well together, like our bodies were made for each other. "Let me see you," I say, my voice breathy with need. My body feels like it's on fire right now, the desire coursing through my veins, my arousal peaking.

I turn around in Sage's arms, taking a step back, drinking her in. Until this point, we haven't been completely naked with each other. I know Sage isn't shy about her body, but I think out of respect for me and my boundaries, she hasn't gone past what I was comfortable with.

But now I want Sage, I want all of her, and I want her now. *God, she looks fantastic.* I knew Sage had an amazing figure, but everything I've seen previously doesn't do her naked body justice. Her long limbs go on for miles, decorated with lines of black and grey, her tattoos covering a large surface area.

Her breasts, though smaller, were perfectly round and perky, the barbells in her piercings drawing my attention to her pink little nipples that were already beginning to harden. My attention rakes further down her body, taking in the neat little landing strip of blonde hair between her legs. Her legs were crossed, hiding her core from me.

"Like what you see?" Sage asks, her voice raspy and full of need.

I nod, giving her a smile. "Absolutely, you're beautiful."

She takes my hand, interlacing her fingers with mine. I tug on her hand, pulling her toward me as I back up against the bed. I lay back, pulling Sage on top of me. She presses her lips to mine, mouth parting, tongue seeking entrance to my mouth. I yield, letting her in, my tongue battling with hers. I get lost in her kisses, her body pressing into mine. I feel her hand skating down my body, running along my hip. I grab her wrist to stop her, knowing where her hand is heading.

Sage looks down at me with a confused expression on her face. "But I thought—" I cut her off, pressing a finger to her lips.

"My turn," I say, grinning ear to ear. "Lay down."

Sage climbs off of me, laying down on the bed as I sit up. I climb on top of Sage, straddling her hips. "Just lay back, and let me take care of you," I say softly, leaning down to press my lips to her jaw, her neck, slowly making my way down her body. My lips skate over Sage's collarbone and shoulders, kissing my way down her sternum.

I kiss my way over to her left breast, reaching out with my tongue and licking Sage's nipple, gently toying with the barbell running through it. I grin as I hear her let out a soft gasp, her hands going to my head, her fingers burying in the curls close to my scalp. I take her nipple into my mouth, sucking gently on the sensitive nub before releasing it.

I switch my attention to the other side, taking that nipple into my mouth and sucking on it firmly until it comes to a peak. My teeth gently scrape against her nipple, catching on the barbell and giving it a little tug. Sage moans loudly, tugging on my hair at the root. I let out a soft groan at the sensation, smiling as I press soft kisses to her right breast. I kiss my way down her torso, pressing kisses along her flat stomach and over her hip bones, kissing from the right side to the left.

I press a gentle kiss to the top of Sage's mound, my nose buried in her pubic hair. I feel her tug on my hair and I look up at her from between her legs. "Are you sure?" she asks, still seeking my consent. I love that about her, constantly checking in with me to make sure I'm okay because she knows this is all new to me.

"Positive," I say, my tongue reaching out and tentatively lapping at her clit. Sage moans loudly, her grip in my hair tightening as I lick through her folds, savoring her taste. She was so wet already, and it turned me on to know that I did this to her. My tongue dips into her entrance before returning to her clit. I insert a finger inside her, pumping in and out as I continue to lick at her sensitive bud.

"Fuck, Naomi, please, I need more," she begs, arching her back and holding my head in place between her legs. I insert a second finger, curling my fingers inside Sage as I thrust my fingers inside of her. She lets out a high-pitched moan, more like a whine, and I know I've found the spot. I continue to brush against that sensitive spot, gently sucking on Sage's clit, and I feel her canal tensing and tightening around me.

I lightly scrape my teeth against her clit, and that sets her off. Sage moans out my name as she reaches her climax, her walls spasming around me. After a moment, I pull my fingers from inside her, licking them clean. There was something about her taste that drove me crazy. I could see myself becoming addicted to being between Sage's legs. Now I get why she's obsessed with going down on me.

I kiss my way back up Sage's body, pressing my mouth to hers, letting her taste herself on my tongue. "How was it?" I ask, laying on my stomach on the bed next to her, propping myself up on my elbow.

She looks over at me in disbelief. "Are you sure you've never done that before?"

I laugh, stroking my hand over the curve of her hip, giving her a lazy smile. "Now you know this is my first time Sage."

She presses her lips to mine gently, returning my smile. "Well, you did fantastic. Seriously, amazing right out the gate. I'm impressed."

"I may have been taking mental notes every time you went down on me," I admit sheepishly.

"Well then. I must not have been doing my job well enough if you were still able to string together any coherent thoughts." Sage rolls over on top of me this time, lowering herself down in between my legs, her mouth descending on my own mound.

I'm so glad my roommates decided to leave for the break, but apologies to my neighbors. Sage and I spend the whole afternoon and evening exploring each other's bodies, trading orgasms like secrets. For someone who barely would kiss another being a few months ago, Sage and I sure were having a lot of sex. And I was enjoying every moment of it.

19

Sage

Ever since Thanksgiving, things have been going well with Naomi and me. It feels good to finally call her my girlfriend, even if it is just in private. Even though Naomi's family is states away, and the likelihood of her parents finding out accidentally is slim to none, she wanted to keep things on the low until she was able to tell them.

Naomi's going home to Georgia for winter break, so she's planning to tell them in person toward the end of her trip. I offered to go with her just to provide some backup and moral support, but she insisted on doing it alone. She warned me that her parents are volatile and that this conversation might go south extremely quickly.

I think Naomi just wants to keep me out of their line of fire, especially after what they said about me during their surprise trip. After she asked me to be her girlfriend, we got to talking more about her life and her upbringing. That's when she finally told me about how their little visit went. Previously, when I've asked, all Naomi would say is that it went fine, but she'd dodge any further questions.

This time, she finally decided to come out and tell me exactly how it went down, including the choice words they had to say about me. While I'm not entirely surprised, their words still stung. I've encountered a lot of people in my life who share the same sentiments as Jackson and Adora Williams, but knowing it came from people that the love of my life holds close, it hurts.

I know I'm thinking far into the future, but I don't want Naomi to have to make a decision between me and them, and I don't have faith that they'll be able to accept their daughter is gay. Naomi told me her grandma is pretty liberal. I think she'd have no problem accepting it. I guess her mom didn't become super religious until she met Jackson, so maybe there's some hope she'll come around.

Knowing that Christmas might end up being rough for Naomi, I wanted to do something special for her before we part for the holidays. While our friends might not know we're dating, my sister Theia does. After making things official right before Thanksgiving, I couldn't contain myself when we were at my parents' house. My mom picked up on the change in our energy almost immediately.

So we just decided to give in and tell my parents, and Theia, and my extended family. Everyone showed us so much love. I think they were all just happy to see me happy, happier than I've been in a long time.

Theia and I were currently at the mall, Christmas shopping. "So, where did you want to pop into Theia?" I ask as we scour the mall directory.

"Braserie Dearie," she says with a sly smile, pointing to the store on the map. Braserie Dearie is an underwear store similar to Victoria's Secret but with a greater focus on affordable, size-inclusive lingerie. The stores I wanted to shop at were in the same general vicinity, so we start making our way to that section of the mall.

"Braserie Dearie? I thought you and Aaron broke up?" I ask, bewildered. She finally dumped that abusive, piece of shit ex of hers, so it caught me off guard that she was shopping for lingerie.

She bites her lip, hesitant to answer. "We did. This is for... someone else," she says, her face heating.

I stop in my tracks, turning toward Theia. "You bitch, you're seeing someone new and you didn't tell me?"

She laughs. "Because I know you'd act like this! Besides, we're keeping things on the DL right now."

"Is that because of Aaron or... ?"

"No, it has nothing to do with Aaron. Our relationship is complicated, and it could put our positions with the university at risk."

"Theia, are you seeing another graduate student?"

She shakes her head.

"One of your students?"

She shakes her head again.

"One of your professors?"

This has Theia pausing, remaining silent.

"A professor? Theia, that's so risky!" I say, my voice getting louder as I try to process the bomb my sister just dropped on me.

"Keep it down!" she hisses, shushing me. "He's not my professor. At least not right now, anyway."

"What's that supposed to mean?"

"Well, I had him as a professor in undergrad. And so did you. He teaches English, including the mandatory freshman English Composition class."

I comb through my memories, trying to think back to the professors I had as a freshman. My jaw drops once I make the connection. "No fucking way, T. You're hooking up with Professor Hottie?"

Dr. Samuel Bennett, a.k.a. Professor Hottie, was one of the most talked about professors among the female student body population at Pinebrook University, and not for reasons related to his teaching abilities. The man was one of the youngest, full-time professors at Pinebrook and very attractive. I might be gay, but even I can appreciate that he's extremely good-looking. His upperclassman elective classes often end up being at least seventy-five percent female because a lot of them will request his courses just to spend the class ogling him. Theia was living every female student's fantasy.

Theia slaps a hand over my face, effectively silencing me. "God, Sage, you're such a big mouth," she says, looking around to make sure there was no one she recognized around us. "Yes, Sam and I have been... seeing each other for a little while now, and I'm going to spend a significant portion with him for Winter Break."

I follow her as we head into Braserie Dearie, hanging back as she searches the racks. "I have so many questions, Theia! Like when did this start? How did it happen? Why aren't you coming home for Christmas? Does he treat you well? How's the sex? And 'Sam,' you're on a first-name basis now?"

She holds up a hand to stop my incessant questioning, laughing at my curiosity. "Yes, his first name is Samuel. Dr. Bennett seems so formal now, especially since we're closer to peers now. I guess it technically started on Halloween," she says softly, her face dropping.

"Wait, wasn't Halloween the night that—"

"That Aaron tried to assault me? Yep. I know Maeve told Naomi what she saw, and Naomi talked to you about her concerns, but what you guys don't know is the man that saved me that night was Dr. Bennett. He pulls late nights at his office on campus a lot and I was trying to walk back to my townhouse. We crossed paths, and he helped me home.

He was very respectful, but he helped me shower and change, and made me some food and water. When I woke up the next morning to a PB&J and iced coffee, he had also left a note, just saying that he was sorry for whatever I went through, and if I ever wanted to talk, I had his cell phone number now.

He was my secondary advisor in undergrad, so I felt comfortable speaking to him. Going for coffee led to nights grading assignments together, and then dates at my place, and then one night, we just started hooking up. And it's been fantastic. Like seriously, better than anything I ever had with Aaron. And not just the sex, but he treats me better than that jerk ever did. Seriously, I've been missing out on so much."

I grin widely, pleased to see my sister happier than she's been in a long time. "Theia, I'm so happy for you! You're practically glowing."

She smiles, picking out a couple of lingerie pieces from the rack. "He makes me this happy! So I wanted to get a little something for him since we're spending the holidays together."

"So what's the deal with that? Why aren't you coming home?"

Theia sighs. "Because Aaron's going to be there and I'm trying to avoid him at all costs. I'll drop by for a few hours on Christmas Day, but the less time I'm in Trenton, the better. Sam's daughter is spending Christmas with him, and then she's spending the rest of the break with her maternal grandparents. So once she leaves, I'll go over there, and we'll spend the rest of the break together."

"Wait, so how old is he exactly? How old is the daughter? What about the mom? Is she still in the picture? Are you a side piece?"

She shakes her head, laughing. "No, I'm not a side piece. Sam is forty-three. His daughter Hannah is eleven years old. His wife, Lily, passed away about five years ago from breast cancer. So, no mom in the picture, but Lily's parents are still a big part of their lives, from what Sam has told me. They've been trying to get him back out into the dating pool for a while. They just want him to be happy."

I smile. "Sounds like he's found that with you, even if he is eighteen years older than you."

Theia winces slightly. "Don't remind me of the exact gap. I try not to think about the fact that he's close in age to Dad."

I laugh. "Please let me know when you guys are doing the 'meet the parents,' I'd love to have a front seat to that exchange," I say as Theia goes up to the register to check out.

Theia laughs. "Yeah, like hey Dad , meet my new boyfriend that you probably partied with in college. And no, Sam, I don't have daddy issues. It just so happens that you're close in age to the people who birthed me."

"Does he know?"

"Does who know what?"

"Sam. Does he know that your age gap is that large and that he's close to Mom and Dad in age?"

Theia smirks. "I'm pretty sure he does. I jokingly called him Daddy once and then he had a brief mental breakdown because of our age difference."

I gasp. "Theia! Do you have a daddy kink?"

She laughs. "No, but I think we accidentally discovered that Sam does," she says, moving her eyebrows suggestively.

"You're so bad," I tease, giving her a little shrug as we exit the store.

"That's enough about me though. What about you? Nervous for Naomi to come out to her parents?"

"Is it weird to say that I'm nervous for her? Like I don't know why I'm nervous. I'm not the one that will be sitting down with Jackson and Adora."

"Are you worried that Naomi might pull back if things go really bad with them?"

"Maybe, deep down, that's what's causing my nerves because I guess there's always a small chance that could happen, but realistically, I don't think she will. Her relationship with her parents was already rocky because she decided to come to Pinebrook. I think she's already shown that she's willing to follow what she wants rather than just blindly following her parents' wishes."

Theia nods, taking in what I've told her. "I hope for your sake that you're right. I haven't seen you this happy since Katie. And if I'm going to be honest, I think you're more in love with Naomi than you and Katie ever were."

I can't keep the grin off my face as she says that. "I really do think Naomi's my person. Like I can already picture us searching for our first apartment post-graduation. Coming home after a long day at work to dinner and night cuddling on the couch with her? I'm honestly so excited, Theia."

She squeals in excitement for me. "Oh my god, you're falling in love with her."

"Yeah, I think I might be. It's a bit early, but I can see myself getting there. That's why I wanted to do something nice for her. I wanted to get her something really sweet for Christmas and then set up something special for when we return after break."

"What did you have in mind?" she asks as we step into the beauty supply store.

"Well, for her Christmas present, I was thinking about making her a little gift basket of things I know she loves or that remind me of her. Is that too cheesy? It sounds really corny now that I'm saying it out loud."

Theia shakes her head. "Not at all! I think it's a great idea actually. It shows that you've really gotten to know her and that you pay attention. You should know, women eat that up."

"You're right. I'm just second-guessing things at this point." I nod, searching the store for what I came in for. I grab a couple of the different hair products Naomi uses, a pack of the braid clips she uses in her hair, and a couple bonnets in different colors, including a peach-colored one.

Theia peaks into my shopping basket as I head up to the register. "Oh, you're getting the good stuff," she says, nodding her approval.

I blush slightly. "I figured I'd get a couple of the nicer products she uses for the basket and then some of her daily stuff just to keep at my apartment when she stays over, like a bonnet. I already switched my pillowcases out after the first time she spent the night, but I figured I could put some things in my room for her."

Theia smiles. "That's so sweet! And props to you for remembering specifically what she uses. Every curly girl has their own product lineup, and not all curly hair has the same needs. I'm sure she and I probably have different routines because of our curl patterns. That being said, I do use a lot of those brands, and they are my absolute favorites."

I grin. "Good, I'm glad I'm on the right track," I say as I check out.

I take my bag from the cashier, and we head out of the store. We make a few other stops while at the mall as I finish gathering the remaining items for Naomi's basket. We both needed to shop for our parents' Christmas presents as well, and we were able to kill two birds with one stone.

Before heading back to campus, we decided to stop at Chipotle for dinner. As we're waiting in line, a voice calls out Theia's name.

"Theia, is that you?"

We both turn around to see Dr. Bennett standing a few people behind us in line. I give my sister a smirk, leaning down to her ear. "Go get your man. I'll take care of our orders."

She gives my arm a gentle squeeze in appreciation before joining him in line. I turn back toward the order counter, telling them both mine and Theia's orders. Once they ring me up, I grab the bag with our food, returning to Theia.

Theia smiles, subtly leaning in close to Dr. Bennett. We decided to go to the larger mall rather than the one close to campus because it had a better selection of stores, but we were still less than an hour from Pinebrook. She was being careful because the chance of someone from university seeing the two of them, while slim, isn't zero. "Sage, you remember Dr. Bennett, right? Sam, this is my little sister that I told you about, Sage."

He gives me a warm smile, holding his hand out. "Sage... The name sounds familiar, outside of your sister bringing you up. You wrote a paper on the archetypes of women in video games, didn't you?"

I shake his hand, pleasantly surprised. "Yes, I did, actually. I'm shocked you remember that."

He gives a small shrug. "Your paper stuck with me. It was one of the most well-crafted papers I've received from a freshman in the last few years I've been teaching that class. Seriously, well done."

I blush, a little bit embarrassed from the praise. "Well, thank you, I appreciate that."

Theia smiles. "Sam, you want to join us to eat? We were going to just head back to Pinebrook, but if you were planning to stay and eat..." She trails off as she looks up at him.

He lets out a deep exhale, giving me a cautious glance.

"She already told me all about you two. And for the record, I highly approve of this," I say, pointing between the two of them.

He gives me a small nod before turning his attention to Theia. "As much as I'd love to stay and spend time with you and your sister, I'm actually chaperoning Hannah and two of her friends. They're at the nail salon downstairs getting pedicures, a bit of a late birthday celebration. I prepaid, so I figured I'd get in line now, and hopefully, the girls will be here by the time I check out."

Theia pouts slightly but quickly recovers, smiling at Sam. "I get it. I won't infringe on your father-daughter time. I'll see you soon?"

He cups her cheek, and she practically melts into his touch. "Of course, mamas. I haven't forgotten about our dinner date," he murmurs, pressing his lips to her forehead before pulling away.

Theia's practically vibrating with giddiness as she pulls away from him. "Bye, Samuel," she says softly.

"Bye, Theia, my love," he returns, dropping her hand.

Theia grabs my arm and pulls me toward the exit, unable to wipe the massive grin off her face.

"Bye, Sam!" I call over my shoulder as I follow my sister toward the parking garage so that we can head home.

"Oh, you're fucked," I say to Theia. "Like I think you're in love with that man."

Theia remains quiet for the rest of the walk to our vehicle, seemingly ignoring my teasing. It's not until we're seated in the car that she turns to me instead of starting it. "I think you might be right. Is that crazy?"

"Crazy that you're already falling in love with this hunk of a man who treats you right *and* is head over heels for you? Not at all. I couldn't be happier for you." I smile, giving her hand a gentle squeeze.

Theia lets out a breath of relief, the tension relaxing from her shoulders before she starts the car, pulling out of the parking garage. "Thank you, Sage. That means a lot coming from you."

"Maybe we should do a double date? You, me, Naomi, and Daddy Sam," I say jokingly, "We could go to Top Golf or something."

She rolls her eyes at my use of Sam's nickname. "Don't call him that, you're going to make it weird," she says, both of us laughing.

20

Naomi

Today's the last day before I return to Georgia for Winter Break, and I'm absolutely nervous to go home. I miss Grannie Mae, so I'm excited to get to see her. But I've been dreading seeing my parents. Knowing the conversation I plan to have with them and anticipating their reactions, it's been eating at me all week. I think Sage has picked up on my off-mood because she decided to plan this big date for us before she drives me to the airport in the morning.

I roll over in bed, expecting to snuggle close to Sage's warm body, but surprised when I find her side of the bed empty and cold. Sitting up, I rub my eyes, looking around. Sage must already be up and moving this morning because her change of clothes that she laid out on my desk chair last night are gone too.

I move to get out of bed when a slip of paper on Sage's pillow catches my eye. Grabbing the envelope, I take the card out, reading the words written inside.

> *Morning Church Girl! These next couple of weeks apart are going to be rough for the both of us, but especially you. I want to take you out for the day, to take your mind off things, and to show you how much you truly mean to me. I hung up some clothes for you on the door of your closet, so once you're ready, get dressed and head into the kitchen.*
> *-xoxo, Sagey*

I smile to myself, letting out a wistful sigh. I still can't get over the fact that Pinebrook's resident playgirl is, deep down, a cheesy, hopeless romantic at heart. And that *I'm* the one who gets to experience this side of Sage. I get out of bed, gently padding over to my closet to see what Sage has picked out for me. She pulled for me a light green cowl neck sweater and a pair of light wash skinny jeans.

I grin when I see the sweater. I've had it for years, but I never wore it much. Now, it's one of my favorite pieces of clothing because the color matches Sage's eyes so well. After putting on the clothes, I do my makeup really quickly—just something light and easy—before pulling my curls into a high, messy bun, letting a few pieces fall free around my face.

I head into the kitchen, expecting to find Sage, but instead, I find another note. Opening the envelope, I read Sage's written words in this next card.

> *Hi baby,*
> *I bet you're disappointed that I'm not there to eat breakfast with you. I had a few loose ends to tie up this morning for our day. I made you some shrimp and grits and left your bowl in the microwave to keep warm. I*

know it's probably not as good as your Grannie Mae's, but I tried my best because I know it's one of your favorite foods.

I'll be back soon, I just have one question: Do you trust me? If so, text me a thumbs-up emoji to agree to my surprise. If you don't want to take the chance, text me a thumbs down. I know you trust me either way, so I won't be upset if you choose no.

- xoxo, Sagey

"'Do you trust me?' Well, that's a loaded question," I mutter to myself. I take my phone out, texting Sage the thumbs-up emoji. I trust her completely, so I'm sure she's planned a fun, exciting surprise for me. Taking my bowl of food out of the microwave, I take a seat at the kitchen breakfast bar, digging into my shrimp and grits.

"Mm..." I say, letting out a soft moan as I eat the food Sage made me. Usually I cook, so to have her make me a proper breakfast, and one of my favorites no less, was such a turn-on. She surprisingly did really good! Don't get me wrong, no one can hold a candle to Grannie's cooking, but this was still extremely delicious.

I'm finishing my food when Sage steps through the door, holding a small bouquet of flowers and holding a large gift bag behind her back. I grin widely, standing up for her. "Hi, baby!"

She matches my grin, stepping into the kitchen, placing the flowers on the counter and the bag on the floor before wrapping her arms around my waist and pulling me close. "God, I can't get enough of that," she says, pressing her lips to mine. I kiss her back before pulling back a little, looking at the bouquet on the counter.

"You got me flowers? That's so sweet!"

"I know you're getting ready to leave, so it was probably silly because they're going to die. But I saw them and I just couldn't help myself."

I scrunch up my nose, taking in the kind gesture. "Aw, thank you, Sage. And they're sunflowers, my favorite!" I pick up the bouquet, gently inhaling the flowers' sweet aroma. She never fails to surprise me.

"I got you something else too. This is an early Christmas present from me," Sage says, picking up the large gift bag off the floor to hand to me. Taking the present, I peek inside, my eyes going wide when I take in the contents.

"There's a lot in here! I have to do this on the couch," I say, making my way to the living room with the bag. I take a seat on the couch, placing the bag on the ground, and Sage sits close next to me, the heat radiating from her body as she scoots behind me, resting her chin on my shoulder.

I pull out the items she got me one by one, laying them out on the couch. It was such a thoughtful gift. Sage picked up some of my haircare products, a couple satin bonnets, a slightly weighted sweatshirt with a satin-lined hood, and an aromatherapy essential oils set to help with my anxiety.

I twist in my spot to look at my girlfriend. *Who knew she was such a softie?*

"Sage, this was so nice. You know me so well! I had no idea you were paying this close attention to the products I use."

She beams, feeling proud of her haul. "I took notes and photos, when I was staying at your apartment over Thanksgiving Break, but I also had Theia give her curly girl stamp of approval before I purchased anything. I got you two sets of hair products and a second bonnet, so that way you could leave some at my apartment. This way, you don't have to worry about bringing anything back and forth between my place and yours."

Happy tears well up in my eyes. "Sage, that's so sweet of you. Thank you. I love it all," I say, pressing my lips to hers. I already had commandeered a drawer at Sage's apartment so I could keep clothes there, but now she was actively encouraging me to leave my things at her place, which was a big step for us.

"And then the hoodie has a satin lining so that it doesn't mess up your hair and it's slightly weighted, so it's like a portable weighted blanket. I know you're always cold, plus the weight can help with your anxiety."

I pick up the hoodie, examining the weight before holding it close to my chest. It was made out of an extremely soft material and smelled so good. I take another whiff of it, enjoying the familiar scent. "Wait, isn't that your perfume?"

Sage nods, rubbing the back of her neck as she blushes slightly. "It is. And I slipped a little travel-sized dispenser of it in the hidden pocket in the pouch. We're going to be apart for the next month, so I wanted to give you something to sleep in or sleep with that reminds you of me since I won't be there."

I can't keep the smile off my face as I reach into the pocket of the hoodie, and sure enough, the travel container was in there, just as she said it would be. I straddle Sage's lap, wrapping my arms around her neck.

"You're so amazing, Sagey. Thank you," I murmur, planting gentle kisses all over her face. She laughs before burying her face in my neck.

"There's more to your surprise if you're interested."

I laugh. "What else could you have possibly gotten me, Sage? This is already too much."

She picks her head up, her eyes searching my face. "So I know when you got your nose piercing, you talked about being open to getting a tattoo at a later date. The shop is closed this week, but Ryan agreed to come into the shop today *if* you were interested. No pressure though. This is completely up to you."

My eyebrows raise in surprise. I knew Sage and Ryan were close friends, but she's willing to come tattoo me on her day off? I'm honored, honestly. "How'd you manage to convince her to do that?"

"She thinks of me as the little sister she never had, plus she really likes you. It'd be a very short session for her since you probably wouldn't get anything big, so she didn't mind," Sage says, rubbing small circles with her thumbs as she holds my hips.

I grin. "Then let's do it."

She raises an eyebrow, as if she's surprised by my answer. "You're ready to go get your first tattoo?"

"You seem surprised."

"I am! I wasn't sure if you'd put any more thought into it. I honestly expected this to just jump-start a conversation about getting tattoos, not that you would be ready to do it."

I bite my lip. "If I'm going to be honest, I'm super nervous. But I know myself, and if I put it off or try to schedule it ahead of time, I'm just giving myself an opportunity to chicken out. Now that there's an opportunity being presented to me, I just have to take it."

Sage smiles. "Alright then, let me just give Ryan a call. You should pack your suitcase for your trip home now. We can stay at my parents' house, and then we'll drive you to the airport in the morning from their house. It'll save an extra trip tonight."

"We?"

"Yeah, knowing my mom, she's going to want to drive with me to see you off."

I grin, pressing my lips to hers. "I guess I'll go get packed then."

She returns my smile, giving me a gentle smack on the butt before allowing me to get up from the couch. I head to my room to pack a suitcase for the next month while Sage makes her call. In the past, I wouldn't have too many clothes with me at school, partially because I was so close to home.

But since things were so rocky with my parents when I left, I took most of my belongings with me to Pinebrook. At least all my clothes. My grandmother has some of my things, and there were a couple boxes left in my childhood bedroom. My plan while I'm home is to finish packing up all my things and give Grannie Mae the rest of the boxes to hold onto. I'll get them once I'm done with school and I've decided where I'm going to go after graduation.

Sage pokes her head into the bedroom. "Almost ready, baby?"

I nod, zipping up my large suitcase. I grab my travel backpack, tucking my electronic devices and chargers into my bag. I pack my headphones and neck pillow as well. Sage grabs my suitcase and I follow her out of the apartment, taking my crossbody bag off the hook by the front door on my way out.

We pull up to Wild Thorn Ink to see Ryan's motorcycle parked out front.

"Ready for this?" Sage asks, turning the car off and turning her attention to me.

"Ready as I'll ever be," I say, nodding and taking a few calming breaths. We head in, making our way to the tattoo side of the shop. Ryan was sitting in the corner at her desk, typing away at her computer. She lifts her head and gives a little wave before meeting us at the door.

"Ryan, thank you so much for squeezing us in before the holidays," Sage says, giving the shorter woman a hug.

She waves Sage off. "Nonsense, you know I'll always make time for you. And for Naomi's first tattoo? I'm definitely clearing room in my schedule."

She turns her attention to me, giving me a big hug. "You ready for this?"

"I think so?"

Ryan laughs at my uncertainty. "It's normal to be nervous. Do you at least know what you want?" She walks over to her desk, grabbing her tablet and dragging a stool over to the station she had already set up.

I nod. "I do, actually. I want a small cross, and then the verse Psalm 94:19 along the bottom of the cross."

Ryan makes a rough sketch of my idea on the tablet, and we go back and forth, making adjustments to the design dimensions and testing out different fonts until I'm completely happy with it. "Alright, I'll go get this stencil made up, and then we'll get started!"

As Ryan walks away, I turn to Sage, the nerves radiating off me. "Oh my god, I can't believe you talked me into this!"

Sage gives me a little shove. "Hey, I gave you a choice. *You're* the one that told me to go ahead and call Ryan in."

I grin. "I know. I just can't believe this is happening. Are you planning to get one too?"

Ryan comes back at that moment with the stencil for my tattoo. "Yeah, Sage, are you going to get one too?"

Sage looks over at me before nodding. "Actually, yeah. I think I will get one this time. Small little idea that I've had floating around."

Ryan claps her hands excitedly. "Yay, good! Let me take care of Naomi first and then we can talk about you, ma'am."

She turns her attention on me. "Okay, where would you like this?"

I run my finger along the wrist bone below my thumb on my left side. "Like right here? Maybe a little bit further up my wrist?"

Ryan nods. "I'm not going to lie, some people say the wrist bone is painful, others don't think it's a big deal. Sage and I both are in the latter group, but you never know how you're going to feel about it. I'll move it a little further up so it's more on the arm than directly on the bone. How does that sound?"

I nod. "Sounds good!" Ryan cleans my arm, shaving it before applying the stencil. She has me check that the placement is okay before instructing me to lie down on the bench. I lie back and hold my arm out to the side, placing it on the little cushioned pad next to Ryan's tray.

Sage pulls up a stool on the other side of the bench, taking a seat and taking my free hand in hers. "You're going to be fine," she coos into my ear, pressing her lips to my cheek.

Ryan starts up the machine, grabbing my arm and going in to make the first line. "How was that?" she asks.

I shrug my shoulder on the free side. "Honestly, not as bad as I expected! It's honestly like if you've ever written on your skin with a super fine gel pen but dug hard into the skin while doing it."

Ryan laughs as she goes in to do the rest of the tattoo. "I've never heard it described that way, but you're absolutely right."

Sage grins at me. "You're doing great, Georgia."

I smile over at her. "Thanks, baby," I say, giving her a wink.

Ryan continues to work on the tattoo on my wrist. "So when did you guys make it official?" she asks, pausing to look up at us. "I'm assuming y'all *are* together now? Just based on how much PDA you've shown since you came in here. It's cute. A little gag-inducing, but sweet nonetheless."

Sage rolls her eyes at Ryan's teasing. "About a month now? We've been making up for lost time though," she says, giving me a wink.

I let out a laugh. "That we definitely have," I say, feeling my face heat.

Ryan shakes her head. "TMI, Sage, TMI." She sprays my arm down before wiping at the tattoo.

"You're all done!"

"That's it?" I ask, looking at the finished tattoo on my arm as Ryan applies some kind of plastic film over the fresh ink.

She nods. "Yep, that's it! This is Saniderm. Leave it on for twenty-four hours, wash your tattoo with unscented antibacterial soap, then apply a second piece of film. You can leave that one on for up to five days, and then after that, just keep it moisturized. But a small piece like this, it should heal super quickly.

I smile, sitting up to look at my new tattoo in the mirror. "This looks great! Thanks, Ryan," I say, giving her a big hug.

She hugs me back. "You're absolutely welcome, Naomi. You sit just as well as Sage, honestly, so it was a breeze."

"That's a pretty big compliment," Sage says with a shrug, "I'm her favorite person to tattoo for that very reason."

Ryan scoffs. "Don't let it go to your head, Sega." She walks back to her station. "Let me clean up and reset, and then you'll be next. Tell me what it is you're looking to get while I work."

Sage blushes, shifting her weight on her feet, seemingly a little uncomfortable. "So I wanted to get this mantra that my therapist gave me, 'It's okay not to be okay,' in cursive down my spine with a semicolon at the end."

Ryan stops in her tracks, her face dropping. "Oh, Sage... You never told me," she murmurs, dropping her supplies to give Sage a tight hug.

I look between them, a little confused. Sage told me that she's been in and out of therapy, but that seems like a strong reaction.

Sage pulls away, wiping a tear from her eye. "I don't talk about it much. It was a dark time in my life." She glances over at me, and seeing the confusion on my face, she bites her lip, rubbing the back of her neck.

"I haven't told you this story either, Naomi. I told you how I ended up in foster care, but not everything that happened in the time between entering the system and being placed with the Davises.

I told you about how I was self-harming, but I didn't tell you that I attempted suicide after a few months with my first placement. That family was awful and they treated me a lot like my mom's ex-boyfriend.

I was at school when I attempted because I couldn't bear the thought of going back to that house. My teacher found me and I ended up in the hospital. After DCF investigated, they removed me from that family and I was in a group home for a while.

After my suicide attempt, there was a note put in my file that I was a tough case. They had a hard time finding a family that they could place me with because of it. That is until the Davises came along. They didn't care, they wanted me anyway.

Project Semicolon is a mental health organization dedicated to suicide prevention. The semicolon is a pause in a sentence, not the end. So the semicolon symbolizes that my story isn't over yet either.

I've been thinking about getting this tattoo for a long time, but what better time to get it than now? If my story had ended then, I never would've met you. And this connection that we have? It's so, so special, Naomi," she says, taking my hand.

I reach up with my free hand, wiping the tears forming from my eyes. "Sage, I had no idea. I'm so honored that you shared this with me and decided to trust me with this moment."

"Of course, I couldn't imagine anyone else I trust more," she says, her voice barely above a whisper as she presses her lips to my forehead.

Ryan sniffles, and I look over to see her tearing up. "Stop, you guys are going to make me cry! Okay, let me collect myself while I go make up your stencil." She walks away, wiping her eyes on her T-shirt.

Sage gives me a small smile, pulling me in tight against her. "You're one of the best things that have happened to me, Naomi, and I'm so happy you're mine."

I sigh happily, nuzzling into the crook of her neck. "Likewise Sage. Coming to Pinebrook has been such a blessing in disguise because I got to meet you."

Ryan returns with her stencil. "Ready, Sage?"

She nods, pulling away from me. "Ready."

Sage takes her leather jacket off, tossing it on a chair. She pulls her hair up into a bun before pulling her long-sleeve shirt off, crossing an arm over her chest. She lays face down on the bench. Ryan applies the stencil to her back, taking a picture so Sage can check the placement before starting on her tattoo.

She rests her head on her arms crossed underneath her, closing her eyes. She hums as Ryan works on her back, tightening her shut eyes at some moments.

"How is it?"

Sage pauses for a moment before responding. "Not the worst I've had, but it's not painless. Like I definitely think my underboob and my thigh hurt more, but this hurts more than most of my arms," she says, her eyes remaining closed.

"It's impressive watching you. You're not moving at all," I say in awe of how calm she is despite the pain.

"Eh, at this point, I'm so used to the pain and sensations of being tattooed. I can get through it pretty easily."

Ryan works efficiently, and before I know it, Sage's tattoo is done. She takes a photo, letting Sage check it for herself on camera and in the mirror, before applying the same film to her back that she applied to mine. As she does so, I look up at Sage, becoming aware that she's walking around topless. "Sage, put your shirt back on," I hiss, not wanting to make Ryan uncomfortable.

"It's fine, nothing I haven't seen before," Ryan says, giving me a wink.

Sage chuckles when she sees the shocked reaction on my face. "It's not what you're thinking, Naomi, Ryan, and I have never hooked up. She's the one who did my nipple piercings," she explains as she pulls her long sleeve back on over her head.

"But I thought James was the piercer?"

"He is, but I'm also piercing trained and certified. James is the one who taught me when we first started dating. It's just not my favorite thing to do, so I focus on tattooing. But every once in a while, he'll pull me in to do nipple piercing or clitoral hood piercing on a woman who's not comfortable having a male piercer do it," Ryan answers, cleaning up the shop.

"A what?" I ask incredulously, crossing my legs at the thought.

"Yeah, you can get just about anything pierced. Some people are into that kind of thing. Sage at the time was not comfortable with being topless around James, and probably still isn't honestly, so she had me do them."

Sage grins. "And thankfully, you were willing and able because I love them. But I love all your work so..."

Ryan playfully shoves her. "Come on, let me cash you two out so you can be on your way to dinner."

"Dinner?" I ask, glancing between her and Sage.

"Oops. Did I ruin the surprise?"

Sage waves her off. "It's fine. We were going to be on the road soon anyway," she turns to me, "I made us reservations for dinner at one of my favorite local spots tonight if that's okay with you?"

I smile wide. "Sage! You're spoiling me today. Of course that's okay."

Ryan rings Sage and me up, individually at first, but I insist on paying for both of our tattoos. "You paid for my nose piercing last time we were here, and you've already spoiled me so much today. Let me do this for you," I say as I sign the receipt and send Ryan a tip through Venmo.

"Thank you again, Ryan, for doing this for us," Sage says, pulling Ryan in for a last-minute hug.

I take a moment to hug Ryan too before exiting the shop with Sage.

"You guys enjoy your date night, and Merry Christmas!"

21

Naomi

S age is constantly surprising me. When I woke up this morning, never
did I expect that we would spend the day getting tattoos, and end the
day out to dinner at a very nice restaurant. I was so lucky to have her, and
I think I needed today. Knowing that I was about to head back home to
Georgia and be back in that extremely conservative community for the first
time in months, our date day was the reassurance I didn't realize I needed.
Regardless of how my parents might react once I come out and tell them
about Sage, I know being with her is right.

Tonight, she decided to take me to this upscale, contemporary Indian
restaurant not too far from her parents' house. We've had many conversa-
tions about how limited my taste buds were, and I told Sage that one of the
cuisines I wanted to try the most was Indian food now that my roommates

have introduced me to sushi. She hasn't tried this place yet, but she did say that Mel and Ken come here often for date nights.

"So, does anything look good to you?" Sage asks, snapping my focus back into the present.

"Hm?" I ask, looking up at her, clearing my mind.

She chuckles. "I've been trying to grab your attention for the last five minutes so we could at least get started with drinks and an appetizer. What's on your mind, Naomi? You've been lost in your own head."

I give her a small smile as she reaches across the table to take my hand in hers. "Sorry, I've just been thinking about the day and trying to anticipate how this Winter break is going to work out."

Sage gives me a sympathetic smile. "Nervous?"

"Very," I say with a nod. "I think I'm going to wait until after Christmas to talk to them. I know it's not going to go over well, so I want to make it through the holidays first, and then I'll come out to them and tell them about us."

"You think it will really be that bad?"

"I would love to be wrong about their reactions, but considering how much they disapproved of you when they dropped by unannounced and the fact that they cut me off financially when I dared to leave High Valley University, I won't be surprised if they had an extreme reaction."

Sage squeezes my hand gently in a comforting gesture. "So what are you going to tell them exactly?"

"That I'm gay and that I'm falling in love with this amazingly kind, smart, sexy-as-sin woman named Sage. So they can either get on board or keep it moving because you are the best thing that's happened to me, and I'm not going to give you up."

There are unshed tears shining in Sage's eyes as she looks at me lovingly. "You really think I'm sexy as sin?" she asks, batting her eyelashes.

"You're such a goober. I'm trying to be romantic, pouring my heart out to you, and *that's* what you focused on?"

She laughs. "I'm kidding, I'm kidding. I feel the same way about you. I mean, sure, you're definitely sexy as hell, and you already know I feel that way about you, but that's not what I'm referring to. I definitely think that I'm falling in love with you too."

I get up from the table, walking over to Sage. I pull her chair back from the table before plopping down in her lap. "I'm crazy about you, Sage Carpenter," I murmur, cupping her face in my hands.

She grins, gripping my waist, rubbing her thumbs over my hips. "And I'm hooked on you, Naomi Mae Williams," she says softly before pressing her lips to mine. I return the kiss, pouring all my emotions into the moment. I had no idea I was missing so much out of my relationship with Josiah, but since being with Sage, I have no doubt that this is true love.

I pull back when I hear a throat clear behind me and look up to see our waitress standing near the table. "Sorry, I don't mean to interrupt. I can come back if you need a minute to order, but I did want to warn you that the kitchen closes in about an hour, just in case you might want to order dessert later."

My face heats slightly from embarrassment as I stand up from Sage's lap, returning to my side of the table and taking a seat. "I think we're okay to order. At least to get an appetizer and drink order in. My girlfriend's going to pick our food, but I want the Indian Sunset to drink." The cocktail was vodka and rum-based, with mango and passion fruit puree and hibiscus.

Sage skims the menu quickly, ordering a glass of white wine for herself, and then vegetable samosas, smoked eggplant appetizers, and some sort of chicken kababs for us to start with. She then orders Lamb Butter Masala and Chicken Tikka Saag, with a side of garlic naan. The server takes our order before heading off to the kitchen.

"That's so much food, Sage," I say in a low voice.

She shrugs. "I figured this way, we could try a few different things. And if there's any leftovers, we could get them boxed to go. I'll eat them tomorrow, or my parents will eat them. Either way, the food won't go to waste. I promise you that."

I nod, taking a sip of my water. "So I have a question..."

Sage pauses as the waitress drops off our drinks, taking a sip of her beer. "Shoot."

"What's your middle name? You know mine, but I don't think you've ever told me yours."

"Olivia. My mom named me after my dad. His middle name was Oliver. I don't think it fits me, but Sage Olive would've been a lot," she says with a laugh.

The waitress comes by, placing our appetizers on the table and we dig in, eating and joking. I loved spending nights like this with Sage, just enjoying each other's company, and I can't wait to spend more like this.

After dinner, Sage and I made our way back to her parents' house. Mel and Ken were still up by the time we got there, so we shared a nightcap with them and showed off our brand-new tattoos. Mel even teared up when she heard the story behind our tattoos. We talk about my plans for the winter break, including my plan to come out to my parents. She was so proud of me, not only for standing up to them but for choosing to out and proudly love Sage.

Mel reassured me I will always have a place in their family, so no matter what happens with mine, I still have them, and honestly, I needed to hear that. I know that no matter what, I'll always have my Grannie Mae, but there's a good chance that by coming out, I'll lose all my family and the community I left back in Georgia. But that's okay because I've got a great family that I've made for myself here in the Northeast.

Eventually, Mel and Ken decided to go to bed, so Sage and I decide to just head to bed as well, since my flight is pretty early in the morning. Sage's room was on the ground floor in their house and Mel and Ken were upstairs, thankfully. We both change into some pajamas before crawling into Sage's bed together. I lay on my side, rolling over to look her in the eyes. "Hi," I whisper, my eyes searching her face.

She scoots closer to me, grabbing my hip and pulling me even closer until our torsos press together. "Hey, Church Girl," Sage says, trying to give me one of her signature smirks, the expression very half-hearted.

"I'm going to miss you a lot," I say, reaching up, my thumb brushing against her cheek as I cup her face. She turns her head, pressing her lips to my palm.

"I'm going to miss you too, Naomi." Her hand skates along my hip, teasing along the waistband of my shorts.

I raise an eyebrow, surprised at her brazenness. "Really, Sage? Your parents are home upstairs."

She shrugs, her fingers dipping below my waistband and drifting down the front of my underwear. "They're not going to hear anything unless you plan on screaming. The house is pretty soundproof, trust me. Theia's snuck boyfriends in here enough nights without getting in trouble."

"Are you sure?" I ask, my breath hitching as Sage's fingers find my damp center, brushing against my clit over my underwear.

She grins, pressing a kiss to the underside of my jaw. "I'm positive. I won't do anything if you really don't want me to, but you can't possibly believe that I'm going to let you leave for five weeks without making you cum for me at least once." Her fingers stroke lazily against my slit, heightening my arousal.

"I want you, Sage," I say with a bit of a whine, feeling desperate for a release. She rolls me onto my back, climbing on top of me and kneeling between my legs.

"God, you're so damn sexy." Sage presses her lips to mine, capturing my mouth in a hungry kiss. My lips part, granting her access as her tongue battles with mine.

She pulls her hand from my pants, grabbing at the hem of my shirt. I sit up in bed, allowing her to pull the top over my head. She immediately reaches to cup my breasts, her thumb brushing my nipples. I lay back in the bed, taking in a sharp breath as Sage's warm mouth closes on my right nipple, her fingers toying with my other nipple. "Sage, I need you so bad."

She chuckles darkly, looking up at me from under hooded eyelids. "I love hearing you beg for me," she says, her voice thick with need.

"Less talking, more getting naked." I reach out for the hem of Sage's shirt, tugging it over her head. Her mouth descends on mine, pressing her lips to mine, capturing my bottom lip in her teeth, tugging on it gently. I let out a soft moan, reaching for the waistband of her shorts.

Sage swats my hand away, shaking her head. "Uh uh, Naomi, sit back. Let me make you feel good."

I give her a wide grin, laying back down. She presses a kiss to my neck, then my collarbone, then in between my breasts, and keeps trailing kisses down my body until she reaches the waistband of my shorts, tugging them down my body as she goes.

I close my eyes in anticipation, grinning when I feel the bed dip in between my legs again. Sage's hands run along the inside of my legs, making her way to my inner thighs. She spreads my legs and pushes them back, exposing my bare center to her. My breath hitches with anticipation as I feel her breath skate over my clit. "Come on, Sage, stop teasing me. Give me more."

"You're so needy, baby. Tell me exactly what you want, and I'll give it you," she says, pressing soft kisses to the inside of my thighs.

"I need your mouth on me, Sage."

She presses a kiss to the top of my mound. "Like this?"

"Sage," I whine, shaking my head. "You know that's not what I meant."

She laughs. "You're going to have to be more specific, Naomi."

"Sage. I want you to eat me out and make me come so hard that I see stars."

She looks up at me from between my legs, grinning at me. "Hearing you talk dirty to me is such a turn-on," she says, her voice raspy. "Your wish is my command."

Sage presses her mouth to my core, her tongue lapping at my clit. "God, yes!" I say, my head dropping back against the pillow. She continues to circle my clit, pressing one finger into me and then a second, curling them to stroke that sweet spot.

"Sage, god, yes, I'm so close," I call out, my fingers tangling in her hair, hold her in place between my legs.

She continues to suck and lick my clit intensely, thrusting her two fingers in and out, bringing me to the edge. "I need more."

She reaches up with her free hand, pinching my nipple and rolling the stiff peak between her fingers. The tug is enough to send me over the edge and I come hard, my thighs clenching around Sage's head. "Oh fuck, yes, that's it!"

Sage lightens up, pulling her fingers out, gently stroking my clit with her thumb as I ride out my orgasm against her hand. My legs finally unclench from around Sage's head, trembling as I come down from the climax, chest heaving as I try to catch my breath.

Sage crawls up my body, pressing her lips to mine, allowing me to taste myself on her lips. "I swear, I'm going to smother you one of these days," I murmur, my hands running down her body and dipping below her shorts to grab a handful of her ass.

"Dying while trapped in between your juicy thighs, with the taste of you on my tongue? I can't think of a better way to go."

I laugh, my hand finding its way to rub Sage's clit. She lets out a soft moan, burying her face in my neck. "That's it, Sagey baby, let me make you feel good now. Ride my hand," I say softly into her ear, nibbling at her ear lobe.

She grinds her hips against me, rubbing her clit against my palm.

"Sit up," I say softly, sitting up and adjusting my position in bed. Sage looks at me curiously, sitting up so she was on her knees, straddling my leg. "Still got that sex toy stash that you were telling me about?"

Sage grins, reaching around me to open the top drawer of her nightstand. "What were you thinking about?"

I look over at the stash next to me, my eyes locking in on the small palm-sized blue vibrator. I grab it from the drawer, examining it in my palm as I try to find an on switch. "How do I turn this on?"

Sage takes the toy from me, rotating the bottom to turn it on. "What do you have planned with this?"

"I want you to use this on yourself and come while I watch."

Sage smirks, her eyes twinkling. "Ooo, that's new and fun. I like it."

"Lay back on the bed next to me."

She lays down next to me, pulling her shorts off and tossing them to the side. She adjusts the settings of the small vibrator, turning it up to a medium speed. Sage lets out a moan as she presses the vibrator to her clit. "Oh fuck, that feels so good. I forgot how powerful this thing was."

I smile, my hand finding its way in between my legs to stroke my own clit while I watch Sage. "You're so beautiful like this," I say softly, rolling over to nip at her jawline. She grinds against the vibrator, her back arching as the pleasure builds. I duck my head down, taking one of her pierced nipples into my mouth, rolling the barbell around in my mouth.

Sage whimpers, turning the vibrator up as her climax builds. "Naomi, I'm almost there."

I reach up with my free hand to grab Sage's other nipple, rolling it between my fingers and tugging on the piercing. "You're so close. Come for me, Sage."

"Fuck me," Sage lets out with a loud moan, the climax rolling through her body as she comes undone.

I smile, pressing my lips to hers as she rides out her orgasm. Sage drops the toy to the bed and I grab it, turning it off before tossing it to the side. "That was intense," she says, out of breath.

"That was hot to watch."

"I'm going to miss you these next few weeks."

"I'm going to miss nights like this," I say with a laugh.

"Well, if you're open to it, maybe we can have a phone sex date?" Sage asks hopefully.

"I think I might be open to it," I say, my face heating, "I've never done anything like that before."

"We don't have to if you're uncomfortable with it, just something to think about."

I smile, pressing my lips to Sage's. "I'll be back before you know it."

"And I'll be counting the days until I'm cuddling with you again."

22

Sage

I love Christmas, or at least now I do. Christmases when I was little were great. We'd watch reruns of the old claymation holiday movies while sitting by the fire, drinking hot cocoa. Mom and I would decorate the tree while Grandpa mostly supervised, stepping in on occasion to lift me up and reach higher branches. Christmas Day, he and I would go out to the local hockey rink to go ice skating with Santa while Mom stayed home cooking Christmas Dinner: oven-roasted chicken with mashed potatoes, gravy and a towering plate of warm, freshly baked biscuits.

It was simple, but it was perfect for our little family. Then Grandpa died and everything changed. Hot cocoa turned into regular milk, and the fireplace was boarded up because it was 'too much to look after.' Gone were our trips to pick out a Christmas tree in favor of a pre-lit, pre-decorated fake tree. Ice skating with Santa and home-cooked Christmas dinner became sad snowmen in the front yard and Chinese takeout. The year Grandpa died was the year that Christmas lost all its magic for me.

That is, until I ended up with the Davises. They brought so much joy back to the holiday season, making me look forward to Christmas rather than dread it. Their silly holiday traditions like matching Christmas pajamas for the family, or opening a small gag gift on Christmas Eve. Or spending Christmas day in our PJs, playing board games with Christmas music playing in the background. They gave me a completely unique holiday experience, unmarred by the negative memories of my childhood.

This year, elf was the theme for our matching family pajamas. We all got T-shirts with the body of an elf and our elf names printed on them and then paired them with matching red and green flannel pants and a goofy elf hat. Mel's said "Mama Elf" and Ken was "Papa Elf." Theia, of course, was "Smart Elf," and my shirt said, "Gay Elf." They gave me an option between Gay Elf and Tattooed Elf, but I loved that the Gay Elf was holding a little rainbow flag on the shirt.

The four of us were gathered around the Christmas tree, exchanging gifts. This year, we opted for a big family gift rather than our normal gift exchange. We all chipped in for a family vacation, a seventeen-day, one-way cruise to Europe scheduled for right after my graduation. When my parents present us with the cruise details, I notice that the reservation was for six adults, a three-bedroom suite.

I remember when we were researching the trips and comparing costs, it was cheaper to do a suite, especially when you factored in Mel and Ken's loyalty program benefits. But I expected them to put Theia and me in a double room or something, not give us each our own room. "This reservation was for six? Would they not let you book a suite with a double? Or two single occupancies?"

Mel shakes her head, glancing over at Ken, who gives her a small nod. "We might have overstepped, but we wanted to extend an invite to Naomi and include her on this trip. And then we didn't want Theia to be the odd man out, so we added a sixth adult to the reservation. For a friend. Or that secret boyfriend she thinks we don't know about."

Theia's head snaps up. "Sage!"

I hold my hands up in defense. "I didn't say anything!"

Mel rolls her eyes. "Please. Do you think we're blind? You've been glued to your phone with that goofy grin permanently stuck on your face since you came home. I know it's not whats-his-face, so there must be someone new in your life."

Theia blushes when her phone pings, then pings again, her fingers flexing as if she's itching to check the notification. "Okay, fine, you caught me. Yes, there is someone new, and no, you *cannot* meet him yet. Things are still really new. I just want to get to know him a little more before I make the introductions with the family."

I shrug. "For what it's worth, I thought he was a pretty nice guy," I mumble.

Theia smacks me on the back of the head. "Ow! What was that for?"

"Not ready to make the introductions, huh?" Ken asks, crossing his arms across his chest.

"It's not like that, Dad. Sage and I just ran into him at the mall when we were doing our Christmas shopping, that's all. I didn't go out of my way to introduce them, he stopped me. I promise I'll introduce you guys to him once *I'm* sure about him. After everything with Aaron, I'm trying to take my time and make sure he's a good guy."

Mel's facial expression softens, giving Theia a sympathetic smile. "Oh, honey, we completely understand. We just want you to be happy, right, Kenny?" she asks, giving him a pointed look.

He nods. "Absolutely."

Theia smiles, giving our mom a side hug. "Now can we open these other presents? I know we said no gifts because of the big trip, but I got everyone something small."

"I did the same thing," I say with a laugh.

"I think we all had the same thought," Ken says as he scans the tags taped to the wrapped presents. Another tradition that the Davises have is wrapping paper. Every year, instead of using one generic, printed wrapping paper to wrap all the presents, we're each tasked with getting a unique wrapping paper to wrap all the gifts we are giving. The only rule? It must be Christmas-related in some way. This year, I got gingerbread man print wrapping paper, except the heads were replaced with my face.

My dad laughs, seemingly having discovered my presents. "Okay, ham, Sage, why don't you go first?"

I grin, standing up to grab my boxes and hand them out.

"Where did you even find this stuff?"

"Google," I say, sitting back down once everyone has their presents, "it was either going to be a great gag or a twenty-five-dollar scam. I'm glad it was the former."

They all begin opening their presents, discovering what I got them. A professional, faux leather, shoulder bag that converts into a backpack for Theia, a cheap sous vide for Ken, and then a set of decorative, stained-glass wine glasses for Mel. They take turns handing out their own gifts, and in the end, I got a set of new hair extensions from my mom, a gift certificate to my favorite salon from Theia, and then a new, used laptop from my dad.

We were sitting down, playing Scrabble when my phone starts ringing, the tone indicating that it was a video. I grin when I see Naomi's face pop up on the screen. While I wanted to give her a call first thing this morning, I knew Naomi was spending Christmas at her parents' house rather than staying with her Grandmother, like she planned to do for the rest of her break. So I told her to call me when she got a private moment rather than the other way around.

I answer the phone, hiding it close to my face, so my parents can't see. "Are you decent?" I whisper. Naomi's already surprised me once this break. A couple days ago, I was lying on the couch, watching TV, when she called. Thankfully, my parents were not around, because as soon as I answered the call, the image of Naomi, laying on her back, fully naked with legs spread, popped up on my screen. While the sight was extremely arousing, and we had great phone sex, she gave me no warning, and it could've gone horribly wrong.

Naomi laughs. "Yes, I'm decent. I'm at Grannie Mae's house, helping her finish the pie. My daddy's leading two morning masses today, plus one after dinner, so I decided to leave with her after the first. I was worried I would spontaneously combust if I stayed at the church for too long."

In the background, I can hear her grandmother playfully scolding her for that joke, swatting at her with a dish towel. "Is that your grandma?"

Naomi smiles, taking the phone with her as she stands next to the older woman in the kitchen, adjusting the camera so that I could see the both of them. "Sage, this is my Grannie Mae. Grannie Mae, this is my friend, Sage."

"Oh, so you're the young lady that's been taking such good care of my grandbaby? Thank you, Sage. I was so worried about sending her up there for school all alone, but you pulled something out of her, a confidence and joy that was buried deep down inside, and I'm so happy that she's free," she says, her southern accent rich and warm as she gives me a genuine smile.

"Well, she makes me just as happy. I hope one day we'll be able to meet each other. I know important you are to Naomi."

"Likewise. We'll make that happen one day, absolutely."

Naomi playfully rolls her eyes, but I can see them shining with unshed tears of happiness as she moves away from her grandmother. "Okay that's enough of that."

My mom pokes her head into the frame. "Is that Naomi? Oh, hi honey! How's your Christmas going?"

I stretch my arms, completely extending them to zoom out as much as possible. "Everyone come in and say hi so I can have my girlfriend back to myself." My parents crowd in, my mom taking the phone for herself. I let them have a moment, stepping away to grab my sweatshirt and slippers. When I return, Theia has the phone, talking Naomi's ear off about the spring semester's mini rush and our COB process.

"All right, that's enough. I'm taking my girlfriend back," I say as I attempt to pull the phone out of Theia's hands.

"Bye, Naomi!" she calls out.

"Bye, Theia," Naomi responds as I regain control of my phone.

"Okay, now that that's over. Hi," I say softly, continuing to talk on video call with her as I head outside. Our parents have a sunroom added onto the back of our house. The windows work just like a storm door in that, we're able to replace the panels with screens during the summer, making it an all-weather room. It's not the best insulated, so it does get cold in here in the winter without the space heater on, but it's private and better than going outside.

"Hi, baby. How's your Christmas going so far? Show me your pajamas!"

I pull the phone back, giving Naomi a scan of my outfit. "It's been pretty good so far. Even better now that I'm getting to talk to you."

She rolls her eyes. "Charmer."

"You know you love it. Mel and Ken got the family a seventeen-day European cruise for after my graduation."

Her face falls slightly, but she recovers quickly. "A European cruise? That's so exciting!"

"Everything okay?"

She nods, waving me off. "Of course. Seventeen days, that's just a long time for me to miss you."

"Well, what if you didn't have to miss me?"

"What do you mean, Sage?"

"The cruise reservation is for six people. My parents wanted to invite you to come with us. *I* want you to come with us."

Naomi gasps. "Sage, I can't accept that. That's too much."

"Come on! It's already paid for, all you have to do is make sure your passport is up to date and that your suitcase is packed."

"Sage, that's way too generous."

"Naomi, please join us. Think of this as your graduation present to me."

"My graduation present to you is a vacation for me?"

"No. Your graduation present to me is to join me in celebrating my graduation."

"Semantics," she says, waving me off.

"Please, Naomi? Don't make me beg," I say, pouting.

"You know I love it when you beg," she says breathily, her eyes hooded with lust.

"Naomi! Stop being horny right now and focus!"

She laughs. "Hello, pot meet kettle."

"Naomi!"

"Alright, alright," she says, putting her hand up in surrender. "I will go with y'all on vacation under one condition. Well, two conditions."

"Name it."

"One, I *will* pay for my own excursions and anything I do on board."

"Okay, and what's the other condition?"

Naomi blushes, a bit embarrassed. "You go with me to get my passport."

I smile wide, happy that she's agreed to come with us. "Deal. We can do it when you return to New York."

We continue to video chat for a bit, catching each other up on our Winter Breaks so far and talking about Naomi's plan to come out to her parents right after the new year.

"Naomi, we gotta head over to your momma and daddy's for dinner! You know how he'll get if we start prayer too late."

She sighs, giving me a sad smile. "I have to go. I'll talk to you soon?"

"Absolutely Church Girl. Merry Christmas, Naomi," I say softly, blowing her a kiss through the screen.

"Merry Christmas, Sagey," she replies, returning the gesture.

23

Naomi

oday was the day. Like *the day*. To say I was scared shitless would be an understatement. I hate cursing, but spending so much time around Sage, her sailor mouth has rubbed off on me, and honestly, I can't think of a more fitting word at the moment. I've been so nauseous since I went to bed last night in anticipation of the conversation I knew I would have today. I kept tossing and turning all night, the nerves and racing thoughts rendering me unable to sleep.

Going into today, I knew this conversation would go poorly. My momma and daddy nearly disowned me for getting kicked out of High Valley University and then deciding *not* to return. I can't imagine telling them, "Hey, I'm staying in New York because I've fallen in love with my heavily-tattooed and pierced 'roommate' Sage," is going to go over very well.

But I can't continue to live a lie. I have to be true to myself, and the docile, submissive, pious woman they expect simply isn't me. I think part of why I struggled so much at High Valley is that I was trying too hard to be someone else and fit into that world. Since coming to Pinebrook University, I've discovered so much about myself that I love. Traits and attributes that I was taught from a young age to keep hidden and suppress. Because a woman is supposed to be seen, not heard, because a woman should follow and let her husband lead.

I'm kind but unconditionally so. Not the contractual sort of love that I consistently witnessed within the church growing up.

I'm passionate and driven to lead a life I want to live. To carve out my own path rather than just do what's expected of me.

I've learned I can be outspoken when I need to be. That I can stand up for myself and what's right rather than biting my tongue time and time again.

I discovered that there's beauty in diversity and individuality. Made friends with some of the most wonderful people I've ever met. Enjoyed new cultures and experiences that I, otherwise, probably never would have discovered had I not become part of this University, this sorority.

Regardless of what may happen with my parents, I know I have a couple dozen sisters backing me up. And realistically, my Grannie Mae will always have my back until she's not here anymore. I just wish I didn't have to choose between my family and a girl I'm falling in love with.

Figuring I can't keep delaying the inevitable, I get out of bed, readying to face the day. It is a few days after the new year begins, so my parents have invited me over to help them prepare for the Three Kings Day feast that the parish puts on every year. What better time to tell your parents that you're gay than while you're preparing food for sixty or so people?

I put on a pair of jeans and a simple T-shirt, pulling the sweatshirt Sage got me for Christmas over my head. I've pretty much been living in this sweatshirt since I left New York, and thankfully, she gave me a little bit of her perfume to spray on it too, because considering how many times I've washed it since I've been in Georgia, there would be no perfume left lingering on it if I hadn't been able to re-spray it. Wearing the sweatshirt, while the weight does help with my anxiety, the familiar scent and the warmth are going to help me get through the day. It'll almost be like Sage was right there with her arms wrapped around me.

I make my way downstairs, pausing to say hi to my grandmother cooking in the kitchen. "Grannie Mae, can I talk to you for a second?"

I wanted to tell my grandmother about Sage first. I figured if she reacted poorly, there would be no point in telling my parents. And if she was supportive, then I wouldn't have to explain when I'm calling her for a rescue later.

"Sure baby, come sit! I'm just finishing up my pie dough for the feast."

"Your sweet potato pie?"

"You know it! Now, what did you want to talk to me about?" she asks as she finishes mixing the dough, putting it in a bowl in the fridge to sit until tomorrow when she'll make the pies.

I take a deep breath, trying to calm some of the nerves building in my stomach. "Grannie Mae, I'm gay."

She looks up at me as she begins peeling the sweet potato. "Oh, sweetie, I know."

My brow furrows in confusion. "I don't think you heard me right, Grannie Mae. I said I'm gay. As in, in a relationship with a woman."

Grannie Mae sets the peeler down on the cutting board, putting her hands on her hips. "Now don't you insult me. I may be getting older, but my hearing is still sharp as a whip. I heard what you said, and I said what I said, I know, baby."

"But how could you?"

"Naomi, honey, the way you talk about that girl you're friends with, Sage? It would be impossible not to tell how in love with her you are."

I blush, a little bit embarrassed I was unconsciously that transparent about my feelings for Sage. "So you knew. And you're okay with it?"

She sighs, wiping her hands on her apron before coming around the table to hug me. "Of course I'm okay with it. You're my favorite grandbaby, and all I want is for you to be happy, Naomi."

I laugh, wiping the tears that have formed in my eyes. "Grannie Mae, I'm your only grandbaby."

"Still my favorite," she says with a wink before returning to peeling her sweet potatoes. "Now if you're planning to tell your parents, I can't promise you that they'll be as accepting as I am. But I think you already know that."

I nod. "That's why I told you first, for practice. Although, it didn't really do me much good since you already knew, apparently."

She laughs, nodding. "Yes, I already knew. Sorry about that, baby."

"You were right, though. Sage and I are dating. We've been officially together for a little over a month now? I actually asked her to be my girlfriend right before Thanksgiving."

She gives me a sweet smile. "Got any pictures with her? You talk so much about her, but I haven't seen you two together."

I grin, taking my phone out to show her my lock screen. It was a photo that Sage and I had Theia take of us when we went on a double date with her and Sam. The four of us had gone ice skating at Wollman Rink in Central Park. Sam and I could barely stay upright while Sage and Theia were skating circles around us. Turned out, she and Sage come out here all the time with their parents. I had come off the rink to take a break and Sage came over to check on me.

The photo was of Sage holding me, her arms around my waist, while I rested my head on her shoulder. We were all bundled up because it was freezing that day, but we were still grinning from ear to ear, faces flushed from the brisk cold. It was one of our first official dates and I loved every moment.

"You two are cute as a button. She adores you, you can see it on her face," Grannie Mae says, handing my phone back to me.

"She really does. Sage treats me like a queen. She got me this sweatshirt for Christmas. Even made sure to get one with a satin-lined hood to protect my hair."

Grannie Mae turns her attention from the pot on the stove she was stirring to me. "You're really serious about her, aren't you?"

I nod. "I am. Or at least I think so. I want to see where things go between us. I think she could be my person."

"So, does that mean you're going to stay in New York after next year? And stay with Sage?"

Shrugging, I let out a small sigh. "We haven't actually discussed that yet. But I know we're going to have to have that talk soon. Sage graduates this year, so I'm not sure what her plans are for after graduation. I think I will stay though, even if Sage decides to go off somewhere else. I love New York, I love New York City. I've been able to grow and thrive so much, I can only imagine how much more I can grow once I've graduated."

"I'm happy for you, baby. But you know that means I'm going to miss you, right? New York's just a little too cold for these old bones."

"I know, Grannie Mae, but you could come visit me during the summer! And I can still come home to see you for Christmas. Even if my parents might not want to see me, I know you always will."

"And don't you forget that," she adds with a wink. "Now, stop stalling and go over there. You might as well get it over with."

I sigh, knowing that she is right. I can't delay the inevitable. This conversation is going to happen sooner or later, and their response likely will not change the longer I drag this out. Better to just rip the Band-Aid off and come clean now.

"Don't forget to grab your momma's pie pans!" Grannie Mae calls after me as I exit the house.

Soon, I was sitting at the kitchen table with my momma, helping her grate cheese for her famous macaroni and cheese. It was the easiest thing we could make when trying to feed as many people attending the Three Kings Day feast, but there's a lot of prep involved, especially since my momma makes it from scratch. My daddy normally helps too, but he was currently in his office, working on his sermon for the pre-feast service.

"Momma, I have something to tell you," I say softly, focusing my eyes on the grater in front of me.

"Of course, baby, what did you want to talk to me about?" my mom asks, her soft voice slightly soothing my nerves.

"I'm gay, Momma. I'm in a lesbian relationship with that girl you met, Sage."

Other than the sound of a block of cheese dropping on the table, the kitchen is eerily quiet as I wait for my mother's response.

Silence.

"Momma? Can you say something?" I ask, finally looking up at her. Immediately, I regret doing that. The look on her face is one that I'll never forget. The way her face was twisted up in horror, her lip curling with disgust. You would have thought that I just told her I killed someone rather than simply coming out as gay.

"Momma, I—"

"Stop! Just stop! I knew you going to school up in New York was a bad idea. You've been led astray from the path to the heavenly kingdom."

"Momma, if you just listened—"

"No, Naomi, you listen to me. Your father's going to have a field day when he finds out," she says, getting up from the table and heading down the hall, presumably to tell my father.

It's not long before I hear my father's booming voice coming from down the hallway. "We said it, Adora, we said if she went away to school, she would be tempted and corrupted from the faith!"

I groan, resting my head on my arms on the table. *Here we go...*

"How dare you come into this house and say such vile nonsense?" my father roars as he comes into the kitchen.

"But Daddy, it's not nonsense. I'm a lesbian, I'm in love with Sage," I say, trying to plead with him. It's futile, but I'm hoping that deep down, there's some part of him that's willing to put me first rather than the church.

"That's the devil talking Naomi. You don't love a woman, you can't love a woman. You won't be allowed to enter the Kingdom of God if you choose to continue on this path of sin and sodomy."

I roll my eyes. "Daddy! It's not sodomy, it's love. What Sage and I have is no different than what you and Momma share."

"Don't you dare compare your father and I to your disgusting lifestyle. I can't even believe that you would think that they could possibly be the same thing!"

"But Momma, please! Don't y'all want me to be happy? To find someone who loves and cares for me, supports me, and pushes me to be the best version of me I could be? Sage does that!"

"Blasphemy! You can find that with a nice, sweet boy in the parish. I'm sure if you apologized, Josiah would take you back. You can drop out of school and come work for the parish's mission organization with your mother. After all, that's what you were planning on doing anyway, right?

You don't need a degree to do that. This whole college dream was foolish, to begin with.

I feel tears prick the back of my eyes, but I quickly blink them away. I was determined to maintain my composure and approach this from a place of rationality, even if they might not see it or feel the same.

"Daddy, I'm not coming back home. I'm going to finish my degree and take a job in New York with a nonprofit organization. You might think the degree is foolish, but I don't. I want to get an education and carve a path for myself. I don't want to marry Josiah, I want to be with Sage. I want to do what makes me happy and be with someone who makes me happy. Why can't you respect that?"

"Naomi, don't talk back to your father," my mother warns me.

"Now you listen here, little girl. You are my daughter, and I am your father, your leader, your protector, your master. You are to heed my wishes, and what I say goes. If you wish to remain living under my roof and continue being part of this family, you will end things with this Sage character and move back home. You will not return to Pinebrook University, and if you wish to go back to school, you will only be able to do so if you return to High Valley University."

If his booming voice wasn't enough, I can clearly see his anger right now. That one vein that always pops up when he's animated is practically throbbing; it's so pronounced on his forehead. The one that's in his neck looks like it's about to burst out of his skin too. I've only ever seen him this angry once—when the old church was broken into and vandalized when I was a kid. While it ended up working in our favor because the insurance and donations from the community allowed us to create the modern building that turned into the megachurch we have now, I remember how furious my father was when he saw what they had done, especially since he knew who did it.

It's heartbreaking that, in his eyes, my developing into my own person and finding love is equivalent to the destruction of his temple. He's willing to turn his back on his only child, all because the future I've crafted for myself is not the one he had planned for me. I knew going into this conversation that my relationship with my parents would change significantly; however, I really didn't think that I could lose them altogether.

"Daddy, please. Calm down. Don't make me choose between you and Momma and my happiness." I try in vain to plead and reason with him, but I know I'm not going to get through to him.

My father's a proud and stubborn man; he rarely admits when he's wrong, and once he's set his mind on something, there's no persuading him to do or believe anything else. Ironically enough, pride is one of the seven deadly sins, but of course, the classic catholic hypocrisy led him to believe that me being gay is the worst of all.

"Don't be so dramatic, Naomi, this is just a silly little crush. You'll find new friends and find true love when you return home and go back to High Valley," my mother says, trying in her own convoluted way to be reassuring.

My father crosses his arms across his chest, foot tapping, signifying to me that his mind is made up and that he won't be going back on this one. "So what is it going to be, Naomi?"

I sigh, getting up from the table. *This is it. No turning back.* "Well, then I guess I'm no longer part of this family. I'll get the remainder of my belongings out of the house by tomorrow. What Sage and I have is real, and I'm thriving at Pinebrook in New York. I'm happier than I've ever been, and I'm not going to give that up just because it's not what you would have imagined for me. I hope you guys can come to understand and accept me for who I really am, not who you wish I was. If you ever change your mind, you know how to get in contact with me."

I turn to head toward the door when my mother grabs my arm. Now it was her turn to convince me to change my mind. "Naomi, wait, think this through," she says, her eyes pleading.

The way Granny Mae tells it, my father's the one who radicalized my mother. She was never this devoutly religious until he came along, and it put a major strain on their relationship. I hope that deep down, my mother realizes this and she finally wakes up. She's already broken the connection she shared with her mother, I hope she doesn't allow my father to completely sever the connection she has with their only child.

I give her a sad smile. "I already thought this through, Momma. I knew this conversation could go this way, though I had really hoped it wouldn't. I made up my mind before I came over," I say, peeling her hand off my arm.

My father stared at me incredulously, I think he secretly hoped I was bluffing and would have just given in to his demands. But I knew if I didn't get out now, I never would. I'd be stuck in this controlling, hypocritical web that is the Church, and I just want more. More out of my life, out of my career, out of my relationships, and that just won't happen if I come back to Georgia.

"I'll come by tomorrow to get the rest of my things while you both are at the Three Kings Day celebration. That way, we don't have to cross paths again. And then I'll be out of y'all's hair for good." I make my way toward the door and open it, my father's voice stopping me in the doorframe.

"You're going to regret this, Naomi," he calls after me.

I shake my head as I turn to look him in the eye. "No, Daddy, I think you're going to regret it," I say before I leave my parent's house, shutting the door behind me. The loud thud of the deadbolt locking the door just emphasizes the end of my relationship with my parents. I can only hope that one day, they will come to their senses.

24

Naomi

True to my word, I went back to my parents' house the day after our fight. I went during the Three Kings Day event, knowing I'd be able to avoid them. Grannie Mae even came and helped me pack up the remainder of my clothes and childhood items I wanted to keep. She allowed me to store my boxes in one of the guest rooms at her house on the condition I come get them once I get a real apartment in New York (not just campus housing).

She even offered to give my mother a call and "let her have it for turning her back on her baby," but I told her it wasn't worth it. Their relationship is strained as is, the last thing she needs is to insert herself into my situation. Knowing Grannie Mae though, she probably will call anyway. She's stubborn, similar to my father, and I think that's partially why they never got along, even before she found out he was a preacher.

I stayed at Grannie Mae's house for a couple more days until I could find an open flight to return back to New York earlier than originally scheduled. I was supposed to stay in Georgia for another two weeks, but with everything that happened, there was no point. I have nothing left for me there besides Grannie Mae. My relationship with my father's side of the family was strained to begin with, but now it was nonexistent. Any "friends" I had were from Bible Study or High Valley, and I distanced myself from just about all of them when I left for Pinebrook University.

I reached out to Alex, asking if she was around to pick me up from the airport. Campus is just a little too far from the airport for Uber, and I'm not ready to see Sage yet. She's the only one at Pinebrook who knew I was planning to come out to my family, and I'm not ready to talk about how it went down. I didn't even tell Grannie Mae specifics. She just saw the look on my face when I returned home and put the pieces of the puzzle together.

Thankfully, my roommate decided to spend the time after Thanksgiving with her boyfriend Matthew, so they were at his apartment in Manhattan. She didn't ask too many questions about what happened and why I asked her and not Sage, but I gave her some lame excuse I didn't want to get stuck in Georgia if a big storm hit New York. I don't know if she bought it or not, but either way, she didn't pry any further.

Now, I'm standing at baggage claim, grabbing my big suitcase, waiting for the text from Alex to let me know that she was here. My phone beeps, and I check it, expecting it to be Alex. It was Sage—again. I've been mostly dodging her texts and calls since I talked to my parents. I feel bad, but I'm still processing, and that's all she wants to talk about. I'm sure if I explained to her that, she'd understand, but I'm just taking the coward's way out and avoiding her for now.

My phone rings again, and this time it is Alex. I head outside, looking for her small sedan, surprised when I see her in the passenger seat of a blacked-out Cadillac XT5. "Hi Naomi, Matt is going to drive us back to campus if that's okay? He has to drive to a last-minute conference in Albany and Pinebrook is on the way." I nod, heading toward the trunk to see her boyfriend rounding the vehicle to open the hatchback.

"We haven't officially met, but I've heard a lot about you, Naomi," he says, reaching for my bag and putting it in his trunk for me next to their bags. "I'm Matthew, but everyone calls me Matt."

"Nice to officially meet you, Matt. I've heard a lot about you too," I say, shaking his outstretched hand.

"Good things, I hope?"

I laugh. "Definitely good. She can't stop talking about how great you are." I get in the car, buckling in behind Alex.

"Naomi!" She says defensively, embarrassed to be called out.

"What? You know it's true."

Matthew glances at me through the rearview. "So Naomi, are you graduating this year too?"

I shake my head. "I was only allowed to transfer in so many credits, so I had to come in as a Junior rather than a Senior. I still have one more year."

Alex nods. "Matt too. He's doing a dual BS/MBA program, so he has to take a fifth year to finish the MBA."

"Oh nice, what are you planning to do after graduation?" I ask, trying to make conversation.

"Probably the same thing I'm doing now. I'm not sure how much Aleka told you about my background, but I created and sold a Smart Home app when I was sixteen, and since then I've created a couple indie games that I've released on Steam, plus I have a pretty decent following as a streamer. I want to fully invest and start my own video game development company, you know, do it full time, on a larger scale. I'm a pretty advanced coder, but my Computer Science degree and the MBA will give me a good educational foundation in some of the technicalities and legalities of the business, not to mention the tools and information I need to run a business."

Alex did tell me about his app, but I didn't know quite the full extent of his coding and gaming success. "Wow, that's extremely impressive. So, the apartment in Manhattan and this sweet car?"

"Bought them both with the payout from the app. And then I put the remainder in my savings. I only use it now to pay my tuition. My rent for my apartment on campus and the money I invest into my game development comes from my Twitch earnings and my appearance fees for conferences and conventions."

Alex is a lucky girl. Matthew must be loaded, though I'm sure she probably doesn't care so much about that. "Do you go to a lot of events?" I ask, genuinely curious about his industry.

He nods. "Yeah, a bit. There's a few I go to every year guaranteed, whether they invite me as a featured creator or if I just go as an attendee. I'm required to attend TwitchCon as part of my monetization contract with Twitch, and then I also go to San Diego Comic-Con, DreamHack, and E3, though they've canceled the last couple of E3 cons since Sony pulled out. Then I usually try to see if I can swing an invite to one of the mega Asian gaming conventions like G-Star in South Korea or Tokyo Game Show in Japan."

Alex grins. "And this year, he was invited to sit on a panel for indie game developers at South By Southwest in Austin, Texas. And since it wonderfully coincides with our Spring Break, I'm going to go with him."

I return her smile; I know she must be so excited to go and be part of his world. "What? No annual Kappa trip to Costa Rica?"

She shakes her head. "Not this Spring Break. We were actually thinking about waiting until after graduation to go this year instead, so it works out."

"That's awesome, Alex. I'm happy for you, for both of you, that should be a fun trip."

Matthew glances over at Alex, looking at her adoringly. "I've never gone to a conference with someone before. Even at my first E3 expo, I was eighteen, so I convinced my parents to let me go by myself. I'll be nice to have you there with me by my side."

She blushes, pecking him on the cheek. "I can't wait. And Tyler The Creator is doing a show at the Moody Center in Austin at the end of South By Southwest, so we got tickets to go to that. A little birthday present for the both of us."

I look at Alex, a little puzzled. "Birthday present?"

She nods. "Matt's birthday is like a week before mine. His falls in the middle of SXSW and mine is right after the festival, so the concert is like midway between both birthdays."

"Aw, that's sweet, you two are Pisces twins, right?" Sage has been teaching me a lot about astrology. It wasn't something I had been allowed to enjoy back home, but I've since discovered I love it. Explains a lot about people's personalities.

Alex nods. "Yep! Water signs generally complement each other well, but Pisces Pisces pairings are so harmonious."

Matthew laughs. "What she said. I'm still trying to get a grasp on the whole astrology thing."

"I teach him astrology, he teaches me the best way to get a victory royale in Fortnite."

"It's the only game you'll play with me on a Twitch stream because you can be off-camera in another room."

Alex playfully rolls her eyes. "I'm warming up to the idea of actually being on camera. You have a rabid following, Mister. Men and women."

Matthew blushes but doesn't respond—Alex was right. It doesn't surprise me at all to hear he gets a lot of attention from his followers. He's an attractive guy. He's got that secretly hot thing going on. Like looking at him from the shoulders up, he's not bad looking, but if he takes off his shirt, you get to see all the tattoos and muscles hidden away. Even I was surprised when Alex showed me a photo of them at the beach from this past summer. You'd never know, just looking at his face, that he looked like *that* underneath.

Soon enough, we were back at campus. Matthew pulls up to the front of our apartment building, jumping out to get our bags from the back. I take my bag, thanking him for the ride and the assistance with my things before heading toward the front door. I look back, waiting for Alex as she says goodbye to Matthew. She smiles up at him, her arms wrapped around his middle as he cups her cheek. He whispers something in her ear that makes her laugh and blush beet red before giving her a sweet kiss.

From what Maeve's told me, Alex has had a mix of some okay boyfriends and some not-so-great ones. This is the first guy who's truly adored her in every way, and you can see it on his face and with how he holds her that he's head over heels. I love the two of them together, they complement each other so well.

Eventually, Alex pulls away from her boyfriend, and she walks to meet me at the door, waving at Matthew over her shoulder as he drives away. "You've got it bad for that man," I say to her as we head up to our apartment.

She smiles, nodding in agreement. "I do. We've been talking a lot this break about what we're going to do after college. Or at least after my graduation. I eventually want to work for the United Nations, and their headquarters are in Midtown Manhattan. Matt would love to have his company based in New York City anyway, so the plan is to move in together into his Manhattan apartment once he finishes his fifth year.

But the question for now is, what am I going to do next year? I have a couple options. I can take the year off, wait to apply for jobs, and just stay with Matt on campus next year. I could spend that time learning another language and trying to get my interpreter certification. I'm afraid that I'm going to feel like I'm delaying my career by taking time off to essentially just wait for Matt to finish school.

Another option is to get a work-from-home job in my field, like interpreting and offering official translations of documents, and then stay with Matt here. It would keep my language skills fresh, but I'm not sure how much it'll help me with getting my dream job. The last option is just getting a job in the city and staying at Matt's Manhattan apartment, but then I'd only see him on the weekends. We could make it work, but to do that for a whole academic year? I'm afraid that could put a strain on our relationship."

I can tell that she's put a lot of thought into this. Matthew seems to be an important part of the future she sees for herself, so she's willing to do a lot to make that happen. Even if that's at the expense of her future career, though I don't think he'd let her do that. I truly think he would move Heaven and Earth to support her in anything she wanted to do.

"I think you two will figure it out, Alex. I have faith that y'all will make it work," I say in an attempt to reassure her. She gives me a small smile before turning her focus entirely on me as we enter our apartment.

"What about you? Have you and Sage figured out what you guys are going to do? I know she's finishing up this year too," Alex asks, dropping her bag near the front door before plopping onto the couch. I shrug, taking a seat on the other side of our sectional.

"Honestly? I have no idea. Sage and I haven't talked about it all that much. I know she was looking at Public Health Masters programs, but I don't think she was trying to stay at Pinebrook University. If I remember correctly, NYU and Columbia were her top two picks, and those programs are in-person in the city.

University of New England, New York Medical College, Cornell, and University of Rochester all had online programs she applied to as well, but she knows her GRE scores and GPA aren't super competitive. It's really a matter of what she gets accepted into. And then we'll just travel to each other between campus and the city if need be."

I wasn't exaggerating when I said that Sage and I haven't talked about what we're going to do, relationship-wise, after she graduates. In fact, the only conversation we've had about post-college plans happened before we started dating. Since we got together, it's been a series of *"I can't wait to spend the future with you,"* and nothing more than that. Just one more reason why I'm avoiding Sage.

"Speaking of the lady, why didn't you call Sage to pick you up from the airport? She's back to campus already."

I sigh, covering my face with my hands. "Because I came out to my parents, and unsurprisingly, it didn't go well. I'm still trying to process everything, so I'm not ready to talk to her yet, because I know she wants to know how it went. And I need to process my own emotions before I have to deal with the guilt and pity she's going to feel for me."

Alex winces. "That bad, huh?"

I look over at her. "My father made me choose between my parents and Sage. He said that if I didn't end things with her, leave Pinebrook and return to Georgia, he'd disown me."

She stares at me in disbelief, the thought of a parent disowning their child unfathomable. "And what did you do?"

"I walked out. I went back to move out the rest of my things, with my grandmother's help, the next day while they were at church, and in two days, I was on a plane back to New York. I haven't spoken to them since."

"Oh my gosh, I'm so sorry, Naomi. That's awful."

"I knew it wasn't going to go well and that being disowned was a very real possibility. I had just hoped maybe my father could realize he was being unreasonably controlling, but silly me."

Alex moves closer to rest a reassuring hand on my knee. "Are you going to be okay?"

I nod. "I think so. I mean, our relationship has been extremely strained since I got kicked out of High Valley. It's not like this was an extreme leap from where we already were. It's just final now, rather than a tiny sliver of hope I could continue to hold onto for a little while longer. Plus, my Grannie Mae still has my back, and she's the one I'm closest to."

"Well, you know you always have us. Maeve, me, the sorority, Sage—you've got sisters for life now. And we definitely don't care if you're gay or in a relationship with Sage."

I smile because I know Alex is telling the truth. The ladies of Kappa Theta Alpha have truly shown me unconditional love in a way that my own family hadn't, and I'm so grateful for them. And I honestly attribute that to why I've been so accepting of what happened with my parents. Because in the back of my mind, I knew I had a family in New York. A family that loves me because they choose to love me, not one that's barely holding up their genetic contractual obligation.

"I know y'all have my back. And that's why I was so ready to return to New York. This is where I belong, with all of y'all."

Alex is about to ask me another question when my phone rings. *Again.* "You should probably answer that. You know she's going to keep calling you until you pick up. Or, at the very least, text her back."

I sigh. I know Alex is right. I just don't want Sage to feel sorry for me. Or to blame herself for what happened.

"Hi, Sage," I say, trying not to sound tired but failing miserably.

"Naomi, are you okay? I've been trying to get ahold of you but you haven't been answering. How did it go with your parents?"

Here we go.

25

Sage

Nervously, I made my way over to Naomi's apartment. For the last couple of days of Naomi's trip to Georgia, she wouldn't answer my calls or respond to my texts. Last I had spoke to her, she was getting ready to head over to her parents' house to come out to them. But now? *Radio silence.* That was until last night. Naomi finally picked up my call, just to tell me that she came back early, unbeknownst to me and that she wanted talk to me in person today rather than talk over the phone.

Now, I'd like to think that Naomi and I have a strong relationship. But the avoidance, the fact that she didn't tell me she returned to New York? My rejection sensitivity has me fearing the worst. That what happened with her parents was so bad she decided to end things between us and wanted to do it face-to-face, rather than over the phone. I'm probably worrying for nothing, but that fear is still nagging in the back of my thoughts.

I use my spare key to let myself into Naomi's apartment. When we started sleeping over at each other's apartment regularly, we had spare keys made so that we could always get in. Thankfully we're all in Kappa (except Cora), so we both know each other's roommates, and no one had any issues. I knock gently on the door frame, letting Naomi know I'm here as I make my way into the living room.

"Hi, Sage," Naomi says, looking up from the book she was holding to give me a soft smile.

"Hi, Church Girl, you're back early," I say, taking a seat next to her on the couch and scooting in so that she's tucked into my chest. She reaches up, pressing her lips to the underside of my jaw.

"Yeah. After I talked with my parents, there was no point in staying in Georgia," she says with a small sigh, turning her attention back to her book.

I gently lift her chin with my finger, turning her head so she has to look at me. "Is everything alright, baby?"

Naomi gives me a sad smile, shrugging. "I came out to them! And then my father gave me an ultimatum: leave my life in New York, leave you, or he would disown me. I'm back in New York, and I don't have bags packed and ready by the door, so I'm guessing you can figure out what I picked."

I'm at a loss for words as I process what Naomi told me. I knew her folks were religious zealots, but I don't think I would ever imagine they would let that get in the way of a relationship with their daughter—their only child.

"Baby, you didn't have to cut ties with your family for me."

"I didn't," Naomi says matter-of-factly, "I did it for myself. Don't get me wrong, I am absolutely falling in love with you, but I did this for me. This image they wanted me to portray, the perfect future preacher's wife? It's just not who I am. And expecting me to forgo my education, to have a menial little office job to keep me busy until I start having kids? I would've been miserable if I stepped into the role he wanted me to fulfill.

I knew it was now or never if I wanted to say goodbye to that life for good, so I did. Unfortunately, that meant saying goodbye to my parents with it. But I have no regrets, that's their fault, not mine."

I watch Naomi as she returns to reading her book, seemingly unfazed by it all. I'm in awe of this woman. The way she's taken everything in stride, the way she stood up for herself, chose herself? Amazing. I know a lot of people who would have just accepted her parents' ultimatum and returned to their previous lives. Because it's easier than dealing with the unknown—being alone. But thankfully for her, she's not alone. And I bet she realizes that.

"You're amazing," I murmur, pressing a kiss to her shoulder. That elicits a smile from her as she keeps her focus on her book but snuggles further into me. As I process what Naomi just told me, it dawns on me.

"Wait, you said you were falling in love with me?" I ask, trying to hold back a smile. I've always said it was love at first sight for me, but to hear Naomi loves me back? I'm ecstatic.

She laughs, shaking her head at how long it took me to process. "Yes, Sage, I love you."

I excitedly grab the book from her hands, tucking her bookmark in to save her spot, trying not to mess up any pages as I toss the book on the coffee table.

"Hey! I was reading that," she exclaims, reaching for the book. I sit up, swatting her arm away as I switch my position so I'm leaning over her.

"You'll have time later to read, but right now? I want to enjoy my girlfriend, who I haven't seen in about a month. I want to make love to her," I murmur, burying my face in the crook of Naomi's neck, my nose running along the column of her throat. Underneath me, I can feel her chest heaving, pressed to mine as her heart rate spikes.

"God, I missed you," she says, her arms snaking around my neck. "Your hoodie and phone sex just wasn't enough."

I smirk, nipping along her jawline. "You're insatiable, Georgia," I murmur, my hand running under her sweatshirt, cupping her bare breast. "Mmm, no bra?"

She playfully smiles before nipping at my ear. "Wait until you see what's under my sweatpants."

I press my lips to Naomi's, toying with her nipple under her hoodie. She moans into my mouth, arching her body into mine. "I love that sound," I say, kissing my way down Naomi's body. She sits up, pulling her hoodie over her head before tossing it to the side.

I lean in, dipping my head to bring my mouth to Naomi's chest, but she pushes me back, forcing me to lie down on the couch. "I'm in charge today," she says, straddling me. I raise an eyebrow, equally surprised and turned on by this dominant side of Naomi. I didn't know she even had it in her.

"Oh? I think I might like this side of you, Church Girl. Have your way with me then," I say, smirking as I prop myself on my elbows, leaning back so I can watch Naomi. She presses her finger to my lips, effectively shushing me.

"You talk too much, baby. When I'm done with you, you won't be able to think straight," she murmurs into my ear, her thumb stroking my bottom lip. I don't know what research Naomi's been doing, but whatever she did, it's working well right now. She hasn't even touched me yet, and I can feel my body humming with its arousal.

She pulls away ever so slightly, and before I can protest, I can feel her soft, pillowy lips brushing along the column of my neck. My breath catches as she traces the muscles in my neck, her mouth ghosting over me, the sensation just enough to drive me crazy. A small whine escapes me as Naomi continues to tease me, not touching me in the way I want. I try to arch into her, to force that contact, but she has a firm grip on my waist, holding me in place.

"You're so desperate, Sage. Tell me what you need," she says softly, finally planting soft kisses along my jawline, her free hand skating up my side, tracing the underside of my breasts.

"I need you to touch me, Naomi," I hear myself say. I almost didn't recognize my voice, so raspy, my throat thick with the desire building inside me. She was doing a pretty damn good job of getting me all wound up.

I feel her smile against my cheek, and she scoots back, settling between my legs, spreading them ever so slightly. *This is it.* I feel her run her hands up my legs from ankle to hips, staying on the outside of my legs, avoiding the place I truly need her.

"You mean like this?" she asks teasingly. I shake my head in frustration. I was extremely turned on and getting nothing from her. "So then tell me what you need, baby. Use your words and tell me what you want from me."

"Fuck Naomi. I need your mouth, your hands, your fingers—touch me. Please. Touch my tits, my nipples, my clit, my pussy, just please touch me," I ramble on, desperate for some kind of relief from her.

Her hand starts drifting up my thighs, moving closer to that spot between them. Ever so slightly, she presses against me through my sweats. "Is this what you want from me?" She asks, softly rubbing my clit over my clothes.

"More!" I manage to moan out, my thighs falling apart, spreading to give her better access.

"Sit up," she says, pulling away and sitting back. I quickly sit up, following her directions. She grabs the hem of my sweatshirt, yanking it over my head before tossing it onto the floor. I feel her eyes rake down my chest, likely taking in my rock-hard nipples poking through my tank top. She gestures to my tank top. "That comes off too."

I grab the hem of my tank, pull it up and over my head, tossing it onto the growing pile of clothes on the floor. She presses her hand into the center of my chest, pushing me back down onto the couch. Naomi lowers herself down to my chest, her mouth enclosing around the stiff peak of my nipple, her tongue lapping at the barbell going through it. She uses her other hand to play with the other nipple, rolling the sensitive nub between her fingers.

Finally. My back arches, pushing my breast further into her mouth as she sucks on my nipple hungrily. "Oh fuck, that feels so good, Naomi." She hums her approval, dragging her tongue in a line across my chest from one nipple to the other. She takes that one into her mouth too, teeth scraping against the nub. Instead of taking the other breast in her hand, she drags that hand down my chest, running over my stomach, until her fingers dip below the waistband of my pants. Her fingers brush over the thin fabric of my thong, feeling the dampness that has accumulated between my legs.

"God, you're soaked, Sage, did I do this to you?" she coos, rubbing my sensitive clit through the thin, wet fabric.

"You drive me crazy, baby," I whine, lifting my hips to try and grind against Naomi's fingers. I can feel her grinding her core against my leg as she applies more pressure, rubbing my clit over my underwear with the same rhythm.

I feel my climax building and let out a cry in frustration when I feel Naomi lift off my nipple and pull her hand out of my pants. "No, I was so close!"

She grins devilishly as she sits back, licking her fingers coated in my juices. "Mmm, you taste so good, Sage," she purrs, "take your pants off, but leave the thong. I want to taste it from the source."

Naomi's never been much of a dirty talker, but the way she's speaking now? I could come in pants from just her voice alone. I heed her request, tugging my jogger sweats down my legs, ensuring my thong doesn't come off with them. I kick the pants to the side and look up to see that Naomi has removed her pants. She was sitting back on the couch, legs spread, using the same hand that was soaked in my juices to play with her own clit. I love how unashamed and free she was now. As if coming out allowed her to rid herself of any religious guilt she bared and fully embrace this new side.

I take a step toward her, but she holds a hand up to stop me. "Uh uh, I'm not done with you yet. Go to my bedroom. I don't want to ruin this couch if things get messy," she says, standing up from the couch.

I raise an eyebrow, trying to keep the smile off my face. "I love this newfound confidence of yours," I say, taking her hand and tugging her along as I slowly back out of the living room.

"Then you're going to love what I have planned next," she says, looking smug as she follows me into her bedroom. She backs me right up to the edge of the bed, reaching around me to grab a hair tie off her nightstand. She pulls her curls up into a messy bun on top of her head. "I want you to get on your knees on the bed, facing away from me, and grab the headboard."

I give Naomi a curious look, wondering what she was doing. But I listen, climbing up onto the bed. I kneel at the head of the bed, holding onto her wooden headboard. It's not until I'm in position that I realize my core is directly over her pillows. *She's not going to do what I think she's going to do... is she?*

My suspicions are confirmed when I feel Naomi grip my thighs, pulling herself up the bed as she slides underneath me. "I want you to sit on my face," Naomi says, her breath hot on my core. *Lord have mercy, she's going to be the death of me.*

I look down at Naomi. "Are you sure?"

"Sage. I asked you to sit on my face, so sit on my face," she says, her tone full of sass. I hesitate, I know Naomi is a grown-ass woman, but I want to make sure she's not pushing herself too far simply because she's trying to "stick it to her parents" in some weird, twisted way. My reservations are dismissed when I feel Naomi grab my hips and pull, yanking me down to her face.

I feel her warm wet tongue immediately lap at my clit, and I let out a loud moan as I grip the headboard tighter. "Fuck, Naomi, that feels so good," she continues, ravishing my pussy as her tongue dips between my folds and circles my clit, always avoiding my entrance. I feel her hands move down to my ass, spreading my cheeks, her thumbs spreading me open, granting her better access to my wet, dripping cunt.

As she sucks on my clit, gently nipping at the sensitive bud, I feel one of her fingers slowly circling my entrance. "God, I need more," I moan out, resting my head down in between my hands on the headboard. My hips lift ever so slightly, allowing Naomi room to slide a single finger deep into my pussy.

She thrusts a single finger in and out, stroking against the front of my inner walls. I feel my thighs begin to tremble as my climax begins to build. I feel Naomi latch her lips around my clit, sucking hard as she picks up the pace of her thrusts. "Yes, yes, don't stop! I'm going to come!"

She inserts a second finger, and that's enough to send me over the edge. I feel myself climax, my walls clenching around Naomi's fingers as I buck against her face, riding out my orgasm on her tongue.

My thighs eventually give out and I slump forward against the headboard. I feel Naomi gently lift up my hips, likely to slide out from underneath me. She gently massages my trembling thighs as she presses soft kisses along my spine, up to my shoulder. "Come back down to Earth yet?" she asks, pushing the hair back from my sweaty forehead.

I look over at her, a sleepy smile on my face as I shake my head. That was probably one of the most intense orgasms I've ever had. It's going to take a few minutes to get my bearings back. She continues to rub my back as I try to collect myself before laying down on my back. "Holy shit, Naomi. Where did you learn to do any of that?"

She laughs, laying down in bed next to me, propping herself up on an elbow. "You're going to laugh at me."

"No, I'm not."

She blushes, unable to make eye contact with me. "I might have watched porn for some pointers."

I raise an eyebrow. "Wait, really?" I ask, a bit surprised. We had discussed porn before, but Naomi said she hadn't watched it. Not that she was against watching it now, but she was always taught that porn (like sex) was shameful and sinful. So I was happy to see her embrace her sexuality.

Naomi nods. "It helped get me through the winter break without you. I even picked up a vibrator of my own while in Georgia."

I smile, pressing my lips to hers. "Well, then we'll have to try it together in the future."

She tilts her head. "What do you mean? Watching porn together? Or using my vibrator?"

I shrug. "Both. Hell, we could even use your vibrator right now. You haven't come yet, right?"

Naomi shakes her head. "I actually did. I may have been using my free hand to play with myself while I was getting you off. Who knew that having a really hot woman sit on your face would be such a turn-on?"

"I definitely could've told you that," I laugh, reaching out to pull her curls out of her bun. Her hair tumbles down into her face, and I brush a couple strands from her eyes, tucking the pieces behind her ear.

She smiles down at me, reaching up to cup my cheek, her thumb rubbing circles on my cheek. "I love you, Sage Carpenter."

I grin from ear to ear, turning my head to kiss her palm. "I love you too, Naomi Williams."

She lays back, flopping onto her back.

"You know, we should probably tell the rest of the sorority that we're dating when classes start back up."

We have other things to talk about too. Like what the hell are Naomi and I going to do when I graduate?

26

Naomi

"It's about damn time!" Stephanie exclaims. "I knew you guys would end up together."

Classes have started back up for the Spring Semester, and today was the first Chapter meeting of Kappa Theta Alpha. The sorority has a tradition where, after the first Chapter meeting of the semester, all the active members will stay for a big group dinner. Since all the sisters were in one place, we figured this was the perfect time to tell everyone we were together.

The reactions were... anticlimactic at best. If anything, everyone just happy we're finally dating, officially. But no one was surprised. Except maybe Penny, but bless her heart, that girl ain't the brightest. I think revealing our relationship helped her finally understand why they were so eager to have me join Kappa—Sage had a big crush on me.

Raven smiles. "I knew you two would get together eventually. I'm so glad everything worked out for you two."

I look up at Sage, who has her arms around me. "I'm glad too, I love this crazy lady," I say, scrunching my nose. She leans down to plant a gentle kiss on my lips. "I love you too, Georgia."

Gabby raises an eyebrow. "No more Church Girl?"

I shake my head. "No, it doesn't really fit me anymore. Sage has corrupted me quite a bit."

Sage laughs. "Guilty as charged."

"I don't think I could ever set foot in church again after you've called me that during sex."

Gabby makes a fake gagging motion. "Ugh, TMI, you guys. It's bad enough that I have to hear you sometimes at the apartment. I don't want to deal with it here too."

"Come Gabs, you know you're happy for us," Sage says, teasing her roommate.

I give Gabby a sympathetic smile. "I'm sorry. I'd say it won't happen again, but I think we all know it probably will."

"Yeah, yeah," she says, waving me off. Everyone else congratulates us throughout dinner, and soon enough, Sage and I are heading back to her apartment. Both Gabby and Cora were not coming back tonight, so we had the place to ourselves. While we did eat dinner at the Kappa house, we decided to stop at the local supermarket on our way to get snacks, drinks, and dessert. We were planning to spend the evening just relaxing and celebrating the end of the first week of classes.

We split up once we get to the grocery store. I grab a basket, making my way toward the front of the store where the bakery and freezer sections are, Sage heads to the back of the store to get our drinks and chips. We agree we are going to meet back at self-checkout in thirty minutes. I'm in charge of getting dessert, so I grab a piece of banana bread pudding with a maple glaze and a piece of tiramisu. Then I grab a couple of mini cookies and cream ice cream cups.

I make my way over to the self-checkout lanes, waiting for Sage to come back. I take out my phone, checking for any missed messages. I have a couple missed texts from my Grannie Mae. We've been trying to figure out my summer plans, whether I'd be staying in New York, coming back to her place in Georgia, or if I were doing something else. But I can't give her an answer one way or the other until Sage and I actually discuss what the status of our relationship will be after her graduation.

Unsurprisingly, my parents haven't contacted me since I reached out to them three weeks ago. I half expected my mother to at least send me a text message, but I knew I wouldn't hear from my father. In fact, I would be surprised if he hadn't blocked me on all platforms.

I sigh, putting my phone away just as I feel a hand snake around my waist.

"What's got you in a sourpuss mood, baby?"

I smile at the comment, turning to see Sage armed with a basket full of bottles and chip bags. "A sourpuss?" I mimic, laughing at the comment.

"Hey, it made you smile, didn't it? My work here is done," Sage says, planting a kiss on my forehead.

We checkout, paying for our items after some brief arguing over who will pick up the bill. Once the snacks are loaded into the car, Sage and I make our way back to her apartment. A few minutes in, Sage turns her attention to me, keeping her eyes focused on the road. "But seriously, what had you upset earlier?"

I shrug. "I guess I'm a little bummed that my momma hasn't reached out yet. I knew my father wasn't going to, but I still had hope that my mother would, especially since I knew Grannie Mae called her to let her have it for letting my father throw me out like that. But it's been three weeks, I think that if she really had any intention of reaching out to me to see how I'm doing, she would've done so by now."

Sage reaches across the center console of the vehicle, taking my hand and giving it a gentle squeeze. "Just give her time. She's probably at war with herself, trying to decide between reaching out to her only baby and preserving her marriage by not going against your father. I think, eventually, she will come around and do the right thing by you."

I give her a small smile, returning Sage's hand squeeze with one of my own. "I hope you're right."

Once back at the apartment, Sage and I make ourselves comfortable on the couch. I snuggle up against her, my head resting on her stomach as she leans back against the couch. She pulls a thick fleece blanket over our laps, cocooning us in warmth as she turns on the TV. We settle on a comedy movie, starting the flick before digging into our desserts. While I got the bread pudding for myself and the tiramisu for Sage, we split them half and half so that we could share.

I pick at my dessert, lost in my own thoughts. The text I received from my grandmother earlier had me stuck in an anxiety spiral. We needed to talk about Sage's graduation and what it means for our relationship, but I have no idea how to broach that subject. Do I just come right out and ask her where does she see us heading? Do I ask her what her plans for the summer are? Do I—?

"Hello? Earth to Naomi! You're not even paying attention to the movie?"

I blink, snapping out of my trance-like state to see Sage looking down at me, concern etched on her face. She had stopped the movie, and I hadn't even noticed.

"Sorry, Sage, I just spaced out for a second."

"A second? More like the entire first fifteen minutes of the movie. I thought you had fallen asleep when I didn't hear you laughing at the jokes, but then I looked down to see you just lost in thought. Still thinking about your mom?" she asks, tucking my curly hair behind my ears.

I let out a soft sigh. *I guess it's now or never.* "No, actually. I was thinking about us."

Sage blinks a few times, her concern morphing into confusion. "About us? What about us?"

I chew on my lip, trying to figure out how to bring this up. "It's the end of January, Sage. In four months, you're graduating. We haven't talked about what you plan to do after. Or what that means for us," I trail off, my voice low.

Sage's face softens, smiling at me. "That's it? Naomi, you could've just asked me instead of getting yourself all twisted up."

"I was nervous, okay? With all the stress of coming out to my parents, I was worried that this might end. Like you're my person, Sage, but I was afraid that if I brought up the future, that maybe you didn't see the same long-term picture I did."

Sage's smile grows as she takes my hands in hers. "You once said to me that I was stuck with you, well right back at you Naomi. I choose you, Naomi Williams. You're stuck with me for forever times a million, because I love you.

I love this bond we share, and this relationship we've created, and I'm not willing to give it up just because I'm graduating. Is it going to be tricky? Yeah, but we can survive. If this year has shown me anything, our relationship is a strong one, and if anyone could make medium-distance work, it's us."

I return Sage's smile, her words soothing my anxiety and fears about the trajectory of our relationship. "Well, in that case, what are your post-grad plans, Ms. Carpenter?"

Sage lets out a laugh, the sound infectious. "Ms. Carpenter sounds so formal. I'm still trying to decide if I'm going to go straight into grad school or if I'm going to go straight into the workforce. I applied for a few different public health programs and then a couple related jobs as well. I did get into a Masters of Public Health program, though not my dream program. I was wait-listed for Columbia, which is really where I want to go.

The only job offer I managed to secure was for a Health Education and Outreach Program Coordinator position at a Planned Parenthood on Long Island. I would be overseeing their peer Sex & Identity educational program they run in collaboration with the local LGBTQIA Center. I love the idea of doing that because that's ultimately what I want to do, design and execute a program like that. I just know that eventually, I should get my MPH, especially if I want to focus on programming and policy. I'm just not sure if it would be easier to do it now or go back later."

I mull over what Sage just shared with me. I was already amazed by her, but her dedication and drive? Her desire and passion to do advocacy work? She's truly remarkable. "Could you do your MPH online and still work? Or switch to part-time and then go back to get your MPH?"

Sage shakes her head. "Columbia has an accelerated Online MPH program, but I don't think I qualify. It's really geared toward PhDs and other post-graduate degree holders. And then if I choose to go back, they discourage working or any other extra-curricular activities during the first semester of the program because of how intense it is. So I might have to step down altogether from my position, at least for a few months, if I choose to do that."

"Well, did you mention your intentions to go back to school to the people you interviewed with at the Planned Parenthood?"

Sage shakes her head.

"Well, you should! If they knew that's what you wanted to do, especially if you wanted to keep working for that Planned Parenthood, they'd probably try to accommodate you best they can."

She chews on her lip for a little while she thinks over her options. "You know, you're probably right. Columbia's Public Health program is my dream, and if I reapply in the future once I've been working for a bit, I'll probably have a better chance of being accepted. And this is a role that I do truly want. I think I'm going to call them this week to accept the position."

"That's great, Sage! So would you commute from New Jersey? Or would you move closer to the clinic?"

"Long Island is so expensive! But the commute to Valley Stream is really long, even if I moved to Jersey City or Hoboken rather than staying in Paterson. My best bet would honestly be to move to Queens, and then I'd be able to take the LIRR from there. Then I'm not too far away from home, not too far away from work, not too far away from Manhattan, and not too far from you next year. Plus, you'd be able to take the train to come visit on your free weekends."

"That really does sound like the best-case scenario," I say, thinking about the fun and adventures we could have exploring the city. "Would I be able to stay with you during the summer?"

Sage gives me a look as if I had asked if the sky was blue. "Of course. We're moving in together. Obviously, you will still have a place on campus, but my apartment is yours. When you graduate, you're going to move to the city with me."

"Oh, am I now?" I ask, laughing at Sage's bossiness.

Sage gives me a large, shit-eating grin. "Yup! I figured we could go apartment hunting and furniture shopping together during the summer, so that way, we're all moved in and settled before you have to be back here."

I let out a contented sigh, a warm feeling building in my stomach. The fact that Sage was actually picturing this domestic future for us made me excited to graduate. Originally I was nervous because I had no idea what I was going to do. But now, the future is beginning to look a little clearer to me. Maybe I'll get a job working for a women's rights charity? Maybe

Sage and I will get a cat or a dog? Maybe we'll get engaged and eventually married? This is the most optimistic I've felt about my future in a long time.

"You're doing it again," Sage sing-songs, reaching up to stroke my cheek with her thumb.

I blink, bringing my attention back to her before giving a sheepish smile. "Sorry, Sagey. I started daydreaming about the future."

She perks up at my confession. "Really? What did it look like?"

I smile, leaning into her touch as I trace circles on her leg. "Us married, both working in the nonprofit sector. You doing sex education, me working for a women's rights organization. Both of us coming home at the end of the day to our cat, Cheeto, and our dog, Murphy. Maybe we'd start thinking about kids? Fostering and adopting, of course. We'd buy a house first, though. Maybe in the suburbs. It'd be a longer commute, but hopefully, I'd be remote or hybrid, and you'd be traveling all over anyway."

Sage laughs. "Cheeto and Murphy? You've already named our imaginary pets?"

"Of course!"

"You've really put some thought into this, huh?"

I shake my head. "Not really. I just got excited and hopeful, and my mind took off."

Sage stands up from the couch, holding her hands out to me.

Curiously, I take her hands in mine, Sage pulling me up from the couch. "What?" I ask, looking into her eyes.

Sage gives me a devilish smirk, pulling me in close, her hand trailing down my back and over the curve of my ass before giving the flesh a gentle smack. "Come on, let me show you how good our future really will be," her voice low and sultry.

I return her smirk with a grin of my own as she tugs me to her bedroom. I brace myself because I already know that with Sage's stamina, we've got a long night ahead of us.

27

Sage

Four months later...

Oh shit. Today's the day.

To say I thought I would make it to this day would be a fat ass lie.

Little twelve-year-old Sage would've never guessed that she'd make it to college and have a family of her own, rooting for her every step of the way.

Thirteen-year-old Sage didn't think she would live to see fourteen, let alone twenty-two.

Fifteen-year-old Sage never would've believe she'd be living as an out and proud lesbian in a relationship with a woman that she loves and adores.

Hell, even nineteen-year-old Sage was unsure if she was going to make it through college in one piece, let alone graduate.

And yet, here I am. Graduating from Pinebrook University on time, with honors, with Naomi, Theia, Mel, Ken, and many of the women of Kappa Theta Alpha cheering me on. I've never considered myself to be an overly emotional person, at least outwardly. I'm sure Naomi would probably disagree, but I don't often allow myself to be vulnerable around other people.

Today, however, I've barely been able to stop crying. I've already had to redo my eye makeup twice, though this last time, I made sure to use all my waterproof products because, clearly, this leaky faucet won't be fixed any time soon.

"Sage! Are you almost ready? We have to meet your parents outside the field house in twenty minutes, and I know it's going to be crazy walking over there," Naomi calls from the living room. We decided to get ready for the ceremony at her apartment since she was located on campus. They anticipated such heavy traffic that the campus shuttle wasn't even making any stops within campus just along the peripheral buildings. So we knew either we had to leave at least an hour early or we were going to be walking.

I give myself a quick once over in the mirror, making sure I look okay. Instead of the traditional white dress, I opted for a light, sage green, strapless romper. It was chiffon, making it light and airy but still lined so I wouldn't flash anyone. New York was deceivingly hot in the summer, and even in May, we're already having some pretty hot, humid days. I paired the romper with a pair of white wedges that have a cork sole.

My hair's grown out a little bit, now reaching my armpits, and right after Spring Break, I dyed my hair back to a neutral, golden brown color in preparation for the new job. I was going to go back to my natural blonde, but between the dark blue in my hair and the amount of times I dyed it, darker was the safer move for the health of my hair. At least this shade would be easier to transition back to my natural color as it grows out. Naomi likes it though, she says it makes my green eyes pop, so maybe I'll keep it.

Speaking of Naomi, she's waiting for me. I tuck the last couple of pins into my low bun, keeping the hair off my neck. I grab my small crossbody purse and the hanging plastic bag holding my graduation cap and gown and head into the living room. "Sorry, sorry, I had to put the finishing touches on my hair. You know how I get if my hair starts sticking to my neck when I'm sweaty."

Naomi lets out a soft laugh. We've been together for almost seven months now, and she's definitely picked up on all my little sensory quirks—things sticking to my neck while I'm sweaty, for example. I look up to see Naomi standing in front of me. She has her hair out and curly, embracing her natural texture. She decided on a pale blue floral halter dress that hit her mid-thigh and a pair of white leather pumps, a sweeter take on a pin-up look.

"Are you graduating or am I? You always look so much better than I do," I say, gently pressing my lips to Naomi's forehead, trying to ensure none of this mauve lipstick transfers to her skin.

Her face heats, embarrassed by the compliment. It's cute how Naomi still gets so bashful around me, even months later. "Stop, you look amazing. And I said it when you bought it, but that romper matches your eyes perfectly."

Now it was my turn to blush.

"Come on, we have to get going now. I still have to find your parents to give them their tickets. You have the card, right?"

I nod. At Pinebrook University, graduations are broken down by degree type and program. Thankfully, we don't have to sit alphabetically, but we do have to sit in the section with our departments. So, when lining up to cross the stage, we have to hand the emcee a card with our name, pronunciation, degree, majors, honors, and so on.

They gave us our cards this morning when we checked in for our ceremonies and picked up our tickets, so it's our responsibility to bring them back for graduation. They have blank cards and pens if you forget your card, but it's much easier to just bring it back. I pinned mine to the inside of my grad cap when I got home so I wouldn't lose it.

Naomi grabs her purse and heads out the door, with me following behind her. Since her apartment is one of the townhouses right along the edge of campus, behind the field house where graduation was being held, we decide to take a shortcut, crossing the street and then walk about halfway around the track to reach the lower floor of the field house. From there, we take the elevator up to the main floor, heading out the front to meet Mel and Ken.

"There's my girl! You did it, honey," Mel says, her face lighting up when she sees Naomi and I step outside.

"Hi, Mom, Dad. Glad you guys made it," I say, bending down to give my mother a hug.

"Of course we made it. We wouldn't miss it for the world," Ken says, giving me a brief hug once my mom lets go.

"So proud of you, Sis, you're finally done here," her voice a little distracted. I follow her line of sight to see her ogling Dr. Bennett, who was standing outside talking with one of the other faculty members, his regalia draped over his arm.

I lean in, unable to keep the smirk off my face. "Girl, you are in love with that man. Stop undressing him with your eyes in front of Mom and Dad."

She blushes before turning her attention to me. "I'm just thinking about the fun we had last night with that cap and gown," she says, grinning. I turn to see Dr. Bennett checking out Theia right back. "Gross."

"Y'all are not being very discreet. Did you finally tell your mom and dad? Or the school?" Naomi chimes in, seeing Theia and Bennett.

Theia nods. "I told them last night about Sam, though they haven't met him yet. We have our meeting with the ethics board this coming week," she says with a small sigh. I can feel the nerves radiating off her.

"You'll be fine, sis. You and Sam don't even work in the same department. Not to mention, it's been what? Three, four years since he was your professor or advisor? Despite the age gap, you guys are colleagues now, and there's nothing against that in University Policy," I say, giving her shoulder a squeeze.

"Sage is right. I'm sure it'll all be fine. They're probably just going to require you to sign some disclosure forms and confirm that there was nothing romantic going on between y'all when you were a student."

Theia adamantly shakes her head. "Oh no, definitely not. He was just a fantasy then, and I don't think he even paid much attention to me at that point. This honestly didn't start until this year when he saved me that night."

My mom pokes her into our huddle. "Sage, I think they're calling for the students to start heading into the fieldhouse."

I give Naomi a kiss on the cheek and Theia a hug before heading into the gym.

This is it.

This is the moment I've been waiting for.

Between going through foster care, my mental health, and my ADHD, I honestly wasn't sure if I would make it through high school, let alone college. But here I am, on my graduation day, being cheered on by an amazing woman I'm in love with and the family that's chosen me. I couldn't be more grateful for where I am right now.

Acknowledgements

Writing this book made a childhood dream of mine come true. It was a long time in the making, a year and a half that I've been writing it, but eight years since I first came up with the original concept that evolved into the book that you just read. Sage and Naomi are essentially two pieces of me: the young teen that was struggling with her sexuality and her faith, and the out and proud college student that I eventually became. While this was fiction, there is a lot of me and my life in this book.

I'd like to thank my friend Daisha, for giving me feedback on the early, early stages of this book. You read my Scrivener files for me at two in the morning, instead of doing the job we both hated and I love you for it. You were the first person I told about this book, about my renewed desire to write and publish a novel, and you supported me at every step of the way. *Gracias por tu ayuda y te amo mucho.*

I'd also like to thank the wonderful women of the Soulful Story Collective, my Writing With The Soul ladies. Y'all have been my craft supporters. I would have never finished this book without having a community of writers I could lean on, and y'all are it for me.

I want to thank my Threads mutuals, but especially Sarah Anne/Anna Noel, multihyphenate extraordinaire. You've been such a wealth of knowledge for me for this process – between the author and marketing side of things, and you're a total badass author that I aspire to follow.

Last but not least, I'd like to thank my parents. While I know my dad's not going to read this, my mom and Grandma will. Momma Bear, Daddy, thank you so much for your unconditional support. You two have supported this dream of mine from the moment I said I wanted to make it a reality. Y'all have never pressured me to do one thing, you've encouraged me to pursue my passions and give it my all. And as of the release of this book, I have. I love you two, and I can't thank you enough.

Also By the Author

Coming September 23, 2025

Bi The Way, I Love You

A charity anthology featuring nine Bi+ love stories, by nine Bi+ authors,
to show the world just how diverse, beautiful and valid Bi+ love is!
If you're interested in getting a glimpse into Gabby's story, check out the
novelette featured in this anthology.
https://mybook.to/x8gCJIZ

About the author

MK Owens is a New Adult and Adult Contemporary Romance author.

A self-proclaimed hopeless romantic, she uses her writing to highlight women's empowerment and female sexuality. With a bachelor's degree in Molecular Genetics and Medical Technology, MK works as a healthcare worker during the day and dedicates her nights to pouring all her energies into her writing.

As much as MK loves to cook, dance, and fall down the true-crime rabbit hole, her faithful German Shepard, Basil, loves to hang out with her in the hopes of receiving a treat. As a side note, Basil would like you to know that it's only a coincidence that his mom loves cooking and named him after an herb.

You can connect with MK on Instagram @mkowensbooks or on her website, mkowensbooks.com

www.ingramcontent.com/pod-product-compliance
Lightning Source LLC
Chambersburg PA
CBHW061953170626
46813CB00006B/2628